He despises you. **Yet he made her heart race whenever he was near.**

And Isobel couldn't forget that kiss. It was as if he'd branded her as the shameless wanton he clearly believed her to be.

The stories that had spread around her time in London only strengthened her sense of being utterly alone—she'd learned to be resilient, and she had built up a stone wall around her heart.

But that didn't mean her heart didn't ache within its defenses. She didn't want the person who took that wall down piece by piece to be Connor Hamilton— Connor, with his cynicism, and his scorn for her family, and most of all for herself. She *couldn't* be feeling what she did for him—she just couldn't!

Author Note

I love reading about the lives of men who were born with nothing, but achieve real success—they owe nobody anything, and they're ideal hero material. My hero in this book, Connor, is a good example—he's what the people of Regency times would have called an "iron master," since through his iron foundries he's made a fortune for himself from building canals, harbors and bridges.

But Connor makes the mistake of moving into the former home of a ruined heiress, Isobel Blake—and then the sparks really begin to fly!

LUCY ASHFORD

The Master of Calverley Hall

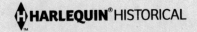

Recycling programs
for this product may
not exist in your area.

ISBN-13: 978-1-335-52281-8

The Master of Calverley Hall

Copyright © 2018 by Lucy Ashford

Printed in U.S.A.

www.Harlequin.com

For Alan

Lucy Ashford studied English with history at Nottingham University, and the Regency era is her favorite period. She lives with her husband in an old stone cottage in the Derbyshire Peak District, close to beautiful Chatsworth House, and she loves to walk in the surrounding hills while letting her imagination go to work on her latest story.

You can contact Lucy via her website, lucyashford.com.

Books by Lucy Ashford

Harlequin Historical

The Major and the Pickpocket
The Return of Lord Conistone
The Captain's Courtesan
Snowbound Wedding Wishes
"Twelfth Night Proposal"
The Outrageous Belle Marchmain
The Rake's Bargain
The Captain and His Innocent
The Master of Calverley Hall

Visit the Author Profile page at Harlequin.com.

Chapter One

Gloucestershire—June 1816

Seven years ago, Connor Hamilton had vowed to turn his back for good on the English countryside. But today, as he felt the warm summer sun on his face and breathed in the scent of freshly mown hay, he realised he'd never actually forgotten how beautiful it could be.

He'd chosen to drive from the Hall in his phaeton, with nine-year-old Elvie sitting at his side and Tom, the elderly groom, perched on the back. His two matched bays set a smart pace along the road to Chipping Calverley, but as their destination grew closer Connor reined them to a walk and took a swift glance down at Elvie. Not that he could see a great deal of her, thanks to that huge sunbonnet her grandmother had insisted the child wear.

'I promise I'll bring her back in one piece, Laura,' Connor had teased.

'I know! I know I'm fussing!' Laura had laughed. But then she'd added, more quietly, 'You realise, Connor, how very much my granddaughter means to me.'

An unspoken grief coloured her words and Connor had replied, 'Of course. She means a great deal to me also.'

Poor Elvie. Poor silent, orphaned Elvie. But she was taking everything in, Connor was sure, with quiet pleasure. And suddenly the little girl tugged at the sleeve of his driving coat and whispered, '*Look*, Connor. There's a fair!'

She was pointing to the colourful tents set out on a grassy meadow in the distance, the spaces between them already thronged with people and stalls. 'A fair?' he echoed teasingly. 'Never, Elvie. Surely not.'

'But there is, Connor. There *is.*'

Connor pretended to lean forward, shading his eyes from the bright sun. 'Do you know,' he said, 'I think you're quite right.'

She didn't say another word, but she gazed intently at the bustling scene as they drew closer. And Connor thought, *Pray God I've done the right thing, bringing the child here.* Meaning not just to the fair, but to Calverley, to the very place where he himself had grown up, the place he had turned his back on all those years ago. Thus, in all likelihood, opening himself up to all sorts of memories and regrets...

Concentrate, he told himself sternly, because by now his horses had come to a complete halt in the solid queue of carriages, gigs and carts all heading for the fairground. Connor turned round to his groom. 'All right if I leave you in charge, Tom, while I walk on with Elvie?'

'All right indeed, sir,' said Tom, lowering himself remarkably promptly for a man of his age from the rear of the carriage. 'You two go and enjoy yourselves, now!'

No one could have been more pleased than old Tom when Connor had arrived at Calverley Hall back in April and told him he was going to buy the place. Its former owner had died five years ago, owing money everywhere; the bank had taken possession and put the run-down Hall up for sale. No buyers appeared. Instead, a succession of tenants had done nothing to reverse its general decline and few of the staff from the old days remained.

But now Connor was the new master of Calverley. 'Well,' Tom had said when he heard the news, 'I was thinking of retiring, to be honest. But since *you're* back—if you need a fellow to run your stables, Mr Hamilton, then here I am!' He'd puffed out his chest. 'It will be an honour working for you, sir!'

And if Tom was recalling how Connor grew up the son of the local blacksmith, and had laboured every day in the heat of the forge, then old Tom said nothing at all.

Now Connor handed the reins to him, then went to help little Elvie down. 'It's a bit of a walk, Elvie,' he told her. 'But you don't mind, do you?'

'Oh, *no.*' She gripped his hand tightly.

'Good girl,' he approved and noted how her eyes were round with wonder as he guided her through the lively crowds. So, he thought to himself, people still came from miles around to the midsummer fair at Chipping Calverley. *'It's the prettiest village in Gloucestershire,'* people always used to say. *'With the best fair in the whole of the county!'*

And he was finding that every sound, sight and scent brought back memories. The appetising smell from the stall selling fresh bread. The music of the

Morris Men with their fiddles and their bells. The laughter of the crowd watching the Punch and Judy show. You didn't see many smiles on the faces of London's businessmen, thought Connor. Not unless they'd just made a vast profit in some big financial deal—and even then, their smiles were only half there, because their brains were already busy counting up the money.

Talking of money, those creatures in the livestock pens had to be worth a fair amount. He steered Elvie towards where the farmers stood proudly by their animals and the crowds pressed against the enclosures to get a better view.

'Look, Elvie. See the calves?' He lifted the little girl up high to get a better view of the cows with their young ones and—firmly chained to a stout post—the muscular black bull that gazed balefully at the awestruck crowd. Elvie gasped in delight, then they moved on because a little way past the cattle enclosure Connor had spotted some colourfully dressed gypsies offering pony rides. He saw Elvie gazing at them. 'Do you want a ride?' he asked her gently.

She hesitated and shook her head; he thought he glimpsed uncertainty in her eyes.

'Perhaps another time, then,' he said. 'Yes?' And she nodded.

Maybe I ought to get her a pony of her own, Connor mentally noted. *A small one, a gentle one. It will give her something to take care of. Perhaps even help her, in a small way, to get over her father's death.*

Connor, too, missed Miles Delafield. The older man had been not only his business partner, but his close friend. Miles would have loved all this, he thought suddenly. He gazed around and realised that if you looked beyond the fairground and up the valley, you could actually see Calverley Hall on the far side of the river. From here you got a heart-stopping view of its acres of gardens running down to the water meadows; of its gabled roofs and diamond-paned windows sparkling in the June sun.

And now—all of it belonged to him. What talk there must have been, when the locals heard he was moving in. What speculation about the money he had made. And if he'd hoped to make his appearance here at the fair unnoticed, he was mistaken, because he was finding himself hailed in hearty greeting by landowners and businessmen who wouldn't have acknowledged his existence in the old days. They came up to him one after another, declaring, 'We must get together soon, Hamilton! It's good to see you back, hopefully to restore the Hall to its former glory. You'll come round for dinner soon?'

And then there was the local Vicar, the Reverend Malpass. Malpass ran a small school for the children of the deserving poor, which Connor had briefly attended before being thrown out for hiding a frog in the Vicar's desk.

Did Malpass remember? Surely he did—but he was almost painfully effusive in his attempts to welcome Connor home. 'Mr Hamilton, it's truly excellent news that you've moved into Calverley Hall. I remember you well—and I'm sure that you're *exactly* what the place needs!'

Connor gazed at him, dark eyebrows slightly raised. 'I remember you, too, Reverend Malpass. And I can see that you've hardly changed in the slightest.'

The Vicar hesitated. *Frogs?* thought Connor. *Was*

he thinking of frogs? Then Malpass, clearly shrugging aside the past, beamed down on Elvie. 'And this young lady is your relative, is she? Charming. Charming, I'm sure. How do you do, miss?'

'I—I'm very well, sir.'

That stammer again. Connor felt Elvie shrink against his side and he gripped her hand. 'She's not my relative,' he stated flatly. 'Miss Elvira Delafield is the daughter of my former business partner.'

'Ah, yes. Miles Delafield—he died recently of a heart attack, didn't he? And I hear this poor little girl's mother is dead, too—most, most unfortunate!'

Connor felt Elvie press closer. He'd *always* thought the Vicar was a blundering fool. 'Indeed,' he replied tersely. 'Now, if you'll excuse us…'

But no sooner had Connor got away from the Vicar than he found himself surrounded by a fresh hazard—women.

Oh, the women. Not just the young ones eyeing him up from beneath their beribboned straw bonnets, but their mothers, too, were coming at him from all sides. 'My dear Mr Hamilton!' they simpered one after another. 'We're truly delighted that you've returned to Gloucestershire. We do hope we'll have the privilege of your company soon…'

And they proceeded to recite a list of church committees, fund-raising fêtes and parish entertainments that all sounded extremely worthy—but he knew, of course, what the tabbies were really thinking.

They would be thinking that Mr Connor Hamilton, at twenty-five years old, was an extremely wealthy man. Had risen from being a blacksmith's son to partner in a highly successful iron business—and now that his partner had conveniently died, he'd got the lot. What was more, he was the new owner of the most impressive house in the district by far—a family home if ever there was one, even if it was somewhat neglected—and he was *not married*!

Connor endured just a few more moments of the mothers parading their daughters, but he was heartily glad to be distracted by Elvie tugging at his hand. 'Connor,' she was whispering. 'Connor, look.'

He looked and realised there was some sort of disturbance over by the crowded ale tent. A cluster of children, none of them older than Elvie, were racing around and he thought he could hear a small dog yapping. There were adult voices as well now, raised in anger and in threat.

Connor, with Elvie's hand still in his, drew closer. The children looked underfed and scruffy—he immediately guessed they were from the gypsy caravans that came every summer to set up camp in Plass Valley, half a mile from here. Their parents would be busy harvesting the hay and the children, he realised, were chasing after a puppy whose rope leash trailed after it. They dived to catch it, failed and tried again, shrieking with laughter as the excited puppy evaded them.

Local people didn't like the Plass Valley children, Connor remembered. Local people didn't like their parents much, either, despite the vital work they did on the farms in summer. The children's appearance didn't help, since judging by the mud splashes on their clothes and bare skin they'd all taken a dip in the nearby duck pond.

And so, evidently, had the puppy. Droplets of water were still flying from its fur as it shook itself, caus-

ing nearby ladies to shriek as their best frocks were
bespattered, while their menfolk blustered. One burly
man caught a little lad by the ear. 'You young var-
mint, you and your kind should be beaten out of here.
And I'll—'

He broke off when Connor stepped forward. 'The
child's rather small for your threats, don't you think?'

'I'll bloody thump him, that's what! Plass Valley
vermin!'

'Try thumping me instead,' invited Connor.

Connor was tall and his well-tailored clothes
couldn't hide the fact that he was extremely well mus-
cled into the bargain. The man hesitated, muttered
something under his breath and vanished into the staring crowd. And then Connor heard another voice, a
young woman's voice, saying calmly but firmly, 'Children, you really shouldn't let your puppy get so excited. He thinks it's all a game—he doesn't understand
that you're trying to catch him.'

Connor could see her now. Tall and slender, in her
early twenties, she wore an old-fashioned cotton sunbonnet and a flowery frock—a frock now generously
splashed with mud, since she'd picked up the excited
puppy and was holding it firmly in her arms.

One of the children—a freckle-faced lad in a battered cap set at a jaunty angle—called out to her, 'We
didn't mean any trouble, miss! He went swimming in
the duck pond and got stuck in the weeds. So we pulled
him out, but then he ran away.'

'But here he is—fortunately,' she said. The puppy
was trying to lick her face with its pink tongue. 'Perhaps you'd better take him home and get yourselves
cleaned up.'

The children looked at one another. 'But he's not ours, miss.'

'Not…?'

'He's a stray,' explained the lad. 'We found him this morning up in the fields, really hungry, so we fed him and asked around. No one wants him. And he's not wanted at home, either, at our camp, 'cos our dads say we've got enough dogs already.'

'Well,' she said. *'Well.'*

And Connor felt the memories surge and connect, rolling into place one after another. The young woman wore country clothes that were clearly homemade and years out of fashion; yet she carried herself with grace and spoke with unusual clarity. And more memories began to pile in. Far too many of them.

Then someone else arrived—that blasted Vicar, Malpass. 'Best keep yourself out of this, young lady,' he said curtly to the woman, looking almost with repugnance at the muddy puppy in her arms. 'As for you,' he declared, turning to the children, 'how dare you run wild here, disturbing the peace and up to no good? Be off with you!'

Connor was about to stride forward and intervene, but the children had a defender already.

'I've spoken to the children, Vicar,' she said, still apparently calm, 'about this little dog. He was in difficulties in the pond and they were trying to help him. Is that really so bad of them?'

The Vicar clearly thought it was. 'You know their kind. They're no better than their parents, living like vagrants, thinking they're beyond the power of the law. And they never attend the church!'

'Perhaps they don't attend *your* church,' the woman

said steadily, 'because they realise how unwelcome they'll be.'

And her intervention—was this what she'd intended? Connor wondered—had given the children the chance to escape, scampering through a gap in the hedge and off into the neighbouring fields. Connor stepped forward, Elvie's hand still in his, and said to the Vicar, 'It seems there's no harm done, Reverend Malpass. But I think we all need to remember that these children's parents are vital to the summer harvest. Don't we?'

The Vicar pursed his lips. 'Of course, Mr Hamilton. But we still need to maintain basic standards of morality in the district.' And—with a curt nod of the head—the Vicar moved on.

If Connor had been wise, he'd have moved on, too, but he didn't.

Everyone else had drifted away, back to the ale tent or the food stalls or the livestock pens—but the young woman remained. She was still soothing the puppy, which had settled gratefully into her arms, and Connor noted that despite her slenderness, she certainly possessed her share of womanly curves. Swiftly he lifted his gaze to her face and saw that her eyes were as intense as ever—green flecked with gold and fringed by thick dark lashes...

Then he realised she was meeting his gaze steadfastly. And she said, 'So you're back.'

The little dog whimpered in her arms, as if suddenly uneasy. And Connor, too, was unsettled, was not quite sure how to handle this. *Calmly would be best*. He nodded. 'Indeed, Miss Blake,' he replied. 'I'm back and you are still—how can I put it?—managing to find yourself in the thick of things.'

He thought he glimpsed a faint flush tinge her cheeks. But she lifted her chin and said, 'In the thick of things? If that's how you choose to see it, then, yes. It's a habit of mine, perhaps an unfortunate one, but one I can't appear to break.' She met his gaze mildly, though he thought he glimpsed a pulse of agitation in her throat. 'And I've heard, of course,' she went on, 'that you've bought Calverley Hall. Now, that is what I'd call a spectacular way of returning to the area where you grew up and I offer my hearty congratulations.'

He felt his breath catch. Just for a moment he'd gone back in time, gone back seven years in fact. He was the blacksmith's son, and Isobel Blake, then sixteen years old, had been heiress to Calverley Hall and all its supposed wealth. He said, 'I would hardly go to the trouble of buying the place purely to make an impression, Miss Blake.'

The puppy wriggled a little; she stroked it, murmuring a calming word, then turned her clear green gaze on Connor again. 'Wouldn't you? Oh, but *I* would. If I were you.' Then she was dipping him a curtsy that was almost mocking and saying, 'With your permission, Mr Hamilton, I'll move on. I have certain purchases to make.'

'You're keeping the puppy?' He'd stepped forward impulsively. 'But how on earth are you going to look after him?'

Almost without realising it, he'd put his hand on her arm. The flowery frock she wore was short-sleeved and a jolt ran through him at the warm softness of her honey-gold skin. She looked at his hand and then at him, so he was able to see how her eyes flashed with some new emotion—anger? Swiftly he removed his hand and waited for her answer.

'Do you think,' she said levelly, 'that I'd leave him to starve?'

'No. But I had heard that you've fallen on hard times.'

'I'm not destitute. I do *work* for my living.'

His mouth curled. 'I'd heard that, too.' He saw her catch her breath; she knew exactly what he was thinking.

'Mr Hamilton,' she said politely, 'I'm disappointed in you. Once, you advised me never to heed the tattle of gossipmongers—'

And then she broke off, because the puppy had scrambled from her arms and was scurrying away, its rope leash trailing. 'Oh,' cried Elvie, 'catch him, he's escaped!'

And Connor suddenly realised that for a moment or two he'd almost forgotten little Elvie, because his past had come surging up to engulf him. Isobel Blake had come into his life again.

Not for any longer than I can help, he vowed to himself.

Elvie had already set off after the puppy, as had Isobel, but Connor quickly overtook them both with his long strides, then scooped the creature up and held it out to Isobel. She was forced to come close and he found himself breathing in her scent. *Lavender,* he remembered, *she always loved lavender...*

'My thanks,' she said. Holding the puppy firmly, she was clearly about to turn and go without another word. But then she became aware of Elvie, who was gazing longingly at the little creature.

'He's lovely, isn't he?' she said to her, in a completely different tone of voice to the one she'd used to *him*, Connor noted. 'Would you like to stroke him? That's it. He likes you. He trusts you.'

'Do you know,' Elvie said slowly, 'he's probably the sweetest thing I've ever seen.' Then she turned to Connor. 'Connor. Do you possibly think…?' Her voice trailed away.

Connor said quickly, 'Elvie, I haven't forgotten. I said you could have something to care for when we came to the country. A pony, maybe? We talked about it, didn't we?'

'But can I perhaps have a puppy instead? One like *this,* all white and small? Please? I promise, I would look after him so well! I'd feed him and brush him and take him for walks every day!'

And Connor, for a moment, was lost for a reply. Since her father died, Elvie had rarely spoken more than a few words at a time, even to her grandmother and Connor. There was that stammer, too. The doctors in London had pronounced it was a result of shock and grief. 'Give the child time,' they suggested, 'and perhaps a change of scene. Even so, it could take many months for her to recover. To react normally to her surroundings, and to other people.'

And yet here she was—still chatting to Isobel Blake!

'Do you think, if I had a small puppy like this one, that he would want to walk very far?' Elvie was asking Isobel eagerly. 'Do you think he'd mind being on a leash? And would he eat the same food that Connor's *big* dogs eat?'

'Goodness me,' he heard Isobel say with amusement, 'how many dogs has Connor got?'

'Oh, at least six. He likes big dogs very much, you see. But I would love a little one, like this…' Her voice trailed away longingly.

Connor broke in, very carefully. 'Elvie, the puppy is in the care of this lady. Her name is Miss Blake.'

Elvie said, 'I'm sorry if I'm being a nuisance, Miss Blake.' She looked crestfallen.

And then Miss Blake—Isobel—was saying to Elvie, 'You are very far from being a nuisance. In fact, you may have *this* puppy, if you wish. I think he would be very happy at the Hall. But only—' she glanced swiftly at Connor '—if Mr Hamilton agrees.'

Elvie turned to him in an agony of suspense.

'Impetuous as ever, Miss Blake,' he said softly.

He saw the flush of colour in her cheeks, but she looked unshaken. Connor met her steady gaze and went on, 'Nevertheless, I think your idea is a sound one. As Elvie pointed out, I've several dogs already—they're all considerably larger than this small fellow, but he'll soon make friends. And I promise you he'll be very well looked after.'

She nodded. Then, very carefully, she handed the small, fluffy creature to Elvie—and as Elvie cradled him, breathless with excitement, the puppy reached up to lick the little girl's nose. *Mud,* thought Connor. *Elvie's bound to get mud on her frock.* But what did that matter when she looked so happy?

'Well,' said Isobel Blake, 'I had best be on my way. But I'm very glad of the chance to wish you joy in your new abode, Mr Hamilton. Is it a permanent move, I wonder? Or will the Hall just be your occasional country retreat?'

'I'm not really sure yet. Most of my business is,

naturally, in London. But I hope to spend as much time here as possible.'

She nodded. 'So you won't be just a summer visitor, then, like the Plass Valley people?' She gave her bright, challenging smile. 'Perhaps,' she went on, 'if you're going to be here for a while, you might be able to do something for them?'

He frowned, not at all sure what she meant. '*Do* something for them?'

'Yes!' Though her smile was still bright, something in her eyes took him back suddenly to the old days at the forge, when as a girl she used to ride over to watch him at work. The girl from the big house—rich and inquisitive, and, he thought, very lonely.

'They come here, after all,' she was saying, 'to do vital work, yet they are treated like lepers. They need someone to defend them, Mr Hamilton!'

'Ah,' he said mildly. 'So you want me to become a local benefactor? Following the example set by your father, perhaps? I remember the summer when the travellers decided to stay on in their camp for a few days after the harvest was over, but your father set his men on them with dogs and whips—*just so they got the message*, I think he explained.'

She drew back as if it were she who'd been struck. Very quietly she said, 'Do you think I've forgotten? Don't you realise I would have stopped it, if I had had any way of doing so?'

'You're right,' he said. 'I apologise.' But he saw now that her cheeks were very pale and her breasts rose and fell rather rapidly beneath her thin cotton gown, as if she was struggling to control her emotions.

'No need to apologise.' She lifted her head almost

proudly. 'It was I who made a mistake, in even mentioning the subject of the travellers. But—' and now her voice was light again '—permit me to offer you a word of advice, Mr Hamilton. I think you'll very soon learn that no one around here *ever* talks about my father.'

She cast one last, almost wistful look at the puppy, then said to Elvie, 'You'll take good care of him, won't you? I feel certain you will.'

'Oh, yes! And thank you!' Elvie's so often sad eyes were shining with delight.

'What will you call him?'

It took Elvie only a moment. 'Little Jack!' she declared. 'I shall call him Little Jack—do you think that's all right?'

Isobel laughed again—that merry laugh he remembered so well. 'I think it's absolutely perfect.' She turned to Connor and gave him the slightest of nods. 'I wish you joy of Calverley Hall.'

And she left.

Chapter Two

Connor thought, *Damn it*. He'd guessed he would meet her some time, but not like this, with Elvie here. And even if they'd met when it was just the two of them, what was there to say? How could they talk about the past or—even worse—the present?

He glanced down at Elvie and realised she was clutching the puppy to her as if she still couldn't quite believe he was hers. Connor took him gently from her, then led Elvie to a leather trader's stall where he bought a proper leash and a red collar with a silver buckle. Connor swiftly adjusted them and handed the leash to Elvie, commenting, 'It's quite a responsibility, you know, Elvie, to own a dog. But I think you'll look after him marvellously.'

For a while longer they wandered round in the sunshine with Little Jack trotting alongside, to see what else the midsummer fête had to offer. But Connor felt as if the climax of the day had already come and gone. He was haunted by his memories of the past. Especially that night seven years ago, when Isobel Blake had ridden from the Hall to the blacksmith's cottage where Connor lived with his ailing father.

'Please, Connor. One of my father's mares is sick. I can't think of anyone else to ask. Will you help?'

It was past ten, but he'd ridden back to the Hall's stables with her in the dark and found the mare suffering from an infected hoof. Really, a qualified farrier was needed—but Connor knew as well as Isobel that no one would come out to work for Sir George Blake, because he was a drunken sot who never paid his bills. So, while Isobel held up the lantern, Connor cleaned out the hoof and poulticed it. He'd all but finished when Sir George arrived.

He'd tried to strike Connor. Connor, eighteen then, was easily strong enough to hold him off, but Sir George had said, 'I'll see you and your father ruined for this. What were you after? My horses? My money? My daughter?'

Connor had left the stables without a word. Two nights later, the forge and their adjoining home were set alight. Connor's father, already seriously ill, died just a week afterwards and Connor set off for London, where he made his fortune—but exactly the opposite had happened to Isobel. Her father took her to London when she was eighteen, presumably to find a rich husband, but instead she brought disgrace on herself by going to live with a middle-aged rake, Viscount Loxley, at his London residence near Hyde Park. Shortly afterwards her father died a bankrupt and Calverley Hall was lost. Her mother had died when Isobel was a child and she had no other family—but even so. Even so...

Society condemned her. *She must have had a choice,* Connor tried to tell himself. There was no need for her to ruin her reputation so thoroughly. And yet she'd done it. He'd not seen her since that night at the Calverley stables seven years ago, but he heard the London gossip. Heard how she'd become Loxley's youthful 'companion'. And when Loxley died, three years ago when Isobel was twenty, she'd moved back to Gloucestershire; she'd chosen to live with an artist, Joseph Molina, who occupied a farmhouse not far from Chipping Calverley and not far from the Hall.

This time, people muttered, *she's not even troubled to find a rich man to sell herself to.*

For some time, Connor found it almost impossible to reconcile the stories about Isobel Blake with the girl he once knew. He'd tried to excuse and understand her. But the evidence appeared indisputable.

Couldn't she have saved herself, *somehow*? It still smote him to remember her as a girl. There had always been something of the rebel about Isobel and once he'd admired her for it. Admired the way she used to ride up to the forge, her blonde hair windswept, her cheeks golden from the sun as she declared, 'I had to escape, Connor. I couldn't bear that house a moment longer! Am I a very great nuisance to you?'

Sometimes she was—but he'd always made time for her. And he hadn't thought twice about risking the forge and his livelihood that night long ago by coming to Calverley Hall at her bidding, to tend the sick horse. Well, none of it mattered any more. If she'd stood any chance at all of redeeming her reputation after Viscount Loxley's death, she'd buried it by moving in with her artist. Connor remembered how Haskins, his steward, had responded when asked if he ever saw anything of her in the neighbourhood. 'Miss Blake?' Haskins had spoken with distaste. 'She's set up house with a foreign painter fellow. She's shameless. Quite shameless.'

And yet, try as he might, Connor still couldn't banish her from his mind's eye. There was something about her that made her unforgettable, yes, even in her stupidly large hat and that shabby, clinging dress. She'd been outspoken, too, about the Plass Valley children. 'They need someone to defend them, Mr Hamilton!'

The Plass Valley people did trouble him—he'd noted their rough encampment on the day he arrived. But Isobel Blake troubled him even more. He felt his anger rising again, his sense of betrayal—because he'd thought she was different from her disreputable father, but he'd been wrong.

Now he gently ruffled Elvie's hair. 'Time to go home?' he suggested. 'Let's take Little Jack and introduce him to everyone, shall we?'

And he carried the tired little puppy with one hand, while holding Elvie's with the other, as they headed for the field at the far end of the fair where Tom waited with the carriage.

Connor took one last look around. This countryside was idyllic and he had a beautiful new home. The only trouble was—he'd forgotten how powerful were the memories that came with it.

Tom batted not an eyelid at the arrival of the puppy, but promptly took up his perch on the back of the phaeton as Connor gathered up the reins and set off at a spanking pace towards Calverley Hall. Connor pulled up the horses only slightly as they passed through the Hall's gates, nodding to the lodgekeeper there, then he let the carriage roll on, following the old road as it wound through ancient oak woods, then over the stone bridge that crossed the river.

Soon afterwards they were clattering into the front courtyard, but suddenly Connor was frowning. There were staff waiting for him there. A ridiculous formality, he thought, since he and Tom could have managed everything perfectly well! But no—there were grooms to take charge of the horses and a footman standing by the front door. And Haskins the steward stood stiffly to attention.

Most of the Hall's staff were completely new. The ones who'd stayed on since the old days, like Tom, were a rarity. Housemaids, footmen, gardeners and grooms had been hired by Connor's business secretary, Robert Carstairs, who'd also appointed the new steward Haskins, together with a housekeeper, Mrs Lett.

Carstairs was highly efficient. But sometimes, Connor regretted not conducting the interviews himself.

A young maid hurried forward for Elvie. 'There now, Miss Elvira! Your grandmother's waiting for you. Have you had a lovely day at the fair?'

Elvie nodded shyly, looking longingly at Little Jack; but Connor had the puppy firmly in hand. 'I'll take him to meet the other dogs,' he assured Elvie. 'The groom in charge of the kennels will see that he's made really welcome.' He stooped so he didn't tower over her and added, 'You tell your grandmother all about your trip out—yes?—and then in an hour or so, when Little Jack's settled, I'll take you to see him.'

So Connor led the puppy out to the stables, then returned to the house and headed for his study—only to find Robert Carstairs waiting for him.

'Some news, sir,' Carstairs said. 'And it's *good*

news. You're ahead in the race to provide iron for the new east London docks project, in Wapping. Your plans have been received most favourably. I have some letters to that effect here.'

'Good news indeed, Carstairs,' Connor agreed. But he wished Miles Delafield could have been here to share in the excitement. *I miss you, Miles,* Connor said silently to himself as he led the way into his study, where Carstairs began eagerly laying out the various documents on his desk.

'All we require now,' Carstairs was saying, 'before the contract is signed is government approval—and you should get *that* without any difficulty.'

'I certainly hope so,' said Connor mildly.

Carstairs glanced at him enquiringly. 'You seem a little quiet, sir. Did you enjoy the fair?'

'I enjoyed it well enough,' Connor replied. 'As a matter of fact, I met several people I used to know.'

'Anyone of importance?'

'No. Not at all.' And he started studying those papers again—but he could not stop thinking about Isobel Blake. She'd faced up to him almost defiantly this afternoon. Perhaps she hoped he might not have heard the stories whispered about the years she'd spent with Loxley. Perhaps she hoped he didn't know she was now living with some artist fellow...

No. She wouldn't be that stupid. She must realise he would have heard how she'd made a complete mess of her life and the best thing Connor could do was forget her. *Completely,* he reminded himself. And yet— her skin had felt so warm, so soft when he'd touched her arm.

He pulled out the chair from his desk and sat down.

'Right,' he said to Carstairs. 'The new docks. We need more figures—charts, maps, suppliers. Let's get to work, shall we?'

It had taken Isobel just over an hour to walk the three miles along the narrow track to the farmhouse that was now her home.

She opened the door into the big kitchen that took up most of the ground floor. At one end of this room was the black cooking range, surrounded by gleaming pots and pans; at the other end was Joseph Molina, sitting in front of his easel, which had a permanent place there. The room's numerous windows caught the light all day long and today the sun glittered on the half-finished canvases scattered around.

Joseph turned from his easel with a glad smile when she entered. 'Isobel! My dear, did you enjoy the fair?' He rose awkwardly, because his knees were stiff with rheumatism.

He was fifty-seven years old. Once, he had been a successful portrait artist, but when arthritis began to attack his hands, he was no longer capable of the precise detail the work required. Isobel had first met him in a London gallery three years ago. Loxley had died and she'd found herself homeless, with nothing to her name but a besmirched reputation.

At that gallery Joseph Molina had noticed her admiring one of his watercolour sketches of Gloucestershire and came over to her. 'I know this place,' Isobel had said, pointing to the picture. 'I grew up in the house that looks out over this valley.'

He'd told her he was thinking of moving there, permanently. 'It's so beautiful,' he said, 'and besides, there are practical reasons. I can't afford the rent on my London studio any more. My sister, Agnes, will be coming with me. Why don't you come, too?'

He was so kind to Isobel that day, at a time when she'd felt surrounded by enemies. She'd been moved almost to tears, but forced a smile, as she always did. 'I cannot expect your charity.'

'No charity,' he'd answered. 'I will find you work, believe me!'

So she'd moved back to Gloucestershire with him and Agnes. She'd learned how to grind pigments and mix them with linseed oil and how to care for his canvases and brushes. She knew, of course, what people whispered about her. She expected to make no new friends in Gloucestershire, but then, she'd only ever had one true friend here.

Connor. *Connor*. The way he'd looked at her today. He'd heard everything. Believed everything. And it hurt, more than she'd believed possible.

'Look,' she was saying now to Joseph. 'Look what I found for you.' And soon she was proudly showing him the sticks of charcoal and hog's-hair brushes she'd bought for him from a pedlar at the fair. 'I enjoyed the fair immensely,' she went on, forcing a merry smile, 'but you should have been there, too, Joseph. It wasn't the same without you.'

'Did you find anything of interest?'

'Yes, indeed.' She laid out the new brushes with care. 'For instance, I found an adorable stray puppy— together with some stray children. Oh, and I met a little girl. A rich and rather sad little girl.'

'Perhaps she reminded you of yourself, Isobel? When you were young?'

She lost her smile. 'Perhaps, yes. But the girl, Joseph! She was very sweet. I gave her the puppy and *that* made her happy.'

It had made her happy, too, Isobel realised—at least for a little while. Until she'd seen Connor Hamilton's face and the way he'd looked at her. Something had wrenched the breath from her lungs at that look of his and she still felt bruised—agonised—from it.

Forcing the memory down, she went to examine the painting on Molina's easel.

'This is beautiful!' she exclaimed. 'It's the sunset over the woods on Calverley Hill, isn't it?'

'It's showing promise,' he admitted grudgingly. 'But the greens I've used aren't quite right. Will you help me to mix the colours, Isobel? I need aquamarine, I think, and yellow ochre. Also a touch of cadmium, though I don't know where the cadmium has got to...'

How quickly she settled into her usual routine. Within minutes, she'd found his precious phials of pigment amidst the clutter, as she always did, and the time flew by, until a middle-aged lady in a grey dress and pinafore—his sister, Agnes—came bustling in and scolded mildly, 'Now, Joseph, it's time for you to be putting away those brushes of yours and getting yourself ready for your tea.'

'Agnes is quite right,' Isobel told him, 'so off you go and I'll put these things away for you.'

'Thank you,' he said. 'I don't know what I'd do without you, my dear.'

'Nor I you,' Isobel replied. She smiled again, though the minute he'd gone she felt despair washing through her.

She'd been stupidly rash to visit the fair today. To

pretend she didn't care about the whispers she heard everywhere.

'That's Sir George Blake's daughter there. Remember her? Just to think, she was once an heiress! But her father died a bankrupt and she went to live with a London rake when she was eighteen—yes, only eighteen! Then, when he died, she took up with this artist fellow—yes, they live just up the valley...'

Whenever she heard the talk, Isobel reminded herself she was content with her new life. The Molinas couldn't have been kinder; she had this home in the countryside she'd always loved and indeed she could almost call herself happy—until something happened, like at the fair today, when Connor Hamilton appeared.

She told the Molinas all about the fair while they ate their supper, describing the livestock tents and the entertainers, and the crowds who enjoyed it all so thoroughly. She told them just a little about the Plass Valley children, at which Agnes broke in, 'Do you mean the children of those travellers, who arrive every summer to gather in the hay?'

'Yes, I do,' Isobel answered. 'And they're lovely, but a little high-spirited.'

She went on to explain to Agnes about the runaway puppy—they both loved the story of the lively creature shaking mud all over the Reverend Malpass. At around nine she washed up the dishes and tidied everything away, then she took a candle to her upstairs room under the thatched eaves. She closed her door and leaned against it.

Then, and only then, did she allow the smile she'd put on for her kind friends to fade away.

She closed the curtains on the fast-gathering darkness outside, then by the light of the candle she gazed at herself in the mirror hung on a nail in the wall. Her dress was made of cheap cotton, the kind any country girl might wear, but she realised now that it was too tight around the bodice. Although her figure was slim, her breasts were full and the way the often-washed fabric of the gown clung to them made her look cheap. And that wasn't all.

Her skin was tinted unfashionably gold from the sun, in a way no lady would permit, and her long, obstinately curling fair hair had tumbled as usual from its pins. Try as she might, her efforts to tidy it never lasted long. All in all, she looked like a girl out for fun—a certain *kind* of fun. Once she'd been the heiress to Calverley Hall—but now her position in society was lowly indeed. Here she was, twenty-three years old and completely without prospects, yet she'd always told herself she was content. But today, at the fair, her safe little world had been rocked to its foundations.

Over the last few years she'd heard all the gossip about Connor Hamilton. In fact, she often suspected the locals took great delight in repeating it in her hearing, loudly, in the town or the market place. She'd heard what must be every single detail of how Connor had risen in the world—the news had filtered back, month after month, year after year.

'He's living in London—yes, the big city. He's proving himself mighty skilled. He's become partner in a major iron manufactory and he's making himself extremely rich into the bargain...'

When someone told her—with more than a little satisfaction—that Connor was buying Calverley Hall, she started hearing fresh flurries of speculation. 'He's weary of London,' people said. Or: 'Now that he has that little girl and her grandmother to look after, he must feel that a country residence would do them both good.'

He was returning to the neighbourhood he grew up in—only instead of a blacksmith's forge, he would be living in a mansion. But hadn't he realised that *she* still lived nearby?

She would never forget the coldness in his blue eyes today at the fair as he registered her presence. She felt branded by it. *Let him think the worst of me,* she thought, *like everyone else!* She was happy here, with the Molinas; she loved helping Joseph with his paintings, she enjoyed his and Agnes's gentle company.

But Connor Hamilton was back. And a chill of fear caught at her heart, because he had become quite formidable in a way that made her pulse pound faster and her lungs ache with the sudden need for air.

How she'd first met him, she couldn't even really remember. It was as though he'd always been there and whenever she could she used to ride over to the forge and watch him as he mended ploughshares or shoed horses. She used to ask him question after question about his work and he didn't seem to mind. She felt *safe* with Connor and, although he said little, she felt that he liked her. Even on that awful night when she'd got Connor into so much trouble seven years ago, he'd told her it wasn't her fault.

Since then, he'd become a rich man. An iron master. They said that to keep his hand in he still forged iron himself in the vast foundries that belonged to him—and, looking at him, she could well believe it, because his clothes, though clearly expensive, couldn't hide the innate strength of his body. A typical rich London gentleman he was not; his face and hands were tanned from the open air; his black hair was thick and over-long for fashion and his deep blue eyes missed nothing, and were fooled, she guessed, by nobody.

The locals speculated that he'd returned to his Gloucestershire roots to find himself a suitable bride. Isobel thought differently. She guessed that Connor Hamilton, poor boy made good, had returned to the place of his birth for revenge on all those who'd thwarted him. As for his feelings towards her, she'd seen how his eyes had widened almost in incredulity when he realised who she was. And how they narrowed again with contempt, a moment later.

Scorn—that was what he felt now, for Isobel Blake. And who could blame him?

Not her, that was for sure. Not her. But his scorn was not deserved.

Chapter Three

One week later

'So,' said Laura Delafield, putting her embroidery to one side and letting a spark of mischief twinkle in her eyes. 'You're intent on refurbishing the Hall in its entirety, are you, Connor dear? I do hope that you're not going to disappoint too many people with your surprisingly excellent taste.'

It was a little before noon and Connor had come to join Laura in her favourite room, which had large south-facing windows overlooking the garden. *Surprisingly excellent taste.* He felt his breath catch for a moment, so primed was he to fend off cutting comments about his lowly background, but no insult was intended here—this was Laura, grandmother to Elvie and mother to his former business partner, Miles. Though confined to a bath chair nowadays, she was lively, shrewd and entirely lovable.

He'd first met Laura when he was hired by Miles in London and he'd quickly become enormously appreciative of her gentle wisdom. The Hall—neglected both by Sir George Blake and by a succession of tenants in the last five years—needed complete refurbishing and Connor knew the entire neighbourhood would be watching to see if he was filling the house with the kind of pretentious rubbish they would expect of an upstart like him.

His mouth curled slightly, but he answered with a smile, 'I rather fear I'm going to disappoint the locals, Laura, since my tastes are remarkably staid. You think I should have gone for a livelier style? Russian, perhaps?'

'Not Russian, my dear,' Laura pronounced. 'That is quite *passé*. No, these days you need to turn to Egypt, to be truly *nouveau riche*.' She looked rather dreamy-eyed. 'As much gilt and jade as you like, with painted pharaohs all over the place…'

He chuckled. 'I'm sorry, but I'm going to give the neighbours absolutely nothing to talk about.'

'Oh,' she replied, 'you've already given them plenty to talk about, believe me. For example, the Vicar called this morning, while you were out.'

'Thank God, then, for my excellent sense of timing. What did Malpass want?'

'He told me that he wished to speak to you about the travellers and their encampment in Plass Valley.' She eyed him with care. 'He feels they *"lower the tone of the parish"*. Those were his exact words.'

Connor fought down a stab of irritation. 'The Reverend Malpass has a short memory. They've been coming to Plass Valley every summer, for as long as I can remember. How would the farmers reap their hay harvest without them?'

'The Vicar,' said Laura mildly, 'claims it's the travellers' children who are the chief problem. He says they're running wild and being cheeky to the ladies of the village who try to rebuke them.'

He sighed. 'Have the ladies been complaining to you, too, Laura?'

'Only in passing.' Her cheeks dimpled with amusement. 'As a matter of fact, the local ladies have something far more pressing on their minds when they make their morning calls on me. Without exception, they have daughters of a marriageable age. You get my drift?'

Connor groaned. 'Heaven help me, I do.' He seized on a fragment of hope. 'But didn't any of them, when referring to me, mention the word "upstart"?'

'Not a whisper.'

'Then there's nothing for it, Laura. I shall have to pretend I already have a fiancée in London. Either that, or feign a dissolute past…'

'*Feign* a dissolute past, dear?' she mocked gently.

He laughed, acknowledging the mild correction by raising one hand in a gesture of submission. Laura pretended to study her embroidery again, then said, after a pause, 'You know, Connor, that marriage does have its compensations. Children being not the least of them.'

And just for a moment Connor could hear the heartache behind her gentle words. Laura, a widow for many years, had no other children but Miles, who had been Connor's mentor, friend and business partner for years. And now she'd lost *him*. A tragedy for all of them, yet Laura was, thank God, as loving and generous-spirited as ever and a vital presence in the life of her granddaughter, Elvie.

'Laura,' he said, 'if I could find someone like you, the decision to marry would be easy, believe me.'

She was laughing. 'Connor,' she said, 'you ridiculous flatterer. But seriously, I've heard—'

'You'll have heard,' he broke in, 'all kinds of nonsense.'

'I've heard something a little more than nonsense lately.' She placed a few more stitches, but now she raised her eyes to his. 'I've heard talk, in fact, about Miss Helena Staithe.'

Connor walked slowly to the window overlooking the sunlit gardens and turned to face her. 'You're right, Laura, to assume that at some point I'll have to consider the matter of marriage a little more seriously.'

'Perhaps you will,' Laura said teasingly, 'if only to put a damper on the talk Miss Staithe's friends are spreading that perhaps your interest in her is becoming significant.'

He suppressed an exclamation of impatience. 'People will always talk. Of course, there are strong business connections with her family—you'll remember as well as anyone, Laura, how Helena's father sponsored Miles's projects in the early days.'

'Of course I remember. Her father was a Member of Parliament, was he not? And now Helena's brother has taken over his seat.'

'He has.' Connor frowned a little. 'But whether my obligation to the Staithe family stretches to marriage on my part is rather questionable. To be honest, a marriage of convenience holds little appeal.'

'You mean,' said Laura lightly, 'that you're waiting for the love of your life?'

'Does such a thing exist?'

She hesitated. 'I believe so, yes. But then, perhaps I was lucky... Oh, Connor, I was completely forgetting!' She put down her needlework again. 'You told me you had to return to London tonight for an important meeting. You must have all kinds of things to sort out and here I am, delaying you with my chatter!'

He laughed. 'The meeting's not that important,' he assured her. 'In fact, I've decided to send Carstairs instead—it's simply a matter of delivering some proposed figures to my chief shareholders.'

'You're hoping for their support in this new project of yours—the docks?'

'That's right and I'm pretty certain I'll get it. But, Laura, as it happens I've got another matter on my mind and it's something I need to deal with here. A few minutes ago you mentioned the Plass Valley children and now's perhaps the time to tell you my plan. You see...' he paused for a moment '...I'm thinking of setting up a school for them.'

'A *school*? For the children of the travellers?'

'Exactly. It would be for the summer season only, of course, since after that they'll be moving on to their next place of work. The older children are kept busy helping their parents with the hay harvest—but for the little ones, there's absolutely nothing to do.'

'Except get into mischief,' said Laura thoughtfully. 'Yes, I see. But—a school?'

'It wouldn't be a very formal affair. The children could be taught basics, like the alphabet and some simple arithmetic.' He was surprising himself by the enthusiasm with which he spoke. 'I realise, of course, that plenty of local people will say I'm wasting my time. But I've met these children and they're not malicious, they're just full of energy—energy that needs direction.'

'So where exactly would you hold this school?'

And he knew he had her approval.

'There's the old chapel,' he said, 'in the grounds of the Hall—you can see it from here, if you look out of the window. It's not been used for years, but I've examined it pretty carefully and I think I could easily have it made suitable.'

'And who would you appoint as their teacher?'

'I'm not sure yet. I need a person who's not just well educated, but is someone the children will actually *like*.' He paused. 'Laura, you know how much I value your opinion. You don't think it's a dreadful idea?'

'On the contrary,' she answered. 'I think it's one of the best ideas you've ever had, Connor. And—'

She broke off, because just at that moment Elvie came running in and Laura held out her hands to her. 'Darling Elvie. I think you've come to remind me it's time for lunch?'

'Yes, Grandmother, I have.' Elvie hesitated, then turned to Connor. 'Connor, *after* lunch, p-please may I play with Little Jack in the garden?'

Her speech was still slightly hesitant—even with himself and Laura. But she was, he could see, shyly eager for the pleasures to come. He crouched a little so he was nearer her height. 'Very well, mischief. You take Jack out after you've eaten your meal and teach him some tricks—oh, and obedience! Don't forget that!'

'I will,' she said earnestly. 'He really will be the best dog *ever*.'

By then a footman had appeared to wheel Laura

through to the dining room and Elvie followed. But at the last minute, Laura turned her head. 'Connor, are you joining us?'

'Very soon—I have one or two things to see to first.'

'Just like Miles,' she said. 'Don't let time be your master, though, Connor. Promise me?' Then—without waiting for his answer—she and Elvie were gone and Connor was alone.

Don't let time be your master.

Miles Delafield had confided to Connor last year that he intended to cut down his own workload in the near future. He'd talked of buying an estate in the country, with acres of land and gardens for his mother and Elvie to enjoy. A heart attack out of the blue had put paid to Miles's plans, but Connor had resolved to see that Elvie and Laura would live out that dream of his. Though what was Connor's dream? What did he really want for himself?

He would never forget those early days when—still bitter from the loss of the forge and the death so soon afterwards of his ailing father—he'd left Calverley as an eighteen-year-old to take the road for London. He'd headed straight for the eastern end of the city, where the new iron foundries were spilling over into the flat Essex countryside, and there he'd tramped around begging for work.

When Miles Delafield took him on, Connor laboured at the foundry as an apprentice by day. But by night he studied and Miles, realising his eagerness to learn, lent him books—Miles owned volume after volume on metallurgy and engineering, and Connor had read them till past midnight, every night, until his eyes burned and his brain was dizzy with new-found knowledge.

And his dreams grew bigger. He didn't just want to be a foundryman. He wanted to make sure that no one would look down on him again—*ever*.

Now he stood by the window of the garden room in Calverley Hall, gazing out at the idyllic landscape. Now no one dared to snub the iron master Connor Hamilton. But should he have come back here? Was it ever wise, to revive memories of the past?

He'd thought it would give him satisfaction, to re-visit all the remembered places of his youth. But there was one memory—one person—he'd not reckoned on.

Isobel Blake.

Just how old he'd been when he first met her he couldn't exactly recall—fifteen, sixteen, perhaps? By then Connor's father was ill and Connor had taken on most of the work of the forge himself. Isobel used to arrive on horseback, as if by chance. 'I was just passing,' she would say.

She was lonely, he guessed. He also knew that she shouldn't even be out on her own, let alone come to visit him. But she didn't seem to care. She loved to watch him work, especially when he worked with the horses; she would linger there in the forge's yard and Connor hadn't minded.

There was no arrogance to her, no concern for her position or her appearance. Her fair hair was always carelessly pulled back in a loose plait and her clothes were often dusty from the stables. He'd never thought of her as a nuisance, even on that last night, when she'd pleaded with him to visit the sick horse at her father's stables and her father had been so angry at Connor's so-called interference that he'd ordered the forge to be destroyed.

She'd tried to defend Connor to her father. And he'd realised, last week at the fair, that she still had the utmost courage; he'd seen it in the way she had stood up to the Vicar over those children. She still had rebellion in her eyes and fire in her blood. He couldn't forget, either, the way that Elvie had instantly taken to her...

Suddenly he wasn't seeing the view from the window any more—he was seeing Isobel Blake. *Children.* She liked them and they liked her. They took to her. Trusted her. Wouldn't she make a good teacher for his school? But her reputation made the notion impossible. She was living with that artist as his mistress! And there was something else—another complication that troubled Connor far more than he cared to admit.

His first reaction, on being close to her, was to feel a harsh and unwelcome stab of desire. Something that couldn't be sated by mere physical contact, because it was accompanied by another urge that was perhaps even more disturbing. He wanted to *talk* to her, to get to know what was really going on beneath that bright and defiant veneer of hers.

She'd deliberately allowed herself to fall just about as far down the social ladder as it was possible to fall. But he, Connor, could so easily conjure up the startling green-gold of her eyes and the luxuriant blonde of her hair as it fell in unruly waves from beneath that absurd bonnet. Could imagine running his hands through it, letting it fall over her bare shoulders...

Fool. It was a waste of precious time even to think of her. Fortunately, he had plenty to keep him busy—if all went well, there was this new contract for the

London docks, for a start. And while he was here, he was determined to set up a summer school for the Plass Valley children—which meant finding someone suitable to run it.

He'd already spoken to the ever-efficient Carstairs about the matter. 'I would suggest an advertisement, sir,' was Carstairs's response.

And so, two days later, an advertisement appeared in the *Gloucestershire Herald*.

Required—temporary tutor for small group of children, to start as soon as possible. Applications to be returned to Mr Connor Hamilton, Calverley Hall.

A week later, Connor sat behind the big desk in his study interviewing one by one the five short-listed applicants with Laura at his side. The candidates turned out to be a diverse bunch, ranging from a plump farmer's daughter who couldn't glance at Connor without blushing, to a retired parson whom Connor assumed, by the state of his nose, to have a drink problem. Connor asked each of them the same questions. 'Since the summer school will be for a few weeks only, what do you consider the most vital topics to be covered? Do you think there should be an element of enjoyment in every lesson? Or is learning a matter of hard work, always?'

What a revelation the answers were. 'The children need to be taught their place, with a good birching every now and then,' one young man cheerfully suggested. He had, he informed them, taught at an expensive day school in Bath for two years. 'After all,' he went on, 'you can't make a silk purse out of a sow's ear, can you?'

Laura glanced at Connor, waiting for the explosion. But Connor merely rose rather abruptly from his chair. *Interview over.* 'Thank you,' he said. 'That will be all.'

There was an ex-governess, too, who happened to catch sight of Elvie out on the lawn playing with Little Jack. 'I take it the girl out there is one of the tinkers' children? Of course, if I was in charge, behaviour like that would cease instantly!'

Connor followed her glance out of the window— Elvie did look untidy, he realised. She was in an old frock and pinafore, and her pigtails had long since come undone. But out there with her puppy she looked as happy as Connor had seen her for months.

'That child,' he said, 'happens to be my ward.'

He caught Laura smothering a smile; the woman's face turned a startling red. 'Oh! Oh, I see. Well, of course, Mr Hamilton, I didn't mean…'

'I have to thank you for revealing your feelings so frankly,' said Connor. 'I have no more questions. Good day to you.'

It was clear, when they came to the end of the interviews, that not one of the candidates was suitable by any stretch of the imagination. And Connor saw that Laura looked tired. Summoning her maid and thanking Laura for her assistance, he suggested she take a rest for an hour or so; then he went out into the garden to join Elvie. She ran towards him with the puppy bounding at her heels. She looked anxious.

'Connor,' she said. 'Those p-people who were here. You're not going to choose one of *them* to work at the school you told me about, are you?'

He'd already explained to her his idea for the school. 'You saw them, then? They were a rather strange bunch, weren't they, little one? Don't worry. I don't think any of them will be in charge of my school—if, indeed, I manage to ever start it.'

'I hope you do,' she said seriously. 'I'm lucky because I've got Grandmother to help me with my lessons—but they've got no one.'

'I'll find someone,' he promised. 'Someone kind. And fun.'

She nodded, then her puppy came rushing up to drop his new ball at her feet, tail wagging. And Elvie was off, running across the lawn with Little Jack racing ahead.

Connor watched. *Someone kind. And fun.* But—who?

'The children must have five hours a day at least of lessons,' one of the would-be teachers had declared.

Five hours? Connor's raised eyebrows had expressed mild astonishment.

'Indeed,' the woman had gone on, 'that is the absolute minimum required to bring an element of civilisation to people of their kind, Mr Hamilton!'

Of their kind. Connor walked back into the house and settled himself again in his study. Perhaps the whole idea was entirely foolish—after all, what difference could a few weeks of learning make to children who would be moving on in no time?

But then again, it might make all the difference in the world. Look at his own past. He'd been thrown out of Malpass's church school early on, but Connor's father owned some books—rare indeed in a poor household like theirs. There'd been travel stories and poems,

and tales of ancient history, which Connor had read by
the light of a tallow candle. He'd found he had a great
hunger for learning that was awakened once again
when he was given access to Miles Delafield's fine
library in London.

Who was to say there wasn't another child like him
somewhere amongst the travellers' families? A child
who would grasp at the tiniest seed of learning?

A knock at his door announced the entry of
Haskins, the steward. 'Sir,' Haskins said, 'some of
the furniture you ordered from Gloucester is starting
to arrive. Could you come and examine the items, and
approve their condition?'

Connor rose and followed him out of the study.
Haskins was precise and orderly, but he still wasn't
sure he actually *liked* the fellow. And when Connor
reached the reception hall, he looked around with a
snort of disbelief. Had he really ordered so much stuff?
All around were not only chairs, tables and sofas, but
also a colourful array of rugs, pictures and mirrors.
Haskins had the delivery notes in his hand and, with
daunting precision, he pointed out each item together
with its price and place of manufacture.

Yes, Connor realised, he *had* ordered all this—after
all, he'd bought himself a great mansion and it had to
be furnished. With a sigh, he took the delivery notes
from Haskins and soon enough everything was dealt
with and signed for. The tradesmen, who'd been hovering anxiously, doffed their caps and hastened back
out to their waiting vehicles.

'And now, sir…' Haskins began.

'I know,' Connor said. 'You want to be told where
everything is going.'

Haskins inclined his head. 'It would be good, sir, to place each item as soon as possible in the exact place for which it was intended. And I have a plan...'

'I thought you might,' said Connor.

Haskins was flourishing a large sheet of paper. 'You'll see, sir, that I've drawn a map of each floor. Do I have your permission to ask the footmen to proceed?'

'You do indeed,' said Connor heartily. And Haskins, in an absolute fervour of efficiency, began to give instructions to his team of footmen.

Connor was assailed once more by one of those moments of doubt that still came upon him rather too frequently. Was this really what he wanted? To be surrounded by belongings and an army of servants? He reminded himself he'd done it for Elvie and Laura—but Elvie was happiest running around the garden, with her new puppy. And Laura—well, she was happy if Elvie was happy.

Perhaps, he thought suddenly, it would be different if he was married and had children of his own to fill the place. He tried to picture Helena here—her brother Roderick Staithe had been making it clear to Connor for some time that an offer of marriage from Connor would be more than acceptable. There were subtle hints and not-so-subtle insinuations at every meeting of the two men.

'Of course, Connor,' Staithe liked to say grandly, 'our father, as a Member of Parliament, was largely responsible for helping Miles to set up his first major projects.'

The implication being, of course, that Roderick—who'd inherited his father's Parliamentary seat—could do the same for Connor. In other words, get him the official backing that was necessary these days for any large building scheme. But Connor relished his independence. He didn't want to be trapped, for the simple reason that he'd fought so hard for his freedom.

He'd been gazing abstractedly at a rather garish Chinese cabinet—*good God, had he really ordered that?*—when he realised a young woman was standing in the doorway, looking uncertainly around her.

He blinked.

It was Isobel Blake.

Chapter Four

The dealers, as they departed, had left the big front doors wide open. The sunshine was bright outside, highlighting the rainbow colours of Isobel's cotton frock and the pink ribbons decorating her overlarge straw bonnet. Already Haskins was speaking sharply to her; Connor walked steadily towards them both, just as Haskins turned to him.

'This person, sir—' Haskins indicated Isobel '—says she needs to speak with you urgently. I am, of course, telling her that you are extremely busy at present—'

Connor broke in. 'That will be all, Haskins. Please leave us.'

He was looking at Isobel as he spoke. Her eyes met his, dark-lashed, green-gold and defiant; he remembered once more the midsummer fair and the way the sun had glittered on her long blonde hair and her cheap dress. Remembered, too, all the things he'd heard about her.

Could she be a possible schoolteacher? No. She was a walking scandal.

'Miss Blake,' he said coolly. 'To what do I owe this honour?'

He saw how she immediately registered the sarcasm of that last word—*honour*. She blinked, then looked at the footmen heaving chairs and oversized mirrors up the stairs. She turned back to him. 'Oh, dear. I'm intruding. Aren't I?'

'You are,' he agreed.

She caught her breath and he thought he saw a flash of vulnerability in her eyes, though it was gone in a minute. 'I couldn't think,' she said at last, 'of anyone else to tell.' And she smiled and shrugged, but he saw how she was clasping her hands together and her voice was a little too bright.

This was how she used to be, he remembered suddenly, *when she used to visit me at the forge. Making a huge effort to hide her emotions, after being upset by something her unspeakable father had said or done.*

'You may as well tell me,' he answered coolly, 'since you're here.'

She nodded, drew in a deep breath and said, 'It's about the children.'

He felt a stab of surprise that her thoughts had been running in exactly the same direction as his. 'You mean the Plass Valley children?'

'I do. The older children have been helping their parents to gather in the hay at Mr Bryanson's farm. But the little ones—they were playing by the river further down the valley this morning, doing no one any harm, when some of the village men came up to them and threatened them, saying…saying…'

She'd lost control of her voice, he realised. 'Saying what?' he prompted.

She steadied herself. 'These men said they were filthy scum and they should get back to where they came from. The children ran, of course. They were very frightened. I'd been shopping in the village and came across them as I walked home…' Her voice faltered again, but she steadied herself and carried on. 'Some of the little ones were crying. The older ones told me what had happened. I didn't know what to do, to be honest, but then I remembered how you defended them at the fair. And I thought you might be able to think of some way to help them, because…' Her voice trailed away.

'Because I was once considered filthy scum myself?' he said levelly.

He saw her flinch. Then she braced herself again and said steadily, 'I'm sorry. Clearly I made a mistake. I shouldn't have come here.' She glanced at the footmen hauling a large *chaise longue* through to the drawing room. 'I can see you have far more important things to see to. Good day to you, Mr Hamilton.' And she turned to go.

'Wait,' he said. 'Were any of the children hurt?'

She pushed back a strand of hair that had strayed from under her bonnet. 'Two little girls grazed their knees as they tried to run away and the youngest boy has a sprained wrist from where a man swung him around. I took them to the doctor in the village, who very reluctantly tended their injuries. But when I asked him if he would help me take action against those— those bullies, he refused. *Nobody* will help them!'

He said, quietly, 'You must have had to pay the doctor. Did you?'

Her eyes flashed. 'Yes, but it really does not matter!'

'Wait a moment,' he cut in, 'while I fetch money

to repay you and to perhaps buy some food for their families.'

She flushed at that and her eyes sparkled defiance. 'Oh,' she said, 'you *are* taking your role as lord of the manor seriously, aren't you? It's very generous of you to offer charity—but they need rather more than charity, Mr Hamilton!'

'I believe you told me so at the fair,' he said.

'Yes, and I'll say it again. They need someone to defend them! And I realise—'

She broke off. She was clenching her hands, he saw. Little spots of colour burned in her cheeks, and beneath that worn and shabby frock her breasts heaved. Clearly she was making a huge effort to calm herself and when she spoke again her voice was so quiet he had to strain to hear her.

'I realise,' she went on, 'that I am probably the last person on earth who should come to you asking for favours.' She lifted her head, and he saw her green eyes were very clear. 'But I do *not* want your money. In fact, I can see that by coming here today I have made another grave mistake and I've already taken up quite enough of your time. I will bid you good day, Mr Hamilton!'

'Stop,' Connor said urgently. *'Wait.'* But she was already hurrying down the steps, that ridiculous pink-beribboned bonnet bobbing as she set off along the drive.

He could have pursued her. But instead he stood there, frozen by memories. *I realise that I'm probably the last person on earth who should come to you asking for favours.*

In his youth he had not borne her any dislike for

being Sir George Blake's daughter—on the contrary, he used to feel the utmost pity for her. But since then, she'd allowed herself to sink so low that even the local tattle-mongers had grown weary of spreading her story.

Yet *still* she was as outspoken as ever. And those clothes!

He had no need to think about her any further. She was nothing to him, of no importance whatsoever; the whole community scorned her. And yet she was the only one of that community to defend those children. She was the only one with the courage to care...

No. He rubbed his clenched fist against his forehead. The faint lavender scent of her lingered in the hall and it was delicate, it was haunting, it made him think things he definitely *shouldn't* be thinking. Like—how sweet she would be to kiss. And to hold, and to caress. And suddenly a vivid picture shot into his mind of him exploring the satiny, secret places of her slender body, possibly on that very bed the footmen were struggling to get up the stairs just now...

'Mr Hamilton, sir!' Haskins's voice banished Connor's vision in an instant. 'Mr Hamilton,' went on Haskins importantly, bustling towards him, 'there are several items of furniture we need to ask you about. We're not quite sure where they belong.'

Again Connor tried to rub the tension from his forehead. Where did *he* belong, exactly? And why did he, all of a sudden, feel so damned dissatisfied with this new life of his? Why did he feel right now as if the acquisition of wealth and power were like prison chains, in which he was becoming more and more entangled?

'Very well, Haskins,' he replied at last. 'Lead the way.'

* * *

Isobel hurried down the drive, feeling quite dizzy with dismay. She had been stupid beyond words to have come to the Hall and Connor Hamilton had looked at her with a coldness that had chilled her blood. She lashed herself inwardly as she walked, remembering with a shiver how his eyes had run with casual contempt over her flowered print frock, her face and her bare arms. All she'd wanted was for him to help the children—because she'd thought he might care.

And all she wanted now was to be as far away from here as possible. But the children! Their plight had upset her desperately and, while wondering last night what on earth she could do to help them, her mind had suddenly flown to Connor. She'd hoped that whatever he thought of *her,* he might still feel pity for the children.

She'd tried to say as much to Joseph and Agnes before setting out on this visit, though they'd expressed strong doubt, saying they'd heard Mr Hamilton was a hard and a ruthless man. But Isobel had carried on regardless—and she was wrong. She should have heeded the Molinas' warning. Now that she was safely away, she paused to glance back at the Hall, with all its daunting immensity, and remembered that this was the place she'd once called home, though in truth she'd grown to hate it.

Billy, who drove the carrier's cart, had dropped her off at the lodge gates. He'd told her he had deliveries to make to a couple of farms farther on. 'But I'll pick you up on my way back, Miss Isobel,' he'd promised cheerily. 'I'll be here at the gates around noon.'

She was early, so she decided to leave the broad

drive and take a slightly longer route through Calverley's parkland. That would, she hoped, give her time to calm herself before meeting Billy. But as she approached a woodland dell, she was halted in her tracks by a child's voice calling, 'Bring it to me, Jack! Good boy! Good boy!'

Hesitating between the trees, she glimpsed Elvie, throwing sticks for her puppy. The little girl's voice was steady, but Isobel could see that her cheeks were wet with tears.

It's none of my business, Isobel told herself. *It's got nothing to do with me. I've done enough interfering for one day.* But the puppy was already scampering towards her and now Elvie had seen her, too. 'It's you,' she exclaimed, 'the lady from the fair! Little Jack, look who it is!'

She'd scooped her puppy up and was burying her nose in his fur, but not before Isobel saw that tears were trickling down her cheeks. Isobel touched her arm gently. 'My dear. Why are you crying?'

The little girl's tears welled up anew as she gazed up at Isobel. 'It's because I—I miss my father so!'

Isobel wanted to hug her, hard. Instead she led her to a nearby bench and sat next to her, while Little Jack settled forlornly at his young mistress's feet. Isobel was trying to remember everything she'd heard about Elvira Delafield. *Her mother died a month after she was born; her father died of a heart attack six months ago. Her grandmother is her only living relative...*

'I think,' Isobel said, 'that you're very brave, Elvie. And I'm really glad you've got Jack to keep you company. You've got your grandmother, too, haven't you?'

Elvie was trying to rub her tears away. 'Yes. Grandmother is lovely, but she gets tired and sometimes I feel lonely.' She swallowed a fresh sob.

Isobel looked around. 'Do you know, I remember a girl who once lived here.'

'At the Hall?'

'Yes. She was sometimes lonely, too, but she did have one friend. He might not have realised it, but she depended on him, a great deal.'

Elvie was gazing up at her. 'And is she *still* friends with him?'

Isobel felt something hot and tight gathering inside her. 'Sadly, no. You see, Elvie, sometimes things happen as you get older. There was a misunderstanding. But when she was young and alone, he was there for her. And she will never, ever forget that.'

Elvie was wide-eyed. 'And has this girl got friends *now*?'

'Yes, she has.' Isobel was thinking of Agnes and Joseph. 'Just like you, Elvie. You have people who care for you very much and always will. Your grandmother, and Connor, too—I could see how good he was to you at the fair—'

She broke off, because she'd suddenly realised they were visible here from the upper storey of the Hall and she thought she'd glimpsed a face at one of the windows.

'I must go now.' She rose swiftly from the bench. 'But as I said, I'm sure Connor wants the very best for you. I'm sure he's extremely kind.'

And Isobel left, with her own words echoing again and again in her head.

He *used* to be kind. He'd been her secret hero. But things had changed—he was a successful man now, with power and money. As for her, whatever kind of future she'd expected for herself, it wasn't this.

Since London, she'd told herself she didn't care in the least what people thought of her. But everything had changed, catastrophically, that day when she'd met Connor at the fair. It was the same again today, when she confronted him so disastrously in the place that used to be her home. She'd felt her carefully built defences crumble away as she stumbled over one word after another. It was plain that he'd formed his own rock-solid opinion of her character, and he'd never given her one chance to defend herself.

She had made a terrible mistake visiting the Hall. And her nightmare day wasn't over yet, because as soon as Billy dropped her off at the Molinas' farmhouse, Agnes came hurrying out. 'Oh, Isobel!' She had clearly been weeping.

'Agnes, what's happened?' Isobel felt her heart thudding. 'Is Joseph ill?'

'No. But we've had a letter from our landlord, saying that our rent is overdue. And this is our last warning!'

'But surely Joseph always pays the rent on time?'

Agnes's eyes brimmed with fresh tears. 'He's just told me that he hasn't paid it for two months—he hasn't the money! And the landlord's letter says the next letter we get will be from his lawyer. Oh, Isobel, if we have to leave here, I don't know where we'll go, how we'll live...'

Isobel put her arm round her. 'Agnes. Don't cry. I'm sure there will be *something* we can do.'

But her heart was pounding with dread.

Chapter Five

Connor Hamilton sat in his study and tried to concentrate on the papers piled up on his desk. Normally, concentration came easily to him. This time—it was absurdly difficult.

He would not, in a million years, have described himself as a sentimental man. But there was something in Isobel Blake's defiant demeanour—a hint of vulnerability, almost fragility—that had caught him completely unawares.

Two encounters, in just over a fortnight. Of course, he'd known it was quite possible he would see her again on returning to Calverley. Local rumour used ugly words about Isobel Blake. *'This time she's not even troubled to find a rich man to sell herself to.'* And yet Connor had felt entangled in some nameless emotion as he'd watched her leave the Hall earlier, with her head held high under that showy bonnet. He'd felt something that was partly pity and partly something else he really didn't want to identify—because it *complicated* things.

'Wait,' he'd tried to call after her.

But she either hadn't heard him or chose not to, because she'd walked steadily out of the door and down the drive and out of his life again. Connor uttered some unseemly words of frustration. Beneath her shabby clothes and that false brightness, he guessed there was a protective wall she'd put up around herself to prevent anyone from getting too close. As if she was expecting fresh hurt or insult at every step.

Connor ground his fist against his forehead. It should have been his final triumph to return to Calverley Hall as its master. Indeed, it *was* a triumph—so why should a foolish girl from his past trouble him so?

He was certainly shaken by the spirited way in which she'd spoken up for the Plass Valley children. The trouble was, it wasn't just her words that had affected him. She'd appealed for his help for them, while apparently completely unaware that some strands of her lovely blonde hair were escaping from beneath that bonnet of hers and there was even a golden dusting of flower pollen on the tip of her nose, from where she'd no doubt paused to breathe in the scent of some flowers in the gardens as she'd marched her way to his front door.

He briefly compared her to the rich girls who were thrust in front of him in London. Girls who'd probably spent all day preparing their gowns, their jewels, their hair. They made him impatient with their vanity and silly chatter. But Isobel? She'd always had courage— he knew that. She'd had to cope from an early age with her father's determination to ruin himself with drink and gambling debts.

And now, there was something else. She had become strikingly beautiful.

She's thrown herself away, he reminded himself.

At the age of eighteen she'd gone to live with that notorious rake Loxley in his secretive Hyde Park mansion and the stories spread about her had been dark indeed. And now, she had her artist. But yet again he felt a spark of self-reproach. *She came here to appeal to you about the Plass Valley children. You could have at least sympathised. You could have told her that you are actually planning to do something to help them.*

But he hadn't and one thing was certain—she wouldn't be calling on him again. As for the school, he'd already arranged for his carpenters to begin work on the old chapel in the grounds. He knew he had to get the project started up soon—in fact, within the next week if it was to be of any use, since the summer days were already passing all too quickly. Yesterday he'd ridden round the farms on the Calverley estate and, as he spoke with his farmers, he'd casually mentioned his idea for the Plass Valley children—with depressingly negative results.

'Teach them to read and write? Now, *that's* a waste of time!' one farmer had declared. 'They'll be picking crops like their parents in a few years, Mr Hamilton, and that's all they're needed for—you don't need an education for that!'

But Connor remembered the chances he'd been given, poor though he was. And just at that moment, there was a tap at his door—it opened and there was Laura. Connor gestured to the footman who attended her to wheel her in, then depart.

And Laura said, 'Connor, dear. You did promise Elvie that you would come to look at a story she's written about Little Jack. At eleven, in the conservatory. Did you forget?'

He looked at his watch. *Oh, no.* Half-past eleven already. 'I'm sorry,' he said quickly. 'I'll go to her now.'

'It's all right! I told Elvie you were very busy after the arrival of all that furniture. But, Connor, I gather Miss Blake called. Now, *that* must have been rather a surprise. The poor girl. How very odd for her, to no longer have a connection to this place.'

A gentle but timely probe—that was typical of Laura. He was aware of his own intake of breath. 'Let me put it this way, Laura. I owe her family no favours.'

'I understand that. But, Connor—' Laura was leaning forward in a way that indicated she meant business '—is her family *her* fault?'

When Connor made no reply, Laura waited a moment more, then went on, in her easy, pleasant way: 'You know what servants are like, dear—they hear everything and talk to me. And so I can't help but know what Miss Blake came to you about.'

'The Plass Valley children?'

Laura nodded. 'She came to ask you to help them, didn't she? And I've been thinking, Connor—why not ask *her* to run your little school? Wait a minute—you look aghast, but I feel sure she'd be wonderful with the children. Just ask Elvie.'

Once more he was taken aback. 'Elvie? What has she to do with it?'

'A little while ago, I was upstairs in my private sitting room, which as you know overlooks the gardens. And I happened to see Miss Blake with Elvie—she must have come across her completely by chance as she walked back through the park after her visit here. And Elvie had been crying a little, I think, because I saw Miss Blake dry her tears and make a great fuss of Little Jack—and by end, Elvie was clinging to her hand as if she didn't want to let go. So I thought—why not hire *her* for your school? She would be perfect!'

He tried—really tried—to explain tactfully. 'Laura, unfortunately her past—and indeed her *present* circumstances—make the notion impossible.'

'What, exactly, do you mean?'

Connor shook his head. Did Laura have any idea of Isobel's scandalous London past? She'd never been one for gossip, but surely she must have heard that the way Isobel was living now did nothing to recommend her for the post in question!

'Well…' Connor spread out his large, capable hands. 'Miss Blake lives with an artist. A man called Joseph Molina.'

'I know that, of course.' Laura's tone was just a little crisp. 'She's his assistant, I believe. Connor, have you ever met Mr Molina? Don't you realise the poor man is in his fifties, is almost crippled by rheumatism and, besides, has never shown any interest in women—in the romantic sense—in his life? Besides, his sister Agnes lives with him, too, as his housekeeper and carer. I believe the Molinas took in Miss Blake as an act of friendship and in return she shops for them and helps around the house, and assists Mr Molina with his paintings. There is nothing at all improper in their relationship. And I must say, Connor, I expected better of you than to listen to malicious tittle-tattle!'

Connor closed his eyes briefly. So he'd perhaps been over-hasty in listening to the gossip concerning Isobel and Molina! But Isobel's time with Loxley… Should he tell Laura about it?

He didn't get the chance, because Laura was speak-

ing again. 'I believe,' she went on, 'that the girl has
suffered from other rumours in the past. But is she
never to be given the chance to redeem herself? And
today I heard that the Molinas have received a new
blow, because their landlord, whoever he may be, is
threatening to evict them for non-payment of their rent.
So it occurred to me straight away that Miss Blake
might very much welcome the income from the teaching post you're trying to fill. It's not, after all, as if
she's going to teach the children of a duke! Her father
was a disgrace, I know—but is that her fault?'

Having already been wrongfooted over Isobel's relationship with Molina, Connor was silent.

'Miss Blake,' Laura continued imperturbably,
'would presumably have been well educated as a girl.
And I think there's something about her that appeals
very much to children. I've only observed her from
a distance, but she has a kind of *sparkle,* don't you
think? As for the town's malicious gossips, I don't
think either you or I need to sink to their level. Now,
I know the final decision rests with you...' Laura gave
him her charming smile '...but I urge you, please, to
consider what I've said.'

After she'd gone, Connor rose abruptly from his
desk and paced the room.

So Laura thought he'd made a huge mistake in judging Isobel so harshly. But, damn it, she didn't know
what he knew. He wished all of it were lies, but even
Isobel herself made no pretence of it—once more he
remembered how she'd whispered, 'I understand why
you find it impossible to forgive me, both for what I
used to be and for what I am now.'

But it appeared now that he'd misjudged her present situation badly. *Give her a chance*, Laura had said. Just as he'd been given a chance by Miles Delafield. He'd been laughed at when Miles first promoted him— laughed at for his country accent, his rough clothes. Yet he'd been given the opportunity to create a new life for himself. Why not give Isobel this chance? She had challenged him to do something to help those scruffy waifs. And since he'd not found anyone else remotely suitable for his school, why not respond by throwing the challenge back at Miss Isobel Blake?

He headed for the conservatory, where Elvie was helping Laura sort her embroidery silks, but she jumped to her feet when she saw him.

'Connor, Grandmother said you would read the story I've written, about Little Jack.' She hesitated. 'But she also said you're very busy, so perhaps you would rather wait?'

'Elvie,' he said, 'I would love to read your story right now.'

'Then I will leave you to it,' said Laura, smiling. She was gathering her silks together. 'I'll go to rest in my room for a while, but I'll see you both at lunch-time, I hope?'

Connor moved to the bell-pull to summon a foot-man for her wheelchair. 'You will,' he said. 'And you'll be glad to hear, Laura, that I've decided to follow your advice.'

And she knew instantly. 'Oh, good,' she said.

'There is no guarantee whatsoever,' he warned, 'that Miss Blake will accept the post—you know? She might loathe the idea of having anything to do with Calverley Hall. She might consider it the greatest in-sult I could possibly offer her.'

'I don't think so. I really don't.'

The footman was there now to wheel her to her room, but Connor was aware of that smile still on her face. *Victory,* it said. *Victory.* He settled himself next to Elvie and together they began to read the story of Little Jack.

That afternoon, Isobel decided to weed the garden of the Molinas' farmhouse. The double blow of her calamitous meeting with Connor in the morning—*all your own fault, you fool, you asked for everything you got*—together with the news that the Molinas faced eviction had shaken her to her core. In an effort to overcome her gathering sense of panic, she'd resolved on an hour or two of physical hard work.

But the strategy just wasn't having the desired effect.

'I'm sure there'll be something we can do about the rent,' she'd said earlier to Agnes. Brave words. Stupid words. Because what real use was *she* to her friends? She did various jobs for them, admittedly, but her presence there was a luxury they could no longer afford. If she moved out, then at least they could replace her with a tenant who actually paid. But what would she do then? How would she live?

She felt the shadows gathering, as they had three years ago when Viscount Loxley was dying and his relatives hovered like crows around a corpse. Only it was Isobel whom they would gladly have pecked and harried to her grave.

She would be alone again. But there were worse things, weren't there? Like seeing the scorn in Connor's eyes this morning.

Trying to push away her growing dread, she'd put

on her thick cotton gloves and gone out into the garden with a basket and trowel. The scents of the flowers reached out to her and the gentle drone of honey bees filled the air. There were vegetables, too, to tend and raspberries to gather, and for an hour or more she was completely absorbed.

Then she realised that someone had ridden up to the house without her hearing and was sitting there on his horse watching her. She rose slowly, for a split second fearing it might be their unknown landlord come with more threats for poor Joseph and Agnes.

But it wasn't the landlord. It was Connor Hamilton. 'Good day,' he said.

Isobel brushed the leaves from her gloved hands against the coarse sackcloth apron she wore. *Oh, no. This was all she needed.*

'I wanted to speak to you, Miss Blake,' Connor went on. 'Is this a convenient time?' By now he had dismounted and was holding his horse's reins.

No, she thought rather wildly. *No time is convenient...*

She adjusted her sunbonnet that had slipped to one side. She was tall, but Connor Hamilton was taller and broad-shouldered, and... She felt hot inside. Hot and bruised and sort of *aching*, because—because of what?

Because of what he'd once meant to her? But that was long ago and she knew now that she couldn't trust anyone, let alone Connor the blacksmith's son, who'd once been her only friend. Isobel gazed up at him. 'As you see,' she said brightly, 'I am rather busy, Mr Hamilton. So far I've collected a full basket of raspberries, but there are still beans to be picked and peas to be watered—really, at this time of year, the work never ends!'

She gestured around the garden lightly, but inside she was desperately afraid. *Why on earth is he here?* Most likely he'd come to laugh at what she was reduced to. Come to gloat.

'I'm sorry,' he said, 'to see you reduced to this, Miss Blake.'

But Isobel could see no sympathy in his cold blue eyes. 'Are you?' Her words expressed mild surprise. 'Really? Do you know, Mr Hamilton, I've found that many people positively *relish* my descent from riches to rags.' She brushed some raspberry leaves from her arm. 'I'm sure you'll know that my story gives delight to the tale-tellers for miles around. But—' and this time her eyes met his in direct challenge '—Mr Molina and his sister have proved to be good, indeed estimable friends to me. And if there is any malicious gossip about them, I will deny it in the strongest possible terms!'

He was silent a moment, his gaze still inscrutable. Beneath her calm demeanour, she felt her heart thudding almost painfully. *Why on earth is he here?*

He said at last, 'You've had to adjust to considerable changes in your life, Isobel.'

Was he referring to the fact that she was once heiress to Calverley Hall? Or was he thinking about the years in between? As for Calverley Hall—she closed her eyes a moment as the memories of her childhood all but overwhelmed her. Memories of formal, silent meals in the great dining hall with her mother and father, while all the footmen stood around waiting to serve each elaborate dish. Memories of the daily torment of lessons in the schoolroom. *You're a disgrace to us, Isobel*, her mother would remonstrate.

She didn't flinch from Connor Hamilton's penetrating gaze. 'I have no regrets,' she said steadily. 'I've found that I have adapted to my new life quite perfectly, thank you!'

She saw him gazing around the garden, then at the dilapidated house. And he said, 'Your friend, Mr Molina, is unable to pay his rent. What will you do if the Molinas are forced to leave this place?'

Isobel flinched then. Visibly. How did he know this, so soon? And how could she possibly answer?

Because, quite simply, she had no idea what on earth she would do next—what kind of employment she could apply for, who would take her on.

'Is this why you came here?' She was dismayed to find that her voice shook slightly. 'To interrogate me and take pleasure in my predicament? To be quite honest, I have absolutely no idea what I will do next, but even if I did, I fail to see why I would discuss it with you.' She picked up her basket of raspberries. 'If you'll excuse me, Mr Hamilton, I have jobs to be getting on with. I cannot stand here chatting all day.'

Voice steady again. Thank goodness.

She made a move towards the house, but he blocked her path. 'Then you could be making a grave mistake. You see, I've come here with a proposition for you that could just be the solution to your problems.'

Her stomach flipped, and her heart began to thud with hard, painful beats. *A proposition?* No. No. Surely, he couldn't mean that he wanted her to be his mistress?

* * *

Connor realised straight away how his words could be interpreted and inwardly cursed himself for his verbal clumsiness. Because, he suddenly thought, despite her shabby clothes and carelessly tied-back hair, she would receive rather a lot of propositions, one way or another.

When he arrived and saw her in the garden, the scene had been idyllic. The flowerbeds were full of colour and scent, and she'd been working away, dressed in her print frock and cotton sunbonnet, utterly absorbed—she was humming to herself.

And something had tugged at Connor's heart. Damn it, he'd thought; she wasn't even trying to be attractive or alluring—yet every time he met her, she disturbed him in a way that made him absolutely furious with himself.

For God's sake, she couldn't even afford a decent gown and her fair hair was tumbling untidily round her face as usual. But all that somehow made him all the more aware of her femininity and, yes, of her vulnerability, even though she offered scarcely a hint of weakness. Didn't she realise how everything about her was guaranteed to fill a man's mind with exactly the kind of thoughts he shouldn't be having? He snapped his gaze to her face—only to find himself fascinated by the way her skin was tinted gold by the sun. He thought, *Her green-gold eyes, with their dark lashes, are the kind you could drown in...*

And they were still wide with alarm. Yes, she was clearly thinking that he was asking her to become his mistress—to her obvious horror.

Connor acted quickly to remedy his own mistake,

before it took too firm a grip on his own imagination and even more directly on his treacherous body, which was already considering how sweet she might be to hold and how tender those full lips would be to kiss. In an effort to push his wayward thoughts aside, he said, far more abruptly than he meant to, 'I've come here today with a specific and practical offer. You visited the Hall this morning to demand that I do something to help the Plass Valley children. I've come here to tell you I've decided to set up a summer school for those children—and I want to ask you if you will accept the post of teacher to them.'

He saw how her eyes widened again, this time in incredulity—then she was backing away, shaking her head.

'No,' she breathed. She actually tried to laugh. 'Oh, no. The idea is *absurd...*'

'Why?'

She spread her hands wide. 'To begin with, I have absolutely no qualifications. I have no experience.' She looked as if she was fighting for words. 'Mr Hamilton, you could find someone more capable than me very easily!'

'I've interviewed several candidates already.' His reply was sharp. 'But all of them were useless—most of them didn't even appear to *like* children. Then I thought of you and how you defended them at the midsummer fair. You challenged me to help them, Miss Blake. Well, I'm handing that challenge over to you.'

'But I've told you. I'm in no way eligible—'

'And what if I beg to differ?' Connor was aware of a damned stubborn streak rising up in him. He did not, in any fashion, want to turn round and just go. 'Won't you at least hear me out, Miss Blake? Do you really find my proposition so very hateful? And wouldn't I be right in thinking you have to make some rather difficult choices, now that your friends the Molinas are in financial difficulties?'

He thought then that her eyes might have misted slightly, just as they used to sometimes when she rode over to the forge when she was a girl. Though if ever he asked her what was wrong, she would always answer, *Nothing. Nothing at all.*

She held herself rigid. 'Mr Molina and his sister have some money difficulties, yes, but I have already started to consider how I might help—'

'Well,' he interrupted curtly, 'I may be able to help them in one easy step and at the same time help you to widen your horizons. Believe me, I speak as a friend.'

'Do you?' she whispered. 'Do you?'

He saw how she'd clenched her hands. He thought, *She is virtually alone and has been for most of her life.* Having to defend herself against the whole world, it seemed. Including him.

And yet, she'd brought so much of it upon herself. She was lucky to be offered a second chance! With fresh resolve, he pressed on. 'You spoke the other day of wishing the past undone. Is it possible, Miss Blake, that you and I should consider a truce?'

She gazed up at him. 'Why?'

And he suddenly saw that her eyes were filled with an emotion he couldn't recognise—hurt? he wondered. Fear? 'Why?' she'd asked and that was a damned good question—what on earth was he thinking of, inviting her into his life again? Was he mad?

Clearly she thought so. But she was a challenge

and he was *not* going to let her off the hook, so he switched tactics.

'Look,' he said. And he smiled almost. 'What I'm trying to say is we could make an effort, you and I, to let bygones be bygones. And I admit I had no business arriving here out of the blue like this—I should at least have given you some advance warning.'

She still looked astonished. Incredulous. 'You think that would have helped?'

'No,' he admitted. 'Probably not.'

And something about his frankness finally reached her, he saw. 'Very well,' she said. She was taking a deep breath. 'Very well. I am trying to consider seriously what you've just said. As I understand it, you're suggesting we start anew. And I think—I very much hope—I can believe you when you say you mean well towards my friends the Molinas.'

'I'm a businessman. And believe it or not, I'm known for fair dealing. I think I can offer you an arrangement that benefits all sides.'

She looked towards the house, then back at him, as if making a decision. She nodded at last. 'Mr Hamilton,' she said, 'I fear my manners have gone sadly astray in not inviting you in and offering you some tea.'

'I would like that very much,' he replied. 'Thank you.'

Chapter Six

She led the way in and he followed. He found the large farmhouse kitchen refreshingly cool after the sunshine outside and saw that the place was prettily if simply furnished, with small vases of flowers sitting on every windowsill. A man he assumed to be Joseph Molina was at the far end of the room in front of an easel. When Molina saw them he was about to rise, but Connor walked swiftly towards him and held out his hand.

'Please stay where you are, Mr Molina. I'm Connor Hamilton, and I'm glad to make your acquaintance. Do carry on with your work.'

Molina gripped his outstretched hand. 'I, too, am heartily pleased to meet you, sir!'

Joseph Molina was indeed a semi-invalid, as Laura had said; his shoulders were crooked with arthritis. Connor mentally lambasted himself for even briefly listening to the rumour-mongers who'd linked his name with Isobel's. Then Molina's sister came in and was clearly rendered almost speechless by Connor's presence; she offered to make tea, but Isobel told her gently that she would do it.

'You could, Agnes,' Isobel suggested, 'bring us some of your almond cakes from the pantry.'

As Agnes hurried off Isobel said quietly to Connor, 'She means well, but she would probably drop the cups and saucers. She is rather awed by you, you see.'

Was Isobel awed? He couldn't tell a thing from her expression as he watched her move swiftly around the kitchen area, putting the kettle on the range, arranging cups and spoons on a tray. Despite her calm, he suspected she was still no doubt wishing him anywhere but here.

'Please, Mr Hamilton,' she said, 'take a seat', and he walked over to where she pointed, to a bay window alcove containing two faded tapestry chairs and a low table. He stood looking out. From here you could see the distant gabled roofs of Calverley Hall and he thought, suddenly, how could Isobel regard his purchase of her former home as anything other than an action of pure, ruthless revenge?

She'd taken a cup of tea over to Joseph Molina first, he noticed. Then she was coming towards him with the tray and he moved to take it from her and place it on the low table. She nodded her thanks and he pulled out a chair for her before sitting down to face her.

Her arms were bare from her gardening and tinted gold, like her complexion, from the sun. She'd washed her hands, of course, before making the tea—he could smell the fresh lavender scent of the soap—and she'd removed her cotton bonnet, so that her golden curls bobbed untamed around her neck. Her frock—cheap and garish as it was—matched her defiance of conventional taste and he felt a sudden pulse of lust. *Forget the frock.* It was far more tantalising to imagine that sweet figure in nothing at all...

The absolute wrongness of his thoughts made him draw back abruptly. *Oh, no.* Stay well away from *that*, you fool.

She'd poured the tea and he nodded his thanks. Then he said, 'Miss Blake. If I may return once more to the subject of the Plass Valley children?'

Her expression, though polite, was unreadable. 'You may,' she said coolly, 'though as I said, I fear I am unable to help personally.'

Connor took his tea. 'Even so, I hoped you may have some ideas. Some suggestions. I estimate, for instance, that the children probably have only another six weeks in this district before their families move on to other work in other places. I imagine they would require lessons, oh, for only three hours in the morning at most—it's doubtful if their concentration would last for longer. But if they could learn their letters and some basic arithmetic—if they were to hear some stories from history, perhaps, and tales of other lands— who knows what spark might be kindled? Who knows if maybe just one or two of those children might decide they want to learn more?'

She was silent a moment. Then she looked at him and said politely, 'So now that you're rich, you feel the urge to do something mildly charitable? As wealthy people do?'

That pulled him up. He replied, with an edge of irritation, 'That is how it might appear, I agree. But I mean it. I want to do something for those children and I want *you* to help me. Please, Miss Blake. I've

advertised, I've interviewed for the post, but as I've
said, time is short and I think you would be ideal...'

She was shaking her head. 'You don't know me,'
she whispered. 'You really don't know me.'

Again he was feeling some emotion that he didn't
want to recognise and it confused him. Whatever it
was, he didn't like it. 'Look...' he was trying to speak
as mildly as he could '...if *I'm* the problem, you really won't have to see very much of me. I've told you,
I thought the school could be held in the old chapel,
in the Hall's grounds—you remember it?—and you
can, for your convenience, have your own bedroom
and parlour in the Hall for the duration, so you don't
have the daily walk—'

She broke in, looking very white. 'I *can't.*'

She was panicking again, he could see. He rose
and walked to the window before turning back to
her, angry and frustrated. 'Is it because of Calverley Hall? Is it because you simply cannot bear the
thought of living as an employee in the place you
once called home?'

He saw a burst of the old spirit flash in her eyes,
followed by a shrug. 'Something like that,' she said.

He'd thought earlier that she'd looked vulnerable—
terrified, even—by his proposition. But now—was she
merely being arrogant? He really couldn't tell.

'Surely,' she was almost whispering now, '*surely*
you could look again and find someone more suitable than me?'

He sat down and leaned forward to face her. 'I'm
not at all sure that I could. I saw you—remember?—
with those children at the midsummer fair. They liked
you. They respected you. And I've heard how you

met and talked with Elvie in the garden of the Hall this morning.'

She flushed. 'I suppose it was presumptuous of me, for which I apologise.'

He stifled an impatient exclamation. 'Miss Blake, I'm not criticising you for being kind to her—far from it! But since Elvie's father died earlier this year, she's hardly spoken a word to anyone other than her grandmother and me. As I said, children clearly trust you and it confirms for me that you would be ideal for the Plass Valley school. Won't you give them a chance?'

She was quite pale again now. 'These children mean a good deal to you.'

He looked straight at her. 'I was born into a society that condemned me to the lower ranks, but I was lucky. Miss Blake, I think we decided outside in the garden just now, you and I, that perhaps we ought to sweep aside our differences and fix our minds on this one objective—the school.'

She was gazing at him still. 'I can't do it,' she whispered. 'Believe me, I cannot.'

Yes, he decided, this was sheer arrogance and it angered him. 'Very well,' he said flatly. 'As I mentioned earlier, I know about your friends the Molinas' financial troubles. I believe they're considerably in arrears with the rent on this house.'

He saw her blink, just once. Then she said, very calmly, 'Why, Mr Hamilton, I rather think that's none of your business.'

'It is, actually.' He rose to his feet again and folded his arms across his chest. 'Because, you see, I happen to own this house. In fact, I own the entire valley.'

* * *

Isobel felt beaten and trapped and afraid. All she could do, by way of defence, was to try her best not to let this man realise it. 'I can see,' she answered at last, 'that it's no wonder you've risen so far. You really have got everything planned out, haven't you?'

'I didn't plan it at all, as it happens.' He looked, she thought, as if he was growing a little tired of the tussle. 'When I bought the Hall, I knew some land came with it, but I didn't realise until extremely recently that this place was mine.'

'So you decided to try a little blackmail, Mr Hamilton?' she queried almost sweetly.

She saw the anger flare in his eyes. '*No.* I'm merely trying to point out that if you accepted the post I'm offering, then as well as helping the Plass Valley children, you could at the same time be of use to your friends the Molinas. And I thought...' He spoke more quietly. 'I thought that being with those children might make you happy.'

She truly didn't know whether to laugh or cry. All sorts of long-buried emotions had been stirred up by this man who'd once meant so much to her as a friend. They welled up inside her like a great, surging tide. And she couldn't let him see what his presence did to her.

She rose again, since he was still standing. At the far end of the room Joseph was completely absorbed in his painting. Of his sister there was no sign, but Isobel could imagine Agnes staying out of the way deliberately, perhaps peeping in every so often with hope in her eyes, thinking, *A visitor. A rich visitor for Miss Isobel.*

Once this man had meant the world to her as a

friend; but for all sorts of reasons there was no chance of friendship now. Especially as she was having to acknowledge that something else had come between them. She'd realised it at the fair; she'd tried to deny it, but his impact on her was something she'd never before experienced. Every time she looked into his face, with its harshly defined jaw and cheekbones, she felt a confused heat stirring inside her like a secret threat; especially if she looked at his mouth, his surprisingly expressive, curved mouth...

How horrified he would be, if he knew the effect he had on her. He would despise her even more.

She met his gaze at last and was relieved that her smile didn't falter. 'You thought being with the children might make me happy.' She said it very softly. '"Sometimes you have to learn to find happiness. Sometimes you never do." You said that to me once, Connor, just before you left your home for good, seven years ago. Do you remember?'

So far he'd hardly moved a muscle—all six foot of him, packed with an iron strength of body and mind. But now she saw him catching his breath. And he was walking towards her and was so near she could breathe in the scent of his fine clean linen and his citrus cologne, could see the almost silver glints in the navy blue of his eyes and the faint stubble of his jaw, where his dark beard was already starting to show.

And she was shaken to her very core, because she'd had the most astounding thought—that if he were to take her in his arms and kiss her now, this minute, she would be helpless. Absolutely helpless.

It was such a ridiculous thought that she almost laughed aloud. Connor Hamilton, rich London iron master, would no more wish to seduce her than he would a Calverley Hall chambermaid. He would have a sophisticated mistress—mistresses, even—in London for his physical needs and, when he *did* marry, it would be for status and fortune, nothing less.

A little shiver ran through her at the term she'd just used—*his physical needs*. Connor Hamilton would, she thought, be as formidable in love as he was in every other sphere of his life—though 'love' was a ridiculous word for her to choose, since she guessed he didn't believe in it.

But… *Connor*.

Again she felt that lurch of her heart. Something about this man made her vulnerable and afraid in a way she'd never, ever felt before, not even during the very worst times of her life. She must have looked as unsteady as she felt, because suddenly he touched her arm. And once more she felt that plunging sensation in her stomach, as if she was falling, falling…

'Miss Blake,' he said. 'Miss Blake, are you listening?'

'But of course!'

'I have no desire whatever,' he went on, 'to force you into the post in question. But I will gift your friends the Molinas the lease of this house for their lifetimes, regardless of whether or not you accept the job.'

His hand was at his side now and there was nothing to remind her of that contact except that her skin still tingled in warning. 'But that's charity. And people will say…'

'People will say what?' he answered evenly.

She didn't reply. She didn't understand any of this—and what frightened her most of all was that she didn't understand *herself.* She swallowed hard and shook her head.

'I'll go now,' he said. He was already making for the door, but he paused a moment. 'I can see that you have little liking for me personally. But if you do agree to take on the post, it might help you if I repeat that you won't see me often, since my business affairs take me regularly to London. Though I'll always, of course, be available if you have any problems. I hope, too, that you'll accept my offer of accommodation at the Hall.' With his hand on the door, he held her eyes with that fathomless blue gaze that transfixed her. 'I shall send someone for your answer tomorrow.'

And he was gone. She sat on her chair, clasping her hands in an effort to steady them.

Trapped. She was trapped, by her own big mouth and by his clever scheming. She felt humiliated and stupid and afraid. Often nowadays she attracted attention from men who repelled her—but Connor Hamilton was different.

He didn't repel her. He wouldn't repel *any* woman, with those blue eyes that made you dizzy if you looked into them for too long. With that lean but muscular body that promised all kinds of things she'd never allowed herself to even think about before. She would be making a huge mistake in more ways than one if she accepted his offer.

And then Agnes came hurrying in, beaming. Isobel said rather wearily, 'You never brought the almond cakes, Agnes.'

'Almond cakes? I knew you would want to be alone with that handsome gentleman for a while! So I went into the garden to be out of the way. And I've got such good news! Mr Hamilton came up to me out there and said he was very sorry to hear of Joseph's ill health. And he told me *he* is our new landlord now and there was a mistake in the letter about the rent, and we can stay here without paying anything for the present, since he sees that the place suits us so well. And he also promised he will get a doctor to come and visit Joseph—a doctor all the way from Bath! Can you believe he'd do all this out of the goodness of his heart?'

No, Isobel thought flatly, *I can't.* 'There's something else, Agnes. Mr Hamilton has plans for me also. In fact, he came here to offer me employment at Calverley Hall.'

Isobel saw Agnes's reaction immediately. The doubt. The shock.

'Don't worry,' Isobel went on, 'everything is perfectly respectable. You see, Mr Hamilton has asked me to teach for a short while at a school he's setting up for the Plass Valley children.'

Agnes's eyes widened. 'And you're going to accept?'

'Yes,' Isobel said quietly. 'I'm going to accept.'

Even though Connor Hamilton really couldn't have thought of a more perfect way of humiliating her.

Connor rode back to the Hall with the bitter taste of a hollow victory in his mouth. He honestly hadn't realised, until Carstairs pointed it out on the map this morning, that the Calverley estate included the Molinas' dilapidated old farmstead. And so he'd gone there and used it to his advantage.

He remembered that when she was younger Isobel Blake had been passionate about justice, both for animals and people. He remembered how once, when she visited the forge, he'd noticed a red weal on her forearm—she'd tried to make light of it, but in the end he got her to tell him how that morning her father had whipped a young stable boy for not having his favourite hunter ready on time.

Apparently she'd tried to stop her father by grabbing at his whip, but that vicious man had struck out at *her*. She'd said no more about it—she never complained, she was completely without self-pity. She took everything life threw at her—including his visit, just now.

She had coped well with him, on the whole. She had been calm and rational when he pointed out the fragility of her situation at the Molinas' home. But he'd also seen a flare of sheer vulnerability in her eyes that had made him want to draw her close and soothe her, and…

And *kiss* her? *And where the hell would that lead to, you fool?* Isobel Blake belonged to his old life and it was best to let that past be buried for good. There would be sneers and criticism enough, God knew, of the fact he was hiring her—he really didn't want any involvement with her at all, other than to ensure that she had—for the time being at least—a useful occupation that might open up some future path for her life to take. As for him, he had his expanding business empire to keep him busy. He had little Elvie and her grandmother to take care of and the Calverley estate to restore.

But all he could think of, as he rode home, was how Isobel had smiled just now, even when she looked as if life was breaking her into tiny pieces.

Chapter Seven

Two days later

Billy with his carrier's cart took Isobel as far as Calverley Hall's lodge. She had estimated she'd have plenty of time to walk along the drive to the Hall, but as she crossed the stone bridge over the river she heard the clock over the stables striking four. *Oh, no.* She was already late.

Yesterday, just the day after Connor's visit, his secretary Mr Carstairs had ridden over to the farmhouse, had introduced himself politely and handed Isobel a sheaf of papers listing her terms of employment. She'd glanced at them and felt her heart hammering. 'This,' she'd said coolly, 'is exceedingly prompt.'

'Mr Hamilton likes to be prompt, ma'am.'

'So he has already assumed I will take the position?'

'Indeed, and Mr Hamilton would like you to start as soon as possible—the old chapel is already prepared as a schoolroom. So if you would kindly read the contract and sign *here*.'

He was laying the papers on a nearby table. She'd gone to fetch pen and ink, and all the time a kind of black panic was tightening in her chest. Ink squirted as she scrawled her signature. 'I am sure,' she'd said, 'that I can rely on Mr Hamilton to ensure everything is as it should be.'

The minute Carstairs had gone, Agnes hurried in and hugged her. 'Oh, Isobel. I couldn't help but over-hear. So soon! We really don't want you to go!'

'And I don't want to leave you and Joseph, Agnes.' Isobel tried to smile. 'But it's all going to be for the best. I will have a delightful new job for a few weeks, working with children. Really, what could be better?'

'You ought to have children of your own,' muttered Agnes darkly. 'With a man to love you and share your life.' Then Agnes hugged her again and cried a little, until Isobel finally got away, and went to start pack-ing her few things for Calverley Hall.

And here she was. She'd hoped the walk along the drive might calm her nerves, but the portmanteau she carried seemed heavier by the minute and she was hot and anxious by the time she reached the Hall's big front door.

She rattled the heavy brass knocker, until it was abruptly opened by a middle-aged man in a dark frock coat who stared at her with a frown. She recognised the steward, Haskins—he'd tried to turn her away when she called to see Connor about the Plass Valley chil-dren. He said, very stiffly, 'Can I be of assistance—ma'am?'

She'd heard from the village gossips how Connor had hired new staff from London. 'They're top-notch,' she'd heard people say. 'Nothing but the best for Mr

Hamilton!' That might be so, but it was far from encouraging to see how Haskins's sharp eyes scanned her drab cloak and bonnet, then dropped to the battered portmanteau by her feet.

She met his gaze steadily. 'I am Miss Blake. I'm going to be teaching the Plass Valley children and I believe a room has been prepared for me, since I'm to stay here for the duration of my employment. You're Mr Haskins, I believe? How do you do?'

She held out a hand for him to take, but he merely looked at it. 'I was told,' he said frostily, 'that you weren't arriving till tomorrow.'

'Tomorrow! But my note of appointment says *today*. I have it here...'

She pulled it from her pocket and handed it to him; he merely glanced at it and handed it back. 'It says you are due to arrive tomorrow, Miss Blake.'

'*Oh.*' The colour flooded her cheeks. 'Oh, how foolish of me...' Her voice trailed away.

'However,' went on Haskins, 'I'm pleased to say your room has already been prepared.' He didn't sound in the least bit pleased about it. 'But before we go in, it's my duty to point out that as a member of staff you should have used the side door. The front door is for Mr Hamilton and the Delafield family only, and their visitors. Please wait while I fetch a maid to show you to your room.'

Isobel felt crushed. 'Shouldn't I report first to Mr Hamilton?'

'Mr Hamilton is away until tomorrow. Which is why he suggested you didn't arrive until then.' And Haskins went inside again, leaving the door half-open.

Isobel stood paralysed with uncertainty. Was she

meant to follow him? All she really wanted to do was pick up her bag and rush back down the long drive to catch up with Billy's cart. *Take me home, Billy, will you? This is all a huge mistake.*

She realised Mr Haskins was calling out to her, his voice this time expressing downright impatience. 'Are you coming in or not, Miss Blake? You may as well use the front door, seeing as you're here.'

She followed.

'Here is Mrs Lett,' Haskins continued. 'She is the housekeeper and she will show you to your room.'

Mrs Lett was small and middle-aged, with narrow dark eyes and a pursed mouth—another of Connor's new appointees from London, Isobel assumed. Mrs Lett said primly, 'Please follow me, Miss Blake.' She glanced at the portmanteau. 'Is that all your luggage?'

'There's a small trunk also. The carrier will bring it tomorrow.'

The housekeeper didn't say another word, but led Isobel up the stairs and along a narrow corridor to a door that Isobel knew only too well. Her throat became dry. 'Is there no other room?'

'What is wrong with this one, Miss Blake? I was under the impression it was perfectly adequate.' *For a mere employee,* Mrs Lett might have added.

Isobel didn't know where to begin. It was, in fact, quite spacious—it was adequately furnished and was better in many respects than her room at the Molinas' house. There was nothing actually *wrong* with it. Except that it was the room in which her mother used to lock her whenever she misbehaved—usually because one of her governesses had complained about her. 'Isobel is simply refusing to do her lessons, Lady Blake! She is such a wayward child!'

Isobel struggled to sound calm. Reasonable. 'Any other room will do, Mrs Lett. Any other than this one, if you please.'

Mrs Lett was clearly *not* pleased, but she took Isobel to another room, which was up an extra flight of stairs and was even smaller. But Isobel said, 'This will suit me perfectly. Thank you.'

Mrs Lett pursed her lips again. 'The servants' supper is served at seven, in the basement hall. I'll send one of the maids to fetch you when it's time.'

And then she was gone and Isobel sank down on the bed, forcing herself to breathe deeply. *This room is fine*, she told herself. Indeed, from its windows she could see the distant woods and hills beyond the park— but what use were the views, when the whole place reminded her what a disaster she'd made of her life?

A maid arrived shortly afterwards. 'I've come to help you unpack your things, miss,' she explained timidly. 'My name is Susan.'

Susan looked extremely young—sixteen at most, Isobel guessed. She also appeared very frightened of her—but then, of course, all the servants would know that Isobel once lived here. Isobel tried to speak lightly. 'I fear, Susan,' she said, 'that I've upset the household routine today.'

Susan glanced at her and hesitated. 'They weren't expecting you till tomorrow, miss. Mr Hamilton is not back from London until then. And Mrs Delafield, she's out visiting, with the little girl—'

A thump of alarm. 'Mrs Delafield?'

'If you please, miss, she's grandmother to Miss Elvira.'

Of course. The mother of Connor Hamilton's dead business partner. Isobel realised Susan was opening drawers to fold away her pitifully few clothes and asked her on impulse, 'Do you like working here, Susan? Is Mr Hamilton a good master?'

Little Susan looked up, her face instantly alight. 'Oh, yes, miss—ever so good! The servants left from the old days say he's much, much better than Sir George, because Sir George was a—oh!'

She clamped a hand to her mouth, realising she was speaking of Isobel's father—and didn't utter a single word more.

By ten o'clock that evening, Isobel was beginning to acknowledge that returning to Calverley Hall was a colossal mistake.

She had gone down to the servants' hall at seven for supper and no one at all had responded to her attempts at conversation. Some might have been tongue-tied because of who she was, but she guessed others viewed her as an unwelcome intruder. Mrs Lett set the tone by saying as soon as she came in, 'Well, Miss Blake? I trust you haven't changed your mind again about your room?'

'The room is perfect. Thank you so much for your concern, Mrs Lett!'

By the time she was halfway through the meal, Isobel had given up any attempt to make friends with the servants on either side of her, who all talked among themselves and completely ignored her. Never having a large appetite at the best of times, she struggled with the plate of beef and boiled vegetables that was put in front of her and when the pudding was served—it was apple pie—she took a spoonful and almost choked.

Her portion had been dusted with a heavy sprinkling of salt. Glancing up, she saw one of the young footmen smirking—no doubt he was responsible. She rose abruptly from her chair.

'Thank you,' she said to them all. 'It's been an *interesting* meal and I've so enjoyed meeting you!' Every eye was upon her. Amidst a chilling silence, she walked out of the room and took a deep, long breath.

She couldn't do this.

She *had* to do this.

Once back in her room she stood gazing out of the window at the velvety night sky, studded with familiar stars. This house had been her home until she was eighteen and her father took her to London. He'd been desperate for her to make a rich marriage; but everywhere she heard the sneering whispers. *'She's Sir George Blake's daughter. That's right—Sir George Blake of Calverley Hall, the gambler...'*

Her mother had died when she was nine. Her chaperon in London was an appalling lady called Mrs Sparlet—who Isobel quickly discovered was in fact her father's mistress. Day after day Mrs Sparlet prepared her for some second-rate party, often to which they'd not even been invited. Isobel had thought the humiliation could not get worse, but it did. It was Viscount Loxley who saved her; Viscount Loxley who'd been her only friend. But then he had died and she really was alone.

Those servants downstairs had been trying to hurt her—but they didn't know that she was used to far worse insults, far worse mockery. She was accustomed to having to be strong—but even so, there were two things that truly, deeply worried her. Tomorrow, she had to begin her duties at the chapel, teaching the Plass Valley children. And tomorrow—Connor Hamilton would be back.

That was what really frightened her. It was one thing keeping up a brave face in front of the staff here. It was quite another to pretend she didn't care what *he* thought. Because seeing him again had not only wakened old memories, it had set completely new sensations sparking like fire through her body, making her imagine things like his lips on hers and his strong fingers caressing her.

Already, just by thinking about him, that tiny explosion of heat had begun again low in her abdomen, as fiery and as dangerous as his harsh gaze when he'd said the other day, *'I've come here with a proposition that could just be the solution to your problems.'*

And she'd thought—just for one heartstopping moment—that he was asking her to be his mistress.

He wasn't, of course. But even so, she dreaded the fact that she would be living under his roof—and whatever he'd said to the contrary, there would be no escaping him. No escaping her own past, either, with the long shadows it cast—especially now she was here once more in the house that had seen her childhood dreams vanish into thin air.

Chapter Eight

The next morning Mrs Lett arrived in Isobel's room a little before nine. 'You didn't come down for breakfast, Miss Blake.'

Hardly surprising. 'No,' Isobel replied. 'I asked the maid, Susan, to bring me some tea and a little toast. I don't have a huge appetite in the mornings.'

Mrs Lett's frown didn't lessen. 'Well, Mr Hamilton won't arrive back till later. But Mr Haskins and I feel he would wish you to start your preparations for the school as soon as possible—so, since you're here, we thought you might like to inspect the chapel.'

'Of course.' Isobel smiled brightly. 'What a delightful idea!'

Isobel followed the housekeeper down the servants' stairs and out of the side door into the sunshine. Five minutes later they'd crossed the courtyard and covered the short distance to the chapel, where Mrs Lett unlocked the door and led the way in before turning to Isobel. 'I imagine you'll know, Miss Blake, that Mr Hamilton has gone to considerable expense to make this place ready so very quickly. Though goodness knows what state it will all be in by the time those children have had the run of it.'

'I take it you don't approve of Mr Hamilton's educational venture?' Isobel had kept her voice calm, but there was enough steel in her words to make the housekeeper suddenly wary.

'Well, now,' Mrs Lett began, 'who am I to pass judgement on Mr Hamilton's decisions?'

'Who indeed?' said Isobel sweetly. 'Thank you so much for bringing me here. But don't let me keep you any longer from your duties!'

As soon as she'd gone, Isobel looked slowly around.

The old chapel had always been airy and spacious, with stained-glass windows that tinted the sun's rays as they fell on the terracotta-tiled floor. Recently the interior walls had been whitewashed—within the last few days, Isobel guessed. The dark oak pews were still there, but in the open area to the front had been placed several child-sized tables and chairs, while next to the pulpit was a blackboard and a desk on which were laid pencils, chalk and books.

She stood there thinking, *How am I going to do this? How can I possibly cope with what is expected of me?*

She walked back to the open door and stepped outside. To her left, across the gravelled courtyard, towered the Hall; to her right lay the gardens, whose woodland paths and secret glades had always been a refuge for her. A little farther on, half-concealed by a tangle of flowering shrubs, was an ancient headstone, a memorial to the distant ancestor who had this house and chapel built and the gardens laid out, long ago.

She was about to return to the chapel when suddenly she caught sight of a small figure in a long brown frock approaching her uncertainly. It was Elvie.

'Has Mrs Lett gone?' the little girl whispered.

'Why, yes! But...'

'Good. You're starting the school tomorrow, aren't you, Miss Blake? I came because I wanted to tell you that the children are talking about it.'

Isobel felt a moment's stunned astonishment. 'The children are... But how on *earth* do you know, Elvie?'

And Elvie told her. Elvie explained how she'd met up with the Plass Valley children regularly, ever since the day of the fair. It started by chance, she said, when she took Little Jack for a walk through the woods to the river.

'On your own?' interrupted Isobel. She'd led Elvie back into the chapel, where they sat at one of the small tables.

Elvie blushed. 'I *know* I'm s-supposed to take a maid with me, but I much prefer it on my own.' She was looking at Isobel anxiously. 'You won't tell Connor, will you? Or my grandmother?'

Isobel hesitated. No point in shattering this little girl's unexpected trust in her. 'No,' she said swiftly, 'of course not. But you shouldn't really stray too far from the Hall, Elvie. And those children...'

'I met them by the river,' Elvie explained. 'Yes, I know it's Connor's land, and they shouldn't be there! But they were playing lovely games, sailing some boats they'd made from twigs and bark, and they asked me to join them. So I did and they taught Little Jack clever tricks—and now I go to meet them there whenever I can.'

Isobel said suddenly, 'Little Jack's not with you now. Where is he?'

'Mr Haskins said he had to be locked in, because he jumped up at a maid and she dropped a jug of milk.' Her eyes welled up a little. 'But he didn't *mean* to. Oh, Miss Blake, I heard him crying for me!' And a tear rolled down her cheek. Isobel saw how Elvie tried to rub it away. 'I feel so sorry for him,' she whispered. 'And I'm sad, too, because I'm lonely.'

Isobel took her hand and squeezed it. 'Elvie. Did you know that once I used to live here, when I was a girl?'

'You *did*?'

'I did. I loved the gardens and the park, and I really want to see it all again. Since it's such a fine day, shall we go and explore?'

Elvie's face lit up. 'Shall I take you to see the children?'

Isobel's heart missed a beat. *Elvie shouldn't be meeting with them like this. Connor would most definitely not approve...*

She saw Elvie's face fall at her hesitation. 'I suppose,' Elvie said despondently, 'you think you won't like them very much.'

'It's not that at all,' said Isobel warmly. 'But, Elvie, you mentioned the children have been talking about the new school. What are they saying about it?'

The little girl looked hesitant once more. 'They say they don't want any lessons.' Her face brightened again. 'But perhaps you can make them change their minds, Miss Blake!'

She took a deep breath. 'Well, let's go and find out, shall we?'

'Now? But what about Little Jack?'

Isobel laughed and replied, 'We shall rescue Little Jack *first thing.*'

Elvie gazed at her in wonder. 'Do you know what, Miss Blake? I think the children will like you very much. And I'll tell you another secret. Sometimes I take them some food from the kitchens without Cook knowing, because they are *always* hungry…'

Of course, Isobel knew she was in trouble from the minute she entered the kitchen. The plump cook was placing a tray of bread rolls in the vast oven. Isobel said cheerfully, 'Good morning, Cook! I'll be taking my lunch outside, today, if you please, with Miss Elvira. I assume it's all right if I help myself?'

And, having already spotted an array of cold foods laid out on a marble slab, she quickly piled some slices of cheese and cold meats in the basket she'd brought with her, adding handfuls of bread rolls, pastries and apples.

'Now, you wait a minute!' ordered Cook. 'Who's all that for?'

But Isobel, waving a hand in thanks, swept from the room.

Elvie was waiting for her out in the main hall and she clapped her hands with glee when she saw the jam pastries poking out of the basket. 'Are you quite sure you're a teacher, Miss Blake? You don't act like one. You don't even look like one.'

And you don't look like the happy carefree child you ought to be, thought Isobel, noting how the little girl was dressed in a heavy serge gown that looked far more suitable for winter. 'Come along,' she said. 'We're going to find you something else to wear, Elvie!'

And so, like a pair of conspirators, they hurried up to Elvie's room where Isobel quickly helped her change into a short-sleeved cotton frock and a sunhat. 'There,' Isobel approved, 'that's better.' She herself was wearing a pink-chintz gown that was several years old, but it was still one of her favourites. 'We look ready for an adventure now, don't we?'

Elvie was laughing. Excited. 'An adventure,' she kept whispering to herself as they hurried back down the stairs. 'An adventure.'

Isobel certainly felt like a conspirator. They crept out of the side door, then round to the stables to free Jack from his kennel, although the groom they encountered there proved almost as unencouraging as Cook—'Mr Haskins gave orders that the creature's to be kept in his kennel all morning, miss!'

Suddenly Isobel found herself speaking in the way she used to in the days when her father owned the Hall. 'I'm afraid Mr Haskins made a mistake,' she announced. 'I'm taking Miss Elvira for a nature walk and Jack is coming with us.'

The puppy was ecstatic to have been released. 'Jack,' cried Elvie. 'Oh, poor Little Jack, you thought you were being punished, didn't you?'

They found the children just where Elvie had said, by the river that marked the boundary of the Calverley estate. There were six of them, barefoot and in patched and tattered clothes. Their ages ranged from around five to eight. They were brown as berries from the sun and laughed and chattered as they paddled in the water and played with some toy boats they'd made from twigs and bark, just as Elvie had described.

When they saw that Elvie had brought someone with her, their faces bore looks of alarm—alarm that swiftly vanished as the freckle-faced boy who was clearly their leader declared, 'It's her. It's the lady who stuck up for us at the fair and who took some of us to the doctor's that day we got chased by the men from the village.'

Elvie beamed. 'That's right. She's Miss Blake and she's nice. This morning Little Jack was locked in his kennel, but she rescued him!'

The boy with freckles nodded. 'You can play with our boats if you want, miss,' he said.

Little Jack had already bounded forward, clearly recognising friends. Isobel made one laughing attempt to join the children by the river and make a boat herself, but it sank straight away. After that she retired to the shade of a nearby clump of alders and occupied herself with a sketchbook and pencil as they played on with their miniature fleets or threw sticks in the river for Jack to fetch.

Then gradually some of the children, overcome by curiosity, drew nearer. 'What's that you're drawing, miss?'

She looked up from her sketchbook. 'I'm drawing a map,' she told them, 'of an island very far from anywhere, where a man called Robinson Crusoe was shipwrecked long ago.'

They gazed down at her map, with its drawings of tiny palm trees and mountain peaks, and fish with sharp jaws swimming in the sea around. 'Did he die, miss? This Robinson?'

'He *thought* he was going to die, yes. But then he started exploring. Shall I tell you more of his story while you eat some lunch?'

She was already taking the cloth off her basket and their eyes widened. The older ones shared it all out very carefully and they ate in utter silence while Isobel told them the story of Robinson Crusoe.

One of her early governesses—one of the few kind ones—had read her the story when she was little. When she'd finished, Harry, the freckle-faced boy, said, 'Wish *we* knew stories like that, miss. Bet it was from a book, but we've not got any books, and anyway, they're no use to us, cos we can't read.'

'Is that so? But I've heard you're to start having some lessons tomorrow.'

She saw them looking at each other. 'Don't want no lessons,' muttered Harry. 'They've told us we'll get beaten if we don't learn things, but we aren't clever, miss. We don't know our letters, or anything.'

'And yet you're learning things all the time,' pointed out Isobel. 'While you were making those boats, you were learning how to make them float. When I told you that story just now, about Robinson Crusoe, you were thinking, "How is he going to find food and water, and shelter?" You were working it all out. *That's* learning!'

Elvie was looking at her questioningly—Isobel knew she was wondering, *Why don't you tell them you're going to be their teacher?* But suddenly the children were on their feet.

'Look out,' she heard Harry say in a low voice. 'Trouble. *Run.*' And they were off as swiftly as a shoal of quicksilver fish, vanishing into the nearby woods.

Isobel had risen, too, and was shading her eyes against the sun to stare along the path.

A horseman was approaching. Elvie was looking, too, then she was running towards him. 'It's Connor!' she cried out gladly. 'Connor, you're back!'

And so he was—he was dismounting and tethering his big horse to a tree nearby. Isobel readied herself. *He was supposed to be in London...*

No, he wasn't, you idiot. He was travelling back today—only Mrs Lett had said he wouldn't arrive till late. Had he caught sight of the children? Whether he had or not, she could see the gathering tightness in the set of his jaw as he strode towards her. And she realised, with a sinking at the pit of her stomach, that she must present an absolute spectacle, with her hair down and her face flushed from the sun, and her flimsy cotton dress clinging to her body in places it really shouldn't.

'Mr Hamilton,' she said. She tilted her chin and smiled. 'This is a pleasant surprise.'

And then Elvie was tugging at his hand. 'Connor, oh, Connor, I'm so glad you're back! We've been having a lovely time. Miss Blake set Little Jack free. He was locked up, Connor, he was so sad! And Miss Blake has just given us a lovely lunch—'

'*Us?* Who's "us", Elvie?'

Elvie caught Isobel's eye. 'Little Jack and me, of course.'

'Elvie,' Connor said, pleasantly enough, 'catch Little Jack and put him on his leash, will you? And then, why don't you collect a posy of wild flowers for your grandmother? You know how much she'd like that.'

'Oh, yes! She loves harebells. And poppies—I saw

some over in that hedgerow.' Elvie went running eagerly off, calling to Jack at the same time.

And Isobel stood there, knowing what was to come. In spite of the warm sun, his gaze froze her to her bones.

'Miss Blake,' he began, 'I've just come from the Hall. I've heard how yesterday you set the whole place in a state of upheaval by arriving on the wrong day, then demanding a different room. And Cook has told Haskins she's going to hand in her notice, because she claims you marched into her kitchen this morning and helped yourself to the food she was setting out for the staff lunch.'

'And?' she said.

'And what, Miss Blake?'

'I can always tell whenever there's an *and* coming. There's clearly something else I've done wrong. Isn't there?'

His cool eyes were still locked with hers. 'You're right. The groom complained that you ordered him to release Little Jack from the kennels against Haskins's specific instructions. You've managed to upset several of my staff all within the space of twenty-four hours. Please, can you try to deal with the obvious difficulties of your situation here with just a little more tact?'

He spoke calmly. But he looked tired, she suddenly thought, so tired; he must have faced non-stop business demands in London and he would have returned expecting at least a little peace…

She felt emotion almost overwhelming her. *There was no way I could have slept in that first room they gave me.* But Mrs Lett must have told Connor all about it the minute he got home and Cook had complained to Haskins about the food; then the groom had rushed to Connor with his tale of Miss Blake's high-handedness. All in all, a disastrous start.

And there was something else especially troubling. As he spoke, Connor had drawn closer—and that didn't help in the slightest. Something about him made her feel as though she wasn't in control of her actions. She'd never registered strongly enough how *imposing* he was.

During the brief and disastrous London Season her father had inflicted on her, she'd seen plenty of men of fashion. Men the other debutantes murmured over, admiring their elegant airs, their graceful manners, the cut of their clothes.

Connor would have scorned the women's chatter. His tall, muscular frame just was not made for fancy evening wear and his dark hair was too long to be fashionable. But then, of course, he wouldn't care. And she found her eyes drawn again to the way his thick, wayward locks emphasised the hard planes of his cheekbone and jaw. *Dark hair, blue eyes,* she found herself thinking. A stunning contrast that emphasised the uniqueness of a stunning man.

And he was a bad enemy to make. Perhaps she'd always recognised that. Of course he despised her— yes, he'd asked her to work for him, but only because she'd talked herself into the job with her big, stupid mouth, by defending the Plass Valley children and by demanding that he do something for them.

Well, he'd obeyed her request by neatly turning the tables and telling her to do something for them herself. Soon she would be utterly humiliated and she ought to hate him for that. Yet in his presence, she felt something—a softening and a longing—that she almost couldn't bear to feel, because it was just too painful. But still she tried to smile.

'You ask me to employ a little more tact, Mr Hamilton.' She tilted her head and arched her brows in mild amusement. 'But you must surely have realised what you were taking on when you decided to employ me. What did you expect but trouble?'

His eyes darkened and suddenly she realised this was no joke any more. 'Listen, Isobel,' he said. 'I always realised it was going to be difficult for you, having to come back to your old home in such different circumstances. But I thought—I actually *believed*—you were intelligent enough to cope with it all. Please, in the next few days, make some effort to demonstrate that I wasn't entirely wrong.'

'Very well,' she said, keeping her voice light. 'I will try. But though I hate to say it, I did warn you that you were making a big mistake in hiring me!'

His expression banished her last attempt at frivolity. 'I didn't think so,' he said. 'And I still don't.'

He was only looking at her, he wasn't even touching her, and she felt hot and awkward and furious. Scalded. *Don't look at me like that, Connor,* she suddenly thought. *Don't look as if you're reading every last thought in my mind. As if you can see what you do to me. How I almost wish...*

'Connor!' Elvie was running up. 'I've picked the flowers for Grandmother! Here are some for you, too, Miss Blake—only now we'll have to get them home quickly, because they're drooping already, do you see?'

She thrust a posy at Isobel. Then Connor, after one last unreadable glance at Isobel, led Elvie to his big horse and lifted the child carefully into the saddle.

'Right, mischief,' she heard him say. 'Let's get you home.'

Chapter Nine

Connor Hamilton was like a kind big brother to Elvie, but to Isobel he was something else entirely. He was dangerous, he was lethal and he despised her. She felt dizzy and her chest was tight. He only had to look at her to set her heart pounding, her senses thudding.

'She's her father's daughter. You know that blood will tell.'

How often had she heard the whispers? How often must Connor have heard them? Slowly she gathered up her things—the now-empty basket, her sketchbook—and began walking after Connor and Elvie back to the Hall.

But she stopped abruptly when she heard a low whistle from behind. 'Miss!'

Connor and Elvie were some way ahead. She turned and realised that Harry was standing there almost shyly. 'Thank you, miss,' he said, 'for the food. It was brilliant.'

'It's been a pleasure, Harry.' Then she remembered just what she'd been about to say to the children when

Connor arrived. 'Harry,' she went on carefully, 'you know this school tomorrow?'

'Yes.' He looked down at the ground, scuffing his battered shoes in the dust.

'Well,' she said, 'I'm going to be your teacher.'

He looked amazed. '*You?* Honest, miss?'

'That's right.' Her heart was thumping, wondering how he would react. 'And I'm really looking forward to my time with you all.'

A broad smile split his freckled face. 'Well,' he said. 'If that don't beat all. This isn't a joke, miss?'

'No,' she said smiling now, 'it's not a joke, Harry. You'll tell the others, won't you? And tomorrow I'll see you at the old chapel, at nine o'clock—is that agreed?'

'Tomorrow,' he said cheerfully. 'Nine o'clock. We'll be there!'

He ran off and only then did she remember she was holding the flowers Elvie had brought her. There were buttercups, ragged robin and wild cranesbill—but then, almost hidden beneath the foliage, she spotted some delicate blooms of speedwell.

And their vivid blue was, she realised, the exact colour of Connor's eyes.

She felt almost an ache of loss. When she'd heard that Connor Hamilton was buying Calverley Hall, she'd thought, *I can deal with this*—just as she'd dealt with everything else that had gone so wrong in her life.

She had thought that she could cope with his return—but she was having to admit that his reappearance in her life was unsettling her more than she'd thought possible.

'*I did try, Connor,*' she'd said to him, '*to warn you that you were making a mistake in hiring me.*' But it was she who'd made the worst mistake of all, in agreeing to all this—because whenever he was near all she could imagine was being in his arms. Feeling his kiss.

She feared she'd wilfully blinded herself to the fact that, despite his scorn for her, she still felt too much for him. Far too much. And worst of all, she'd now put herself in a position that could only lead to her total and utter humiliation.

Isobel made sure she didn't catch up with Connor and Elvie until they reached the courtyard of the house. A groom came running to attend to the horse and Connor lifted Elvie down, holding her hand as they began to climb the steps to the front door.

Little Jack bounded after them. Isobel turned to take the path that led round to the side.

'Miss Blake!'

Connor's peremptory voice cut through the air. She halted and looked round at him. 'Yes, Mr Hamilton?'

'Where, precisely, are you going?'

'To use the side door,' she announced. Her voice was quite calm. 'Your steward told me on my arrival that I was on no account to use the main entrance. He explained it was for family, not servants.'

She saw an unidentifiable emotion working in his jaw. 'You are not a servant,' he said at last. 'You are here in a specific if temporary role and as such you will use the front door. I will have a word with Haskins. Come inside with us now, if you please.'

Elvie quickly ran on and was out of sight, but Connor waited in the hallway and, as Isobel drew near, he said in a milder tone, 'Are you ready for your first day of teaching tomorrow, Miss Blake?'

As ready as I'll ever be, thought Isobel rather wildly. 'Oh, absolutely.' She lifted her chin. 'Don't let appearances deceive you, Mr Hamilton—I shall be very firm with the children. I will stand no nonsense!'

He looked a little startled. Isobel let the smile fade from her face and said, this time very quietly, 'Tell me—what, exactly, do you expect them to achieve in such a short time?'

'A few basics, I suppose,' he answered. 'For example, it would help if they could write their own names, for a start. Then you could move on to the days of the week and the months, that sort of thing. Some basic arithmetic would be useful, too, perhaps familiarising them with common weights and measures. Do you agree?'

'Indeed,' she said heartily, though inside her heart was sinking as fast as that little boat she'd sent to a watery death in the river. 'But tell me.' She tried to keep her voice light. 'You clearly think a formal education will be of value to these children, even though you didn't have any yourself?'

'I did go to school, as a matter of fact,' he replied. 'The Vicar's school, for the children of the deserving poor in Chipping Calverley. I think I was there about a week, when I was seven.' A glint of a smile lurked in his eyes. 'That was how long it took for the Reverend Malpass to boot me out.'

'Not deserving enough?' she quipped.

Again she saw how he almost—*almost*—smiled. 'Actually, I put a live frog in his desk. He wasn't in the least amused. But my father taught me to read and write—he loved reading. And when I moved to London and Miles Delafield gave me a job in his iron foundry, Miles offered me access to his library. He had shelves full of books about mathematics, architecture and metallurgy—and I think I read every single one.'

'I do hope, she said, 'that you found time in London for pleasure also?'

Oh, no. That was a mistake. Because thinking of Connor Hamilton and pleasure was like lighting a beacon in her wayward mind; she had sudden visions of Connor whispering sweet nothings in some girl's ear, Connor taking a girl in his arms and kissing her and more…

Her cheeks flamed. He was watching her. 'I gain,' he said, 'great satisfaction from my work.'

Oh, good for you, thought Isobel rather hollowly. And her attention was suddenly drawn by the sound of a door opening at the far end of the hallway; Connor looked, too, and said to Isobel, 'I told you, I think, that there was someone else I wanted you to meet. Elvie's grandmother, Laura Delafield. And here she is.'

Isobel felt her heart sink even further. Someone else to disapprove of her.

But before she could conjecture any more, she realised that a small, neatly dressed lady with a beaming smile and gentle eyes was being wheeled in a bath chair towards them across the hallway. Elvie was skipping at her side and calling out in delight, 'Here is Miss Blake, Grandmother! Little Jack and I have had such fun with her by the river today!'

No mention of the Plass Valley children, thought Isobel, *thank goodness.*

And Elvie's grandmother was saying warmly, 'My dear. How delightful to meet you! Now, I hope Connor wasn't too heavy-handed in persuading you to take up your new post? He can, I know, be somewhat frightening!'

Before Isobel could think of a reply, Elvie, who was still holding her grandmother's hand, explained, 'Grandmother, Miss Blake told me about someone called Robinson Crusoe and how he was lost on an island hundreds of miles from anywhere. Do you know that story? Shall I draw a picture of Robinson Crusoe for you? I could let him have a dog, like Little Jack.'

'I would love a picture of Robinson Crusoe—and his dog.' Laura Delafield looked warmly again at Isobel. 'Miss Blake, I will be taking tea in my parlour in an hour—would you perhaps join me there?'

Isobel couldn't see Connor's expression, but she could *not* believe he would approve of her taking tea with Mrs Delafield in her private parlour. 'Thank you for your generosity, Mrs Delafield, but I fear I must decline, since I have so much to prepare.'

Laura nodded sympathetically. 'You will be planning tomorrow's lessons for the children, no doubt. But some time soon, perhaps, we can spend a little time together. My dear, I think you're going to be ideal for Connor's project.'

It was then that Connor stepped forward. 'And so do I,' he said quietly.

If Laura's praise startled her, Connor's words of approval took any remaining words from her mouth. Silently she curtsied and turned to go up the servants' stairs to her room.

There she found the young housemaid Susan rubbing away at the mirror with a polishing cloth as if her life depended on it.

'Susan? What on earth are you doing?'

The little maid spun round when she heard Isobel come in and stammered a few incomprehensible words—but there was no need, because Isobel had already seen. An image and some writing had been scrawled on her mirror in chalk—a crude sketch of a young woman with her nose in the air and a bonnet just like Isobel's stuck on her head. Thanks to Susan, the writing had almost gone, but Isobel could guess the kind of thing it might say.

She felt rather sick.

'Miss,' Susan said, 'I'm sure it was just a joke. But if I find out who did it, I shall say what I think! And shouldn't you tell Mr Hamilton that this has happened? Let *him* sort it out?'

'No.' Isobel spoke a little too sharply and forced a smile to soften her words. 'I really would prefer, Susan, for him not to know a thing. Let's just pretend it never happened, shall we?'

Susan nodded, clearly unhappy. 'If you wish. Oh, and I've unpacked your clothes that came today.'

Isobel nodded—that trunk had arrived, then, that Billy had promised to bring over.

Susan was still speaking. 'Will you be joining us for supper tonight, miss, in the servants' hall?'

Isobel suppressed a tiny shudder. 'May I just have a tray in my room this evening? Would that be too much trouble?'

'Not at all, miss. You must be tired, after being out so long with Miss Elvie.'

Susan and the others had no doubt spotted her leaving the house with Elvie this morning.

As long as the servants didn't know she and Elvie

*had spent a large part of the day with the children
from the travellers' camp...*

She realised Susan had paused by the door to say,
'It's good to see Miss Elvira so happy. I'm glad that
you're here, miss.'

Did many others share their feelings? Isobel rather
thought not.

Her supper arrived an hour later, but she found she
didn't have much appetite. She was still picking at it
when there was a knock on her door and Elvie entered
shyly. 'May I come in, Miss Blake? Oh—I see you're
having your supper! I didn't mean to interrupt.'

'Come in, by all means,' said Isobel warmly. 'Have
you had your meal?'

'Yes. But I'm still a *tiny* bit hungry.' The little girl's
eyes settled longingly on the dish of fruit jelly that Isobel had left untouched.

'Take it,' said Isobel, laughing, 'please do. I find,
you see, that I'm quite full.'

So Elvie sat on the bed and carefully ate every bit
of the jelly, then put the dish back on the tray and settled down with a sigh of happiness. 'Today,' she said,
'has been a *good* day.'

'I think so, too. A delightful day.' Isobel hesitated.
'Elvie—you didn't tell Connor or your grandmother,
did you, that you regularly meet those children?'

'Oh, no! I think the children are really nice, and
so does Little Jack—but Connor and Grandmother
wouldn't understand.' Elvie's expression suddenly became anxious. 'You liked them, though, didn't you,
Miss Blake?'

'I liked them very much. I liked your flowers, too,

Elvie—you see?' Isobel pointed to the bunch of wild flowers which she'd put in a vase on her windowsill.

Elvie nodded. 'I didn't know that the countryside would be as nice as this. My governess in London told me that it rained all the time.'

'So you had a governess in London?'

'Yes—Miss Paulson.' Elvie settled in the chair by the window. 'I didn't like her at all and I was very glad she didn't come here with us. Once I heard the London servants talking about her and they said she was *after Connor*. What does that mean, Miss Blake?'

'It probably means,' Isobel said carefully, 'that your governess was making a little bit of a nuisance of herself.' Quite a few females would be 'after' Connor, she suspected. 'Though,' she continued calmly, 'your Miss Paulson was right about one thing—it does rain in the countryside, quite a lot. But when you get a beautiful sunny day like this, you simply have to get outside and enjoy it, just as we did today.'

'I did enjoy it, so much. And Little Jack did, too.'

Elvie is delightful, thought Isobel. *Delightful, but sad.* And no wonder. She had no mother, no father, and now the poor child had been hauled away from the life she knew in London and isolated here, at Calverley Hall...

Suddenly she realised Elvie was watching her. 'What is it, Elvie?'

'Nothing,' said the little girl, frowning a little. 'Except that—I was thinking, Miss Blake. You're not at all like a teacher should be. I thought that Connor would pick one of the teachers who came for the interviews last week, but they looked horrid—I don't think they would have liked the travellers' children *at all*.

I'm really glad he picked you instead of them!' Elvie hesitated. 'Sometimes, I think Connor's unhappy. In London he's always very busy, but I don't think he has much fun. I think he's a little lonely.'

Isobel spoke carefully. 'Some people prefer to lead a private life. They like to be in charge—and other people can stop you being in charge. But one thing is for sure. Connor has got a very good brain and is excellent as a businessman.'

'Is that why he's got such a lot of money?'

Isobel smothered a chuckle. 'Now, Elvie, it's not really considered polite to talk about people's money.' She got to her feet and reached out to wipe a speck of jelly from the little girl's chin. 'It's been lovely to talk to you, but I've just realised the time. Won't your grandmother and Connor be wondering where you are?'

Elvie jumped to her feet. 'Oh, yes! And Grandmother promised she would read me a bedtime story. Thank you for a lovely day out, Miss Blake!'

And Elvie raced happily away.

Isobel sat there in the sudden silence. *I'm really glad he picked you instead of them.*

Little, innocent Elvie thought it was because Connor was kind. Of course, Isobel would let the child continue to think it. But she had made her own decisions about Connor Hamilton and she guessed he did nothing at all without weighing up all the consequences with the utmost precision.

She guessed he would never have bothered to buy Calverley Hall, which was so far from London and his business interests, had the place not preyed on his mind. And now that the Hall was his, he was able to hold the deeds and the keys in his hands and declare, *I'm back. And see what I've made of myself.*

Once, he'd been her friend. Even when she'd been the unwitting cause of his and his father's expulsion from the forge, he'd said, *It's not your fault, Isobel.* But now everything had changed.

Isobel knew she had to work for her living, one way or another. Marriage, for her, was out of the question. But Connor Hamilton had some catastrophic effect on her which resulted in her normally swift reactions drying up at his approach and her pulse rate leaping each time he looked at her with those blue eyes, blue as the speedwell flowers in the vase on her windowsill. She acknowledged she was afraid of him and what he did to her, whether he knew it or not. He'd offered a truce and had declared her position at the Hall to be of benefit to both of them—but she suspected that his overriding motive was to get his revenge on her and everything she represented, such as the aristocracy and all the old, unjust ways of life.

Who could blame him? Slowly she walked across to the window and pulled back the curtains a little so she could gaze out at the moon, rising low and full. Tomorrow, she would have to start giving the children's lessons—proper lessons—and her stomach somersaulted with dread at the thought.

What a fool she'd been to agree to all this. What a fool.

'You look rather thoughtful, Connor dear,' pronounced Laura Delafield later that evening. The two of them were sitting alone at the table in the vast dining room. Laura had read Elvie's bedtime story and the footmen had cleared away the last of the dishes and left. 'Could it,' Laura persisted gently, 'be anything to do with Miss Blake?'

Connor had been sipping his wine slowly. 'I'm a little concerned about her, yes. Haskins tells me that she has—as he puts it—been throwing her weight around.'

Laura was folding her napkin carefully. 'But Miss Blake appears the least arrogant of people to me. She appears unsure of herself. Shy, even.'

'You think so? Haskins informed me that she upset the staff almost the minute she arrived, by demanding her room be changed. And Mrs Lett says she infuriated Cook by commandeering lunch for herself and Elvie today. Of course I told Haskins and Mrs Lett that Miss Blake has my complete backing. But perhaps I should have been firmer with her for taking Elvie out without your permission.'

Laura toyed for a moment with her own small glass of wine. 'Do you know,' she said at last, 'today, when Elvie returned from her outing with Miss Blake, the child looked happy. As happy as I have seen her since Miles died. Surely that's important to you?'

'Of course.' Connor nodded his assent. 'It's the most important thing of all.'

'Undoubtedly,' Laura went on, 'Miss Blake is in a difficult situation here. But she accepted the post willingly enough, didn't she? And I like her. Please give her a chance, Connor.'

Laura left soon after that. Tonight, he knew he had tired her—good God, he had tired himself. What with old memories and old hurts rising to the surface almost faster than he could deal with them, it seemed that his past was threatening to engulf him again.

He'd been unspeakably stirred on seeing Isobel Blake after all these years—first at the fair and then on the day of the interviews, when she'd come to protest about the treatment of the Plass Valley children. And as Laura had said to him, 'Why not hire her as their teacher?' he'd thought, *Yes. Why not?*

But what, precisely, were his motives?

He'd dreamed for years of doing something for children who were denied a proper education for one reason or another, usually poverty. It was very likely, Connor knew, that only a small proportion of children would seize the opportunity for learning as hungrily as he had—but the point was, that they should be *given* that opportunity.

Noble words, he mocked himself. But what about Isobel—were his motives towards her anything like as noble? Laura had put her finger on it. Laura had said to him just now, 'She accepted the post willingly enough, didn't she?' And Connor hadn't contradicted her—but he should have done. He'd used that business of the Molinas' rent to practically force Isobel into a situation that clearly horrified her.

And there was something else.

Connor didn't allow himself much time for emotion of any kind. He saw emotions as a weakness, a crucial fault in a man's armour through which an enemy could probe. The only people he allowed himself to really care about were Elvie and Laura—otherwise, his work was his life. He'd always lived and breathed ambition, always worked towards the acquisition of power, because that meant nobody could get the better of him again, ever.

But was that really all that life was about? He fingered the stem of his glass and stared unseeing across the room.

He was in complete control of his business, his money and his emotions. Then why had Isobel Blake sent his thoughts into freefall? The moment he'd seen her at the fair, after seven years—*seven years!*—he'd felt something slamming against his chest as he'd taken in her slender figure and her face that—always pretty—had matured into a beauty shadowed by inner sadness. Though clearly she had no time whatsoever for self-pity. He'd found himself floored by her quick wit and he'd almost chuckled over her sturdy defence of those children at the fair.

Her reputation, of course, was non-existent. He accepted now that he'd misjudged her relationship with Molina, but everyone knew of the years she'd lived with Loxley. No decent family in the neighbourhood would acknowledge her; she knew it, and clearly didn't care. She dressed carelessly, she behaved outrageously. And yet he'd hired her! He'd invited her to live under his roof! Was he mad? He reached to knead his temples with his fingertips—*talk about playing with fire*. As the local blacksmith's boy, he of all people ought to have known better.

He'd assured himself he was merely doing her a favour by offering her the opportunity to do something she clearly felt strongly about—improving the chances, in however small a way, of the travellers' children.

But when he came upon her with Elvie by the river bank—when he saw her laughing and carefree with her blonde curls falling loosely around her face—he'd realised he desired her. Lust had jolted him as if he'd burned himself, like a moth fluttering too close to a candle. And he knew that thinking of her in that kind of way—noticing her firm, high breasts and her long legs beneath that thin summer frock of hers, wondering what it might be like to take her in his arms and kiss her soft lips—was a stupid, even dangerous thing to do and it had to stop. Especially since she doubtless knew exactly what she was doing to him.

Pushing his chair back, he abruptly got to his feet. He'd tried to convince himself that there were moments when he saw a shyness, almost a fragility in her laughing green-gold eyes—but that would be part of her act, too. You couldn't live with a rake like Viscount Loxley without learning a few tricks. And yet, knowing all this, he still found himself thinking, *What would it be like to really get close to her? To gain her trust, to arouse her desire even?*

Now, that thought sent the blood pulsing to his loins. *You fool, Connor. You fool.*

The next morning Isobel was at the chapel in the grounds by eight, a whole hour before the children were due to arrive. She'd taken no more than a few brief sips of the tea Susan had brought to her room, then she'd dressed in her plainest gown, secured her wayward fair hair tightly back with a black ribbon and hairpins and hurried from the Hall.

In the cool fresh air with the birds singing around her, she remembered her own governesses. There had been many of them and none had lasted long. They used to complain to her mother: *Isobel is impossible to teach. I give up with her...*

Pulling out the big iron key from her pocket, she opened the chapel door and went inside. At least Connor hadn't ordered her to use the old schoolroom in the Hall with its tiny windows that let in hardly any light. That was something. But there were still reminders of the schoolroom aplenty, because—at Connor's orders, no doubt—most of its contents had been transferred here. She looked round, feeling slightly ill.

There was the blackboard with a box of chalk. There were slates for the children and a pile of neatly stacked paper and pencils. There were even those books she used to hate—musty spelling primers, guides to punctuation and grammar.

Her spirits sank even lower as she reached into her pocket and pulled out a folded sheet of paper on which, last night in her room, she'd written out the months of the year. Carefully, painstakingly, she started copying them on to the blackboard. By the time she'd finished it was nine o'clock and there was the sound of boisterous chatter outside.

The Plass Valley children had arrived and excitedly they took their seats. 'Miss! Will you tell us another story, miss, like the one about Robinson Crusoe?'

'Perhaps. But first, children, you're going to learn the months of the year.'

There was a collective groan.

'Do you know the alphabet?' she persisted.

'A bit,' one of them called from the back. 'We got sent to school last winter. But the schoolmaster gave us all the cane so we left.'

Some of them started giggling and Isobel had to raise her voice to be heard. 'Well, children, you can be sure I'm not going to give you the cane. But you're here to learn, so please take up your slates and chalk, and you can practise writing the months—you see how I've written them on the blackboard?'

'Do we have to?' someone said.

'Yes, you do.'

They looked crushed. *Isobel, you're a complete fool,* she told herself bitterly. *You actually thought you could do this, didn't you?* Here she was, about to subject the children to three hours of misery—and this was only the first day!

Suddenly she noticed another shelf, on which sat some dusty wooden boxes. As the children gazed downcast first at the blackboard and then at their slates, she lifted one down. The box clearly hadn't been opened for some time and the clouds of dust billowed as she prised up the lid. Coughing a little, she eased aside some sheets of yellowing newspaper—and saw, with dawning surprise, that the box was full of games. *Children's* games...

Chapter Ten

Four days later, Connor happened to be riding close by the open door of the chapel as he returned to the Hall. Over the last few days he'd been making visits to his tenanted farms and that very morning he'd been to one of the largest, to discuss with the farmer the crops he was thinking of sowing next season.

He knew Isobel would be in the middle of giving the children a lesson and he'd had no intention of eavesdropping. But he couldn't help pulling his horse up sharply when he heard a child's merry peal of laughter and the excited cry, 'My turn. It *must* be my turn next, Miss Blake!'

He frowned. Heard more laughter.

He dismounted, tethered his horse and quietly climbed the steps to the open door. The Plass Valley children—there were eight of them—were seated around three of the small tables, which had been pushed together. On the blackboard were written out the months of the year, but no one was paying any attention to *them*. And Isobel Blake was sitting amongst the children on one of the little chairs, rattling a dice box—'Wish me luck, girls and boys!'—and everyone, apart from a small lad who was crawling around under the tables for some reason, was watching as she threw. A tousle-haired girl called out gleefully, 'You've got a three and a two, Miss Blake! Three and two make five, so you have to let us move a yellow goose!'

A yellow goose? What the...? And now Connor could see that everyone's attention was on a square wooden board set with an assortment of yellow and blue pegs, plus one red one. He cleared his throat, loudly; Isobel looked up, turned as scarlet as that peg and jumped to her feet. Utter silence fell as the children, too, registered his presence.

'Mr Hamilton!' She was straightening her crumpled skirt. 'I did not expect to see you here!'

'Clearly not.' His voice was extremely cool. 'Would you mind telling me, Miss Blake, what exactly is going on?'

Her gown, he saw, had chalk on it. Her hair had fallen from its pins as usual—and that sudden colour had drained from her face. Clearly she had noted his expression.

'I was trying,' she said, 'to make maths fun.'

He raised his eyebrows. The lad who'd been crawling around the floor emerged just then with a blue peg in his hand. 'Found it, miss!' he called triumphantly—then he saw Connor and crept back into his seat. Isobel had adopted that light-hearted, almost flippant look again, though her face was still very pale.

'Yes, fun!' she declared. 'We're playing a game—it's called Fox and Geese. I imagine you know it?'

'No. I don't know it.'

Undaunted, she chattered on. 'The person who is

the fox—that's me—has the red peg. The rest are the geese and the geese—that's the children—can move the yellow pegs and the blue pegs—'

'And this is a lesson?' Connor cut in with unconcealed harshness.

Her chin tilted in defiance. 'We're practising addition and learning about odd and even numbers. I've told the children that if anyone's dice add up to an odd number, they can move a yellow peg, but if they get an even number, they must move a blue one. And if anyone throws two numbers the same, then I can move the red fox. They've picked it up extremely quickly.' She faced him squarely. 'I believe I told you that my methods are a little unorthodox, Mr Hamilton. You can't claim I didn't warn you.'

The children were watching and listening openmouthed.

There was no point, decided Connor rather grimly, in making a scene in front of her pupils. So he answered, 'Would you come outside with me, Miss Blake, for a private word?'

A merry-looking, freckle-faced boy broke in. 'Sir, Miss Blake's been teaching us all sorts! We've learned the months, too—we've been practising them, hard!'

'Very good,' answered Connor coolly. 'Miss Blake. Outside, if you please?'

She followed him to the door, her head held high. And Connor, as he descended the steps into the sunshine, was thinking, *Is this games nonsense her way of rebelling against the position I've virtually forced her into?*

Perhaps the servants were right to complain about her. Demanding that her room be changed, helping herself to food from the kitchen—and now, fun and games in the schoolroom. It looked as if she was going to cause trouble for him every step of the way.

They stood a few yards from the chapel beneath some ancient yews, not far from the memorial stone to her once-proud ancestors. A sudden breeze ruffled her hair, making her look younger and reminding him of the girl she once was. She'd been a rebel even then, because by riding out so often to see him she'd been breaking all the rules of her heritage. Always, she'd had that bright smile on her face—*Here I am again!*—but he guessed that often she'd been lonely and afraid.

What must it have been like, living with that father? Most likely she'd have known everything that was going on—her father's gambling, his womanising, his debts. And that knowledge must have been agonising for her.

Suddenly, as they stood out there beneath the yews, Connor wanted to cancel his stupid bargain with Isobel Blake. He'd been a brute to force her into this. He wished he'd never seen her, that day at the midsummer fair…

Something caught at his heart. *No.* He couldn't wish that.

Damn it, he didn't know exactly why, but something had changed in him, the day that he'd noticed her there. Connor had come across numerous women over the years who had used their so-called fragility to try to manipulate him. He was bored by the wiles that had been used by heiresses angling for his affection; he was irritated by their pleas, their tears even.

Without a doubt, he enjoyed the company of a carefully chosen mistress or two—rich women who were safely married, but bored with their husbands, women who thoroughly relished his company in bed and had no foolish dreams of anything more permanent. If they did start making demands on his emotions, he ended the connection swiftly.

But—*Isobel.* Whether it was the memories that bound them, or her unusual and outright carelessness as to what society thought of her, she had him trapped in a wave of feelings that knocked him sideways.

Deal with it, you fool. And quickly.

He cleared his throat. 'So,' he said flatly. 'The children spent what—an hour?—this morning learning the months of the year. And then you let them play a game?'

'We spent some time on arithmetic, too.' She gazed up at him. 'For example, we worked out how many days are in each month and how many hours are in a week. From that, we calculated how many hours a week their parents work...'

He was looking at her in frank disbelief. 'Are you sure? I saw no evidence of this on the blackboard.'

She met his eyes defiantly. 'That's because I don't need the blackboard to work the figures out. The children use counters and their slates, but I just use my head. I always liked arithmetic.'

And he suddenly remembered how once Isobel, at the forge, had been glancing at the book Connor's father kept of income and outgoings. 'These figures are wrong,' she'd pointed out. 'Your father has missed a whole day's earnings from the weekly total—do you see?'

Isobel was right—and quick though Connor was,

he'd needed to use pencil and paper to make the calculations. She had done it all in her head.

What an extraordinary person she was. What a *liability* she was.

He cleared his throat, aware that two of the children were peeping out from the chapel doorway. 'I think it best, Miss Blake,' he said, 'if you concentrate on rather more conventional lessons from now on. If you're not careful, your pupils will take advantage of you.'

'If they don't enjoy themselves,' she pointed out calmly enough, 'then they simply won't turn up. And they *are* learning, even though it might not be conventional.'

He felt his jaw tighten. 'If you say so.' He indicated the open chapel door. 'Perhaps you'd better return to them and continue with this morning's lesson.'

'Or what's left of it,' she retorted sweetly. She made a mocking half-curtsy. 'Your most obedient servant, Mr Hamilton.' And she turned to go.

But just at that very minute there was the sound of yapping and a bundle of white fluff came hurtling towards them—Little Jack, with Elvie racing along behind. 'Connor!' Elvie was calling. 'Grandmother told me I could come out to meet you!' Elvie came to a halt, breathless. 'Miss Blake, how do you do? Connor, Grandmother said to remind you that we are due to visit Mr and Mrs Phillips and their family in Chipping Calverley for lunch today.'

Connor groaned inwardly—and he judged by Elvie's expression that she wasn't entranced by the idea either. 'I'd not forgotten. Don't you like the prospect, Elvie?'

The little girl hesitated. 'They are very polite, I suppose. They play the piano and recite poems. But they *don't have any fun.'* She looked hopefully at Isobel. 'Couldn't Miss Blake come with us?'

Connor wasn't sure how to point out that an employee did not make social visits alongside her superiors—especially if she was determined to make a damned nuisance of herself. It was Isobel who broke the awkward silence by saying, with her light laugh, 'I really won't have time to come with you, Elvie. I'll have so much to do to prepare for tomorrow's lesson with the children.'

'Yes,' Elvie eagerly blurted out, 'and I hope you've been having fun with them, Miss Blake, just like we did last week…'

Her voice trailed away.

Connor felt the sudden anger explode. 'Last *week*? Do you mean your day out by the river?' Elvie looked utterly dismayed. He turned to Isobel, his expression dark with disbelief. 'Am I really to understand, Miss Blake, that your trip with Elvie involved meeting with those children?'

She only hesitated fractionally. 'Yes,' she said.

'A *deliberate* meeting? Is that why you took such a large quantity of food from the kitchens?'

Again the hesitation. 'Yes.'

'And this was your idea, Miss Blake? On your very first day at Calverley Hall?'

He was aware of Elvie moving slightly at his side. 'Yes,' said Isobel for the third time.

Connor dragged in a deep breath. He said to Elvie, 'Run off home now, will you? And tell your grandmother I'll be back very soon.'

Elvie cast one last, distraught look at Isobel and left, with Little Jack at her heels. Connor turned back to Isobel. 'Miss Blake, what possessed you to take Elvie to meet the Plass Valley children? My God, this is beyond a joke...'

'I apologise.' She faced him squarely. 'If you wish, you may have my resignation immediately.'

'*No,*' he said abruptly. 'Damn it, no. But—how could you? You know they're entirely unsuitable company for her!'

'Perhaps as you were for me?' she said steadily. 'Or so they told me. But I, as you must have realised, took absolutely no notice.'

He stared at her, speechless. *I was different,* he could have tried to say. But was he? Might she be quite right, and he *wasn't* different to those children who would be waiting for her inside the chapel?

Before he could think what to say, she was speaking again. Shrugging, even. 'Of course, you are right, Mr Hamilton. It was very wrong of me to take Elvie to meet the children and you must act as you see fit.'

He sighed. 'I am not going to call a halt to this venture now. If we tell the children that the school is finished, they'll never attend any sort of schooling again.' Once more he indicated the open door of the chapel. 'You'd better continue with what's left of your lesson. And the less said about that outing with Elvie, the better.'

She nodded and Connor felt like the clumsiest bully on earth.

But damn it, she'd acted in the most reckless fashion! Taking Elvie to meet with the Plass Valley children, ordering Elvie no doubt to keep silent about it! And yet he *still* couldn't help but have his emotions

tugged by her. By her outright dignity, despite all that
beset her. Despite all that was said about her...

Isobel, who'd been standing beside Connor very
white and still, was at last turning to go. That was
when he realised a scrap of paper had fallen to the
ground. He picked it up. Someone had been writing
the days of the month and struggling with them, it
appeared. The early attempts were incorrect and had
been crossed out—*Janury. Janueryy*...

And then Isobel was almost snatching the paper
from him.

'That's from my lesson,' she said swiftly. 'I told
you—we've been learning the months of the year and
some of the children found it rather difficult. Now, if
you'll excuse me, I must get back inside—'

He stopped her by grasping her wrist. 'But that
writing—surely it doesn't belong to a child!'

'Your hand,' she whispered. 'You're hurting my
wrist, Mr Hamilton. Please let go.'

And he did; but as he released her, he saw that her
bright smile had vanished and instead there was on
her face was an expression that shook him to his very
core—because it was a look of utter despair.

He watched her hurry back inside. And before she
closed the door, he heard her say cheerfully, 'Very
well, children. Shall we learn some history next? I'm
going to tell you a story that I'm sure you'll love...'

Connor cursed silently. This time, he was *really*
angry with her. How dare she take Elvie to meet the
Plass Valley children? Was it yet another act of deliberate mischief-making? He knew how quickly she'd
antagonised the household staff, but to have involved
Elvie in such a foolish jaunt almost straight away was

going too far! Hopefully Laura would never find out.
He ought to have dismissed Isobel on the spot...

But he hadn't. Why on earth not?

Rubbing his hand across his temples, Connor Hamilton acknowledged that she drove him mad. Whenever he tried to point out the error of her ways—indeed, the outright *foolishness* of some of her actions—she was always ready with some careless retort, some act of defiance.

And yet he couldn't help but notice that when she forgot to put on her bright smile and to produce those swift quips of hers, she looked lost. Quite lost. And then it was he, Connor, who was aware of his usual rock-steady composure shifting beneath him, as if the ground he was on was suddenly crumbling, cracking even. It always happened, whenever she was near. It was almost, he thought, like laying his plans for some new feat of engineering—you had to be sure of all your equipment, of all your calculations, and above all that your foundations were rock-solid—but where Isobel Blake was concerned, all his uncertainties seemed founded on quicksand.

Connor led his horse slowly into the Hall's courtyard, feeling as if he was tearing himself away from a situation that was actually becoming perilous. He realised that something about her was enmeshing him in its coils: her quick tongue, her flash of a cool smile and above all that sudden look of vulnerability. The haunting sadness ever-present in her eyes—always she blinked it swiftly away, but not before something inside him had surged into life: the basic male impulse to stand at her side and defend her against the whole world.

And then—to kiss her.

He ought never to have begun all this. He ought to let her walk away right now—but he found he couldn't bear the thought of it. And he didn't like to consider the implications of *that*.

Chapter Eleven

Isobel continued with the lesson till noon, then she bade the children farewell. 'We'll see you tomorrow, miss!' they called out as they left one by one.

Isobel nodded cheerfully. 'Goodbye, Mary—don't forget your sunbonnet! Goodbye, Peter—I'm glad you enjoyed yourself. Goodbye, Reuben. You'll all be here tomorrow, won't you, at nine?'

''Course we will, miss,' called Harry, their spokesperson.

She stood by the door, her hand raised in farewell until they were out of sight. Then she went back inside and sat at the desk, motionless. The crisis she'd been dreading had arrived even sooner than she'd feared.

She'd been intelligent and inquisitive as a child. She was eager to learn from an early age, reading simple texts before she was four and enjoying mathematics, too, loving the way everything fitted.

But she was an atrocious speller.

The problem had begun when she was six and her governess had sternly told her mother, 'I'm afraid your daughter has an issue, Lady Blake. You see, she uses her left hand to write.'

Her mother had been horrified. 'Then she must be stopped. By whatever means you think necessary!'

And Isobel realised that this was a terrible secret which must, at all costs, be concealed. She had tried desperately hard to use her right hand, as her governess instructed, but her handwriting was abysmal. Secretly she used her left hand, but one day she was caught and her governess fetched a leather strap and bound her left hand behind her back. 'You mother has ordered me to do this,' she said.

And so Isobel used her right hand, but her writing was crude and unacceptable, and her spelling skills suffered, too. Whole words and sentences became muddled up in her brain, with each letter taunting her as if it had a life of its own. Her reading was perfect, her capacity for mental arithmetic quite astounding, but no one was interested in *that*.

She was nine when her mother died, so the scolding stopped and the governesses stopped after a while, too—her father refused to pay for them. But the damage had been done.

And she'd agreed to be a teacher! In her stupidity, she'd thought she could cope with this—after all, it was only for a few weeks. Connor had issued his ultimatum—*'You challenged me to help them, Miss Blake. Well, I'm handing that challenge over to you.'* And his generosity to her friends the Molinas had forced her hand, but now it looked as if she might fall at the first hurdle.

She stared almost blindly at the empty tables and the blackboard she'd wiped clean.

What else had Connor wanted the children to learn? He'd talked about weights and measures—oh, no, yet more long and difficult words! Her brain already over-tired, she went to the bookcase and found a primer with pages full of measurements—feet, rods, furlongs, acres. Pulling a sheet of paper towards her, she began slowly copying the words one by one.

She didn't realise how the time had gone by until the door opened and Susan the maid came in.

'Beg pardon, miss, but it's well past one o'clock. Mrs Lett's been expecting you to take lunch with us in the servants' hall these last few days. And she wants to know, will you be coming there today?'

Isobel rose to her feet. Lunch? She'd simply done without it—and in the evenings she'd eaten in her room. 'Could you possibly bring me something here, Susan? That is, if it's not too much trouble?'

'Not at all, miss.' Susan bobbed a little curtsy, then hesitated by the door. 'Miss Blake, they say how this was your home when you were younger. And it's a real shame that you've lost all this. You must have been broken-hearted...' She pulled up, blushing furiously. 'I'm sorry, it's not my place to say it, I'm sure. Begging pardon, miss.'

And she was gone. Isobel sat down again slowly. Did Susan but know it, her memories of those last years at Calverley Hall were so painful that she'd all but blotted them out. Memories of how after her mother's death her father's life had sunk further and further into ruin as he drank and gambled with his friends for night after night. Memories of his debt-ors virtually laying siege to the Hall, which was why he'd taken Isobel to London when she was eighteen. 'You've got to make a good match,' he'd told her. 'You've got to bring some money into the family—do you understand?'

London. A rented house in down-at-heel Bayswater. The awful Mrs Sparlet dragging her to one party after another. Doors often being slammed in their faces. She recalled her father's increasing desperation and his final illness only two months after their arrival in the city. He was still being hounded by debtors on his deathbed. Viscount Loxley had actually been Isobel's saviour—but no one would believe that.

When Loxley died two years later, Joseph Molina's kind offer had meant Isobel could return to the Gloucestershire countryside she loved. But now—with Connor's return also—everything had gone wrong again. How *could* she have been so stupid as to accept this job?

She suddenly remembered something else that troubled her. This morning, one of the children had told Isobel that her father had been involved in a fight last night—over the school.

Isobel had frowned. 'Are you sure about this, Mary? That it was about the school?'

'Miss,' Harry put in, 'it started outside the alehouse. Some of the men around here don't like us. *"A school isn't for the likes of you lot,"* they said. But my dad thumped them and Mary's dad thumped them, and they ran.'

Isobel would have liked to know more, but that was when Connor had arrived. She remembered the story again now, though, and it troubled her. Perhaps Connor ought to be informed? Then Susan came in with some cold lunch on a tray; Isobel thanked her and made herself eat it, even though she wasn't really hungry. She expected the maid to come back for the tray—but it wasn't Susan who came in next. It was the housekeeper, Mrs Lett.

'Will you be long in here, Miss Blake? I've not said anything for the last few days, but I really must tell you that the maids need to clean the chapel. It's on their afternoon duty rota.'

Isobel gave the woman her brightest smile. 'Oh, Mrs Lett! I simply have to get this work done for the children's lesson tomorrow. Can the maids wait another half-hour, perhaps?'

'That would be most inconvenient for them.'

'Even so, I'm afraid I must insist. Thank you *so* much, Mrs Lett!'

The housekeeper departed, her rather sharp shutting of the chapel door showing exactly what she thought of this interference with her staff's schedule. Isobel worked on, lighting a candle as the shifting afternoon light left her desk in shadow, practising the spellings over and over, then at last standing up to transfer all those fiendish words on to the blackboard, ready for tomorrow.

And then she heard the door opening, yet again. She glanced at the clock on the wall—it was five o'clock. The housekeeper, she thought wearily, come to order her out of here, so the maids could get on with their work. She turned round, resigned. But it wasn't the housekeeper. It was Connor. She dropped the piece of chalk and reached to pick it up, and in doing so she sent books and papers flying from her desk. *Oh, no. Please not him again. Not now.*

* * *

Since visiting the schoolroom that morning, Connor had escorted Laura and Elvie to the Phillips's family home, staying just long enough to be civil before going on to visit two more farms that lay on the Calverley Hall estate. The tenants were full of gratitude for the new equipment and stock Connor was providing, though to him, the money he was spending was simply a business investment. He wanted to make something of this place and he had a limited time in which to do so. Soon, his commitment to the docks work in London would be making far more demands on his schedule, so he was determined to make the most of the summer here.

After returning from his visit to the farms, he'd gone to his study to start checking the estate's accounts, but his mind was elsewhere. His mind was on Isobel, in fact. There had been yet more rumbles of discontent about her from the servants this afternoon—Haskins had reported that she was proving reluctant to adjust to the household routines.

'Miss Blake is only here for a short while,' Connor had replied, 'and I'd be glad if you and Mrs Lett would allow her some leeway.'

'Yes, sir,' said Haskins rather woodenly.

Now Connor frowned at the memory. Of course, what Haskins and the others meant was that Isobel in no way looked or acted like a servant, but Connor didn't really expect her to—he'd hired her to run a school and the children clearly liked her, very much. Wasn't that vitally important to the process of learning? He was extremely eager for his scheme, small as it was, to prove a success, because he was hoping he might be able to use it to encourage various business colleagues to set up similar projects for their own workers' children.

But if there was going to be any sly innuendo as to why he'd hired such a young, attractive teacher, then his project might be dragged through the mud.

He'd been a fool to take her on and not only because of the scandal attached to her name. He was a fool because whenever he was close to her—even when he was blazingly angry with her, like this morning—he couldn't help but imagine how soft her skin would be to touch and how sweet her lips to taste. In the chapel, even as the children stared at him in awe, he'd actually longed to slide his hands around their teacher's slim waist and draw her close, and kiss her…

Connor almost thumped his desk. How could he be so foolish as to even *think* it? She had no place in his life. He enjoyed the company of women and he knew that some day he would do what was expected of him and get married. As Laura had recently pointed out to him, there were plenty of suitable candidates—the chief amongst them being Helena Staithe, who would bring her family's proud heritage to the match.

Isobel Blake was just the opposite. Her family heritage was a tale of headlong ruin and disgrace. But there was something else—something that he just couldn't get his head around.

She was always cool and calm with him, as if it didn't matter that she had lost everything; in fact, sometimes she was so flippant that it appeared as if she didn't even care! Yet just occasionally, like this morning in the chapel when he'd questioned the unsuitability of what she called her *lesson,* he'd seen a glimpse of raw vulnerability. And when he'd picked up that crumpled sheet of paper, she'd looked almost terrified.

Why? What on earth was going on?

He should just let her get on with the job he was paying her for and leave it at that. It was safer to feel nothing for Isobel Blake—no anger, no scorn, just nothing. That was the only possible course. Because otherwise, his rampant thoughts about her sweet face and soft lips and lush figure would cause absolute mayhem in his body and his brain.

It was gone five by the time Connor had packed away his papers in his study and went out to the stables to inspect the horses and enjoy a chat with the grooms. But as he left the stables to return to the Hall, he happened to glance in the direction of the chapel and he noticed candlelight shining from its windows.

Surely Isobel wasn't still in there? Doing *what*, for God's sake?

He was still frowning when he opened the chapel door several minutes later. She almost jumped from her seat when he came in, knocking a book and some papers to the floor. Her face was flushed with confusion.

Connor found himself, as usual, utterly perplexed by her. Had she been in here all afternoon? Why did she look almost afraid to see him? Was she doing something she ought not to be doing? But what *could* she be doing wrong in a schoolroom, on her own, for heaven's sake?

And why did he feel that sharp tug in the region of his heart, as he observed the effort she made to pull herself together, to pick up those papers and scrape back some loose tendrils of her fair hair and try to smile?

'Why, Mr Hamilton,' she said, 'what a surprise to see you.'

He replied, 'Miss Blake. What a surprise to see *you*. What on earth are you doing here at this hour?'

She gestured towards the books and pieces of paper on the desk. 'Oh, I take my duties most seriously— whatever you may think to the contrary!'

She was being her usual flippant self, but she looked tired. Frightened, almost. She didn't want him to be in here. Didn't want him to know what she was doing…

He moved closer to look at the book on the table— *Barnaby's Guide to Weights and Measures.* On the blackboard behind her, he realised, were rows of carefully written words.

4 rods = 1 chain
40 rods = 1 furlong

He turned to face her. 'I take it you're preparing tomorrow's lesson? I don't expect you to work non-stop, Miss Blake. There's absolutely no point in exhausting yourself.'

She waved one hand airily. 'Oh, it was just a little something I was checking on. Tomorrow, I've decided we'll have a mathematical lesson, using various measurements—poles, perches, rods and everything! Just as you requested!'

Even as she spoke, he noted that she was scooping up the pieces of paper from her desk and transferring them to a folder. But she'd dropped one. He picked it up, glanced at it and frowned.

What the devil...?

Someone had been ruling lines and writing the same word over and over, sometimes incorrectly, just like that sheet of paper he'd picked up earlier with the months on—*Janury. Januery.* Yet again, the handwriting was laborious, awkward. It was the work of the children—it had to be!

But all the words had been written in ink. And the children only had their slates and pieces of chalk...

There was something odd going on. He put the paper down. 'Well,' he said. 'You've had a few days to settle in now and the children appear to be very much enjoying themselves. The question is, are you?'

'It's been wonderful,' she enthused. 'The children are so eager and engaging!' And she chattered on, but Connor was still puzzled, and more than a little troubled. *All afternoon. She'd been in here all afternoon.*

Just after lunch, as Elvie and Laura had prepared to set off on their visit to the neighbours, Elvie had anxiously clutched Connor's hand and said shyly, 'You won't frighten Miss Blake away, will you?'

'Me? Frighten anyone?' he'd teased.

'You are frightening sometimes, you know,' Elvie said seriously.

She was right, of course, thought Connor. Otherwise he wouldn't have got to where he was.

'And sometimes,' Elvie had gone on hesitantly, 'it means people are scared to tell you the truth.'

He'd been taken aback by that. 'Do you think so? I really hope not, Elvie.'

'Connor,' she'd said, 'w-what would you do if someone got into trouble b-because of something *you* had done wrong?'

Oh, no. That stammer again. He'd thought very carefully before replying. 'I think,' he'd said at last, 'that I would feel happier if, however scared I was, I told the truth. Because it would be bound to come out some time, you know?'

And then Elvie had looked as if she was about to tell him something important—only at that precise moment Laura had called for her.

Connor knew Elvie was afraid that he would frighten off Isobel Blake. He had no intention of doing so—*though I am going to keep a damned close eye on her,* he resolved to himself, watching her now as she tidied up her desk. Unfortunately, keeping a close eye on her might involve certain risks he hadn't anticipated.

What had Elvie wanted to tell him? he wondered. But really, it was impossible to concentrate on the question, because Miss Blake had started putting her books away on the shelves and he couldn't help but see how her vigorous movements revealed the delicious curves of her all-too-feminine figure. He found himself distracted yet again by the fact that, despite her drab gown and rumpled hair, she looked quite lovely.

She was struggling now to put the blackboard and chairs away. Swiftly he went to help, but her arm unintentionally brushed his and he felt the sudden shock of her warm, fragrant body so close to his. She must have felt it, too, because she shied away from him like a terrified filly.

He should have backed away, but instead he felt impelled to move closer until he was virtually towering over her. And there was something pulsing between them that was totally powerful and totally dangerous and impossible to resist. He could feel the pounding of his heart, he could hear the ragged rasp of his own breathing. And suddenly raw desire throbbed inside him, crazy and out of control. All he could think was, *What would she taste like if I kissed her?*

He forced himself, literally, to take a step backwards. And he said, in a voice that sounded far harsher than he meant it to, 'Miss Blake. On consideration, I was rather sharp with you this morning, over your choice of lesson material. I just wanted to report how I've heard that your somewhat unconventional teaching methods are already having excellent results. Some of the travellers came to me an hour ago to express their gratitude. I thought I'd let you know.'

She still looked very pale. 'Well,' she said brightly, 'that's satisfactory, at any rate. It would have been rather awkward for you, wouldn't it, if you'd been forced to dismiss me so very swiftly?'

'Yes,' he said, 'it would. And that brings me to another point—please try, will you, not to antagonise my staff?'

She put her head on one side, arching her eyebrows. 'Oh, dear. I take it you've had more complaints?'

'One or two. Though I've reminded my staff to treat you with the respect you deserve.'

She'd started gathering her books together. '*So* understanding of you! Believe me, I'll really try to remember my place.'

He swallowed his exasperation. 'Miss Blake, is it time to remind one another of that truce we agreed to?'

'Why not, Mr Hamilton? It's always such fun to see who breaks it first!'

He smiled back—he couldn't help it. *Keep things light. No danger in that, surely?* 'There was something else I was meaning to ask you,' he said. 'Laura—Mrs Delafield—suggested to me that you might like to take your meal with us this evening.'

She looked stunned. 'You no doubt reminded Mrs Delafield that her invitation, though kind, would in no way be appropriate?'

'I didn't, as it happens. I agreed that it was an excellent idea. So perhaps you will join us to eat in the dining room at seven tonight? As you'll realise, we keep country hours here.'

Isobel closed her eyes briefly, then opened them again. 'I really, really would rather not.'

'And I would prefer it,' he answered, 'if you did.'

He turned to leave. And—as if something was prompted in his brain—he suddenly remembered what Elvie had asked him earlier. *What would you do if someone got into trouble because of something you had done wrong?*

And he faced Isobel again. He said abruptly, 'That expedition to meet the Plass Valley children. It was *Elvie's* idea, wasn't it? Yet you let yourself take all the blame! For pity's sake, Isobel, why?'

She said nothing, but he knew he was right by the way she held herself so very still.

'I'm sorry,' he said between gritted teeth, 'to have misjudged you. Please accept my apologies.'

And he left; but he was still aware of her standing there looking quite lost, with that stray lock of fair hair trailing down her cheek.

Truly, there was something about her that grabbed at his heart. *Damn it.*

* * *

After he'd gone, Isobel didn't move for a long time.

Connor had said he was sorry that he'd blamed her for that meeting with the children—but he'd still been angry with her. *You let yourself take all the blame. For pity's sake, Isobel, why?* As if she would have dreamed of loading the blame on to poor Elvie!

He'd proposed a renewal of their truce—yet the gulf between them was so vast, it was hopeless. She should never, ever have agreed to this arrangement. Not only was their past an insurmountable problem, there was also the present to consider, because some time soon, she'd be caught out—she couldn't spend every afternoon and evening practising her spellings and memorising them for the next day's lessons. Sooner or later, she'd be exposed as being entirely unsuitable for this post—and a liar into the bargain.

There was something else, just as bad. Worse, in fact. She had thought she could cope with the way Connor Hamilton made her feel. Thought she could laugh and joke her way through her conversations with him. But it was getting more and more difficult.

She'd been frightened when he'd drawn so close just then, because at first she'd feared he might be about to guess those clumsy spelling attempts were hers. But then she'd felt another kind of fear. With his taut body so near to hers, and his dark, lean features hovering too close, her mind had become dizzy. She'd known she ought to back away, but she couldn't, because her body was paralysed with a helpless yearning.

Connor the blacksmith's son had become a powerful man, a formidable man—and she'd been fervently imagining his kiss. She'd been *longing* for it.

The young man she'd once hero-worshipped had become something else entirely—and it was making her position here impossible.

She rose and walked over to the chapel window, staring blindly out. Six weeks was the bargain and time and time again she'd mentally lashed herself for agreeing to it. She could easily have backed out—after all, he'd let the Molinas off their rent regardless of her decision. What really disturbed her now was the suspicion that she'd accepted his offer because, from that first day of meeting him at the midsummer fair, he'd worked a kind of dark magic on her.

He didn't even try to look attractive, yet he'd developed a kind of masculine grace that the son of a blacksmith just should not have. He made no effort with his clothes or his grooming; sometimes he looked almost disreputable—his scruffy breeches and boots, his open-necked shirt and his sleeveless leather jerkin were the kind of garments a farm labourer might wear.

His dark hair was long and often unkempt. He really ought to shave twice a day, but clearly didn't—and Isobel found, to her horror, that her wayward fingers longed to tangle in his dark locks and feel the rasp of his strong, stubbled jaw. And to touch the silken softness of his mouth, preferably with her own…

She felt her breasts tingle and the sudden heat bloom low in her belly. She was confused and ashamed, because she felt herself wanting things she'd only heard about before. She thought she'd grown used to those stories about her time in London; she'd told herself she didn't care what people said. But she was wrong.

She was devastated to think that Connor believed them. And perhaps she really was secretly shameful, in her thoughts at least—because as she left the chapel and walked out into the lush greenery of the garden, her body still trembled from his nearness and her lips still imagined his kiss.

Chapter Twelve

The evening meal she was supposed to share with Connor and Laura developed into yet another disaster. Firstly, a footman she met on her way down to the dining room warned her that she wasn't expected there until a quarter past seven.

'I thought I was meant to join Mr Hamilton and Mrs Delafield at seven,' she said, confused.

'Oh, no, ma'am,' the footman said earnestly. 'It will look most odd if you arrive before a quarter past, I assure you.'

He was one of the young footmen whom she suspected of salting her supper that first night. She should have known he wished her ill. By the time she arrived, the first course was already being served—and she also realised, to her horror, that there were two guests: a fashionably dressed couple who regarded her with polite surprise.

What an atrocious start to the evening.

'My apologies to everyone,' Isobel began, colouring as they all turned to look at her. 'What a scatter-brain I am, to be sure!'

Connor had risen the moment she entered. 'It

doesn't matter, Miss Blake. Though I did send a message to inform you we had guests.'

No doubt he'd sent the message via that smirking footman, telling her not to come. Then she realised, with another sickening lurch, that there wasn't a place set for her. She wished she could vanish into thin air, but Connor had already given a signal to the staff and another chair was being brought, another place set. *'It doesn't matter,'* Connor had said. But she knew it did.

Connor was dressed formally. He looked superb in his black evening coat and white cravat, and for a moment, as he held her eyes with his own penetrating blue ones, she felt unable to speak or even breathe. She could guess what he was thinking. No doubt he was wishing the pesky Miss Blake a million miles from here. At least her chair was next to Laura's—that was a small mercy—and Laura couldn't have been kinder, pointing out the dishes and the condiments, asking her what she wished to drink.

It was quite a few minutes before Isobel had time to take further notice of the two guests. The man was around Connor's age; he had fashionably cropped blond hair and his languid gaze flickered over Isobel curiously. The woman was a little younger, raven-haired and elegant in a dark green silk gown. Before Isobel had time to wonder who they were, Connor announced the guests as Roderick Staithe and his sister Helena. 'They are London acquaintances of mine,' he added.

'And we arrived rather unexpectedly,' put in Roderick Staithe in a drawling voice. 'We're on our way to Bath, my sister and I. We have a house on the Crescent and thought we'd spend a little time away from London. All that heat and dust in the capital in summer, you know? But when we realised we would be travelling close by Calverley Hall, we thought, we really must call in and see how our friend Connor's faring. He astonished us all, by buying this place out in the wilds!' He was staring at Isobel. 'So you're a governess, are you?'

Isobel flushed because his pale eyes were devouring her. 'Not quite. I'm a teacher, Mr Staithe.'

Staithe nodded. 'Same thing, surely? Connor's told us a little and I must say I thought, "Now, is the country air getting to Connor's head? Setting up a summer school for the children of tinkers?"' He laughed. 'Though Connor's notions are often surprisingly good. He and my father and Miles Delafield once dabbled in quite a few projects together. Connor supplied the ideas, Miles provided the experience and my father, who was in Parliament and knew all the right people, made sure that everything they set their minds to— bridges, roads, whatever—got the official go-ahead. My father's dead now, but I've got his seat in Parliament. So I can speak up for Connor just like my father did.' He savoured a mouthful of wine. 'I've always found Connor knows exactly what he's doing. And aren't *you* lucky, to be invited to live in a place like this, if only for a short while?' He looked around the superb dining hall appreciatively.

He doesn't know, realised Isobel. *He doesn't know my father used to own this house.*

She found she didn't care at all for Roderick Staithe. He was loud and full of himself and all the time he kept staring at her with those pale eyes.

She had prepared herself with care, changing into

a dress that was made of grey wool, with a narrow
lace collar its only adornment. She had pinned back
her unruly blonde hair almost severely, but Staithe
still stared. 'A teacher, eh?' he kept saying between
mouthfuls of food and wine. 'Now I wonder where
Connor found *you*?'

Connor said, 'I advertised, Staithe, as one does.'
His voice was cool. He had decided, Isobel realised,
to keep quiet the fact that she once lived here. For her
sake, or for his? She wasn't quite certain. Surely he
didn't actually like this man? But in Connor's world
of money and towering ambition, no doubt business
interests came above everything.

And then Staithe's sister Helena spoke up. She must
have been travelling all day, but her gown was fresh and
uncreased, and her dark ringlets were immaculate—no
doubt she would have her own maid travelling with her.
And Isobel realised, with a painful tightening in her
lungs, that there was only one person in the room to
whom Helena was paying any true attention—Connor.

'Really, Connor,' Helena was saying to him now in
an amused voice, 'don't you think it's a little much to
expect this poor girl to deal with the children of tinkers, day after day? And what, exactly, is the point?'

At Helena's words Isobel felt her pulse begin to
pound and gripped her hands tightly together under
the table—then she heard Connor's calm voice. 'The
point is, Helena,' he said, 'that I believe every child
should be given the chance of an education.'

'But surely…' and Helena Staithe spread out her
elegant hands '…these children are simply destined
to work in the fields, like their parents?'

Connor was silent a moment. Then he said, 'I

started my working life at my father's forge, shoe-ing horses. Thanks to Miles Delafield, I was given a chance to better myself—through work and through education.'

Roderick Staithe nodded. 'Of course, Miles Delafield was a sound fellow. What a great deal we owe him!' He looked at Laura and raised his glass. 'A toast! To our departed friend, Miles!'

'To Miles,' said Connor. They all lifted their glasses, then Staithe turned his attention to the food again. 'By Jove, this lamb is excellent—mind if I help myself to another slice or two? And are you quite sure, Mrs Delafield, that it's not a problem if my sister and I stay the night?'

'My dear Mr Staithe,' said Laura, 'your rooms are being prepared this minute.'

A brief silence followed as the footman served the next course, then Isobel heard Helena Staithe address-ing Connor in a cajoling voice. 'I must tell you, Con-nor, that you were sadly missed at the small party Roderick and I held two weeks ago to celebrate our move into our new house in Mayfair. Later in the sum-mer we'll be returning there, of course, and you really must visit us—you'll surely be coming back to town before long, won't you? After all, what is there to *do* here? Who is there to talk with?'

'Well, he has me,' said Laura, her smile belying a certain sharpness in her voice.

'Of course, Laura!' Helena said quickly. 'And there's also your delightful grandchild—Miles's poor orphaned daughter. But, Connor, how on earth do you fill your days?'

Connor looked straight at her. 'I'm hoping,' he said,

'to revitalise some of the farms that belong to this estate. For too many years, they've lacked investment and good management. I plan on making them prosperous again.'

Helena pulled a face. 'Oh, Connor. Tinkers' children and farms! Whatever next?'

Then Roderick, who'd been emptying his glass yet again, beckoned to a footman to refill it and said, 'My God, old fellow, if you're looking for somewhere to put your money and see it grow, you need to get back to your London foundries as soon as possible. After all, you're ahead in the running to supply iron for the new east London docks, aren't you?'

'I am,' Connor replied, 'and the matter is well in hand, believe me.'

For the next ten minutes the two men talked about the price of iron and the various building projects going on in and around London. Isobel noticed that Connor showed a real warmness, enthusiasm even for the topic, and in spite of herself she, too, was fascinated to realise just how much business Connor controlled, how much influence he had.

At last, as the desserts were removed, Laura bestowed her sweet smile on the company and said, 'Now, gentlemen. Will you forgive me if I retire to my parlour?'

The men rose from their seats. A footman had already stepped forward to take charge of Laura's bath chair and Isobel was preparing to take her leave, too, the sooner the better. But then she felt Staithe's touch on her arm. He was blocking her way to the door and she realised with a shiver that he was scrutinising her even more closely.

'Do you know,' he said, 'you really are far too pretty to be a teacher. And I could swear I've seen you before! London—it *must* have been London…'

She felt a sudden sick lurching at her stomach, but she opened her eyes wide in mild surprise. 'I truly doubt our paths can ever have crossed, Mr Staithe!'

He sighed. 'Yes,' he said. 'Yes, I suppose you're right.'

Isobel made for the door again, but not before she heard Staithe's sister saying to Connor, 'Now I know you always act with the best of intentions, but that poor girl over there really is out of her depth in more ways than one, isn't she?'

Isobel couldn't hear Connor's reply.

Her intention was to retreat to her room as quickly as possible, but Laura, out in the hallway, had dismissed the footman and was beckoning to her. 'I am so very sorry about the misunderstanding, Miss Blake. When I invited you to dine with us, I'd no idea the Staithes would be arriving. And of course neither Connor nor I would have dreamed of mentioning to them that you once lived here. That your poor father…' Her voice trailed away.

Isobel looked at her steadily. 'My father was a bankrupt. Did Connor tell you that?'

Laura looked startled. 'No. No, he didn't.'

'Then it's only fair that you should realise it, before feeling too sorry for my father or me. He drank, he gambled, he borrowed, then finally he lost the Hall. He would have ended up in a debtors' jail had he not died.'

'Even so,' Laura said. 'It must be very hard for you,

my dear, to come back here like this. And I tried to say as much to Connor…'

'Mr Hamilton offered me a job and I accepted. I do have to work for my living.'

Laura nodded, but she still looked anxious. 'I suppose this teaching post was the best way Connor could think of to help you. But I'm really not sure he was right. And *were* you in London? Did you have a coming-out there?'

Isobel felt her pulse thudding. 'It was several years ago and it was not a success, I assure you.' She looked around. 'Mrs Delafield, you've been most kind, but I really would prefer to retire to my room before your guests join you—'

'No. Please!' Laura reached out for her hand. 'Do join me in my parlour, if only for a little while!'

But just as Isobel hesitated—*how to escape?*—the opportunity mercifully arrived. Elvie's maid appeared and bobbed a curtsy to Laura. 'Begging pardon, ma'am.' She glanced at Isobel also. 'Miss Elvira, bless her, can't sleep. And she asked if she could see—Miss Isobel'

'May I have your permission to go to her?' Isobel asked Laura.

'But of course.' Laura nodded. 'First let me say, though, that all in all, my dear, I think we're *extremely* fortunate to have you here at Calverley Hall.'

Isobel left—just as Helena Staithe was sweeping towards them from the dining room.

Roderick Staithe, clearly intrigued by Isobel, continued to ask Connor questions as the two of them drank their port after the ladies had departed. 'That young woman,' he pronounced, 'doesn't look in the slightest bit like a teacher if you ask me. Damn it, she'd be as pretty as a picture in the right frock and with her hair primped up a bit!' He winked. 'This wasn't some sort of ruse, was it, to get your latest paramour living here? Right under the nose of Miles Delafield's mother!'

'You've been drinking too freely,' Connor answered flatly. 'She's here to temporarily teach the travellers' children and that's all there is to it.'

'She's got an enchanting face. And that figure!' Staithe shook his head in admiration. 'You know, I really could swear I've seen her before—I just can't get the notion out of my mind. Well, no doubt the delights of the country will fade fast enough for you and my sister and I will see you when we're all back in London...'

Roderick Staithe was nothing like his father, to whom Miles Delafield had owed so much in his early career. Now Staithe was changing the topic to some race meeting he'd recently attended and Connor listened with only half an ear.

The trouble was, he couldn't afford to alienate Staithe—at least, not yet. The docks project would require the approval of a Parliamentary committee and Staithe was the man to see it through. But that didn't mean Connor had to like him! And Isobel's arrival at the dinner table had set up all kinds of further possible problems.

Staithe wasn't likely to forget about the young woman Connor had employed to teach the travellers' children. Staithe hadn't realised yet who she was, but if—*when*—he did, the gossip would spread like wildfire. Isobel had coped well with a damnably awkward situation and it was Connor who'd been thrown side-ways almost, because he'd felt nearly overwhelmed by the urge to protect her and save her from further hurt.

Yet he was the one responsible for all this. He'd been recklessly stupid to choose her for his school and, to add insult to injury, he'd virtually forced her to come back here and live in such changed circum-stances that every minute of every hour must be tor-ment for her.

Yet up till now she appeared to have coped stead-fastly. He suspected she might even be rather enjoying ruffling the feathers of his senior staff, and himself, too. But once or twice already he'd glimpsed a raw vulnerability when her guard was down, a vulnera-bility that Roderick and Helena's arrival had brought to the fore.

Roderick, of course, hoped Connor would offer for his sister. The Staithe family was of noble heritage, but lacked ready cash—Connor would bring money in plenty and Helena clearly wasn't averse to the idea. Helena had good breeding, beauty, too, if you liked her kind of immaculate, chilly style. A few years ago Connor could only have dreamt of such a fine match.

But seeing Helena again tonight had made him re-alise that she just didn't compare with Isobel. Tonight must have been agonising for Calverley's former heir-ess, yet she'd endured it all with dignity, and as she'd sat there in her plain, long-sleeved dress he'd suddenly realised she'd never looked lovelier. She wore no frills or fripperies to distract from her slender figure and the neutral colour of her gown somehow seemed to heighten the warm gold of her skin and the sheen of her silky fair hair, which had been escaping from its ribbons as usual to trail in tempting disarray down the delicate nape of her neck.

And all those sickening stories Connor had heard about Isobel, that he'd perhaps just been starting to hope were lies, came flooding back.

They must be true. Yet it frightened him how strongly he felt about them. Worst of all, she'd made no attempt whatever to clear her name—done nothing at all to dispel the rumours about her and Loxley. And Connor offering her this job would in no way help her either, because once the news spread that she was living under his roof, the gossips would have yet more fuel for their talk.

Staithe was still rambling on about racehorses, but when he broke off to reach yet again for the port decanter, Connor put out his hand to stop him and said, 'Shall we join the ladies?'

Fortunately Staithe seemed to have forgotten about Isobel. And Connor was hardly surprised, when they reached Laura's parlour, to find that Isobel had vanished. *No wonder.* She probably couldn't wait to escape. Helena was there, of course, and she was playing some tinkling tune on the piano while throwing an inviting smile in Connor's direction. Connor moved close to Laura and said quietly in her ear, 'I take it Miss Blake has retired for the night?'

'No. There was a message from Elvie's maid—Elvie couldn't sleep and wanted to see Isobel. So Isobel, bless her, went up to her straight away. But perhaps I should go, too, to check all is well—'

'No need for you to disturb yourself,' Connor interrupted. 'I'll go.'

* * *

Isobel had reached Elvie's bedroom to find the child tearful and anxious. 'I'm so sorry, Miss Blake,' Elvie whispered as Isobel settled herself in the chair at her bedside. 'For getting you into trouble, because of our day by the river with the children!'

Swiftly Isobel reached out to stroke back her hair. 'Elvie, there's no need to cry. Connor knows the truth now and he's not cross with you. He understands.'

'But I let you take all the blame for meeting the children! I lied to Connor!' Elvie's voice broke. 'The V-Vicar says that t-telling lies is one of the very worst things of all.'

Sometimes, thought Isobel, *I could do something drastic to that Vicar.*

'Well,' she said, taking Elvie's hand, 'the Vicar told me, when I was about your age, that I was an abomination.'

Elvie's eyes widened. 'What's an abon…abom…?'

'It means he thought I was very naughty, because, you see, I didn't attend his Sunday afternoon Bible classes when I was a girl. Instead I used to run away and wander around the countryside.'

Elvie was chuckling. '*Abomination.* I like that word. Will you write it down for me? There's my little book and a pencil, just there—see?'

Isobel hesitated. *Oh, no.* But Elvie was waiting, expectantly. How could she lie to her?

'Elvie,' she said, 'can I tell you something very private?' Elvie's eyes widened. 'In the Vicar's classes,' went on Isobel, 'we were expected to write answers to lots of questions about the Bible. And I knew I wouldn't be able to spell most of the words—so I just didn't turn up.'

'You couldn't *spell*?' Elvie looked awed.

Isobel tried to laugh. 'Yes. And, Elvie, I still can't. Ridiculous, isn't it? You see, I'm naturally left-handed, but my governesses and my mother made me use my right, so by the time I was your age my hands and my brain were all mixed up. I've never had a problem with reading or with arithmetic—just spelling. But this is our secret, Elvie. I've told you this to explain why I don't take much notice of what certain grown-ups say. People like the Vicar, for example.'

Elvie was still round-eyed. 'Did you get punished for missing the Bible classes?'

Isobel hesitated. 'A little, yes.'

'Were your mama and papa unkind?'

'In some ways, I suppose they were'

'I don't remember my mama.' A lone tear was trickling silently down Elvie's cheek again. 'But my papa was very, very kind—and I miss him so much!'

'Of course you do. Of course.'

Isobel held her, stroking her hair until Elvie swallowed hard and said, 'I'm lucky to have Grandmother and Connor. But what about *you*, Miss Blake?' She pulled away a little. 'Do you have any family?'

'No, Elvie, I don't. But I'm used to that.'

'Used to being on your own? But you shouldn't be!'

'Well, I'm not on my own entirely. I have some lovely friends called Joseph and Agnes—and now I've got the Plass Valley children to think about.' She smiled. 'Which reminds me that I really must be starting to get my things ready for tomorrow morning's lesson. Are you all right if I leave you, Elvie? You don't want Connor or your grandmother to come up to you?'

'No, I'm really sleepy now.' Already Elvie was

snuggling down under the covers, yawning. 'Thank you, Miss Blake. I saw that Miss Staithe was here, with her brother—she wants Connor to marry her, I think, but I hope he doesn't. He should marry you instead.'

Isobel felt her breath catch tightly in her throat. 'Elvie. Elvie, that's nonsense...'

But the little girl's eyelids had closed and within moments she was fast asleep. Isobel rose from her bedside, suddenly weary.

And at that very minute, she realised Connor himself was standing very still, in the half-open doorway. *Oh, no.*

What, precisely, had he heard?

Chapter Thirteen

Connor had moved back out into the corridor, so Isobel was able to leave Elvie's bedroom and quietly close the door.

'How is she?' Connor asked in a low voice.

'She was over-tired, I think,' she replied. 'But she's sleeping now—I asked her if she wished to see you or her grandmother, but she said she would be all right. Now, if you'll excuse me, I really must retire to my own room. Goodness me, these may not be town hours, but to me, it's still late!'

He nodded, unsmiling. 'I wanted to say that I had no idea, when I asked you earlier to dine with us, that Roderick Staithe and his sister would be arriving at such short notice. But I did send a message to fore-warn you.'

'And I never got it. Foolish of me, I know.' The smile she'd put on faded, though she still kept her voice steady. 'It was an awkward situation for you, I fear. Did Mr Staithe eventually realise I was Sir George Blake's daughter? Or—did you feel obliged to tell him?'

'The answer to both your questions is no.'

'But he will realise soon. He's *bound* to...' She made a big effort to steady herself and say lightly, 'You know, Connor, you really should have listened to me when I told you that hiring me was not a good idea. But you're accustomed to getting your own way, I suppose—no wonder you've fared so well in business. Now, if you'll excuse me...'

She was attempting to push her way past him, but he gripped her wrist. 'Once more, Isobel, I apologise. You coped well with Staithe's questions. Whatever you say to the contrary, any enquiries about your past must be painful for you.'

She looked pointedly at his hand on her arm, and he let her go. 'I'm used to it,' she said. 'The stories about my father's ruin. And you'll have heard, no doubt, that during my time in London I managed to bring about my own kind of downfall.'

He was regarding her steadily. 'And are the stories true?'

'Why not? Everyone whispers them, so they must be, must they not?'

She saw a muscle tighten in his jaw. 'For God's sake, Isobel. I'm trying to give you a chance to explain!'

He'd clenched his hands and was stepping closer. She was thinking that if he drew only inches nearer, he could kiss her. Her heart was thudding with hard, almost painful beats as she imagined the feel of his lips on hers—*would they be hard or soft, cool or warm?* His eyes were dark and heavy-lidded, and his whole body radiated tension, as if beneath that cool exterior he was perhaps as agitated as she.

'Explanations,' she said, 'often do more harm than good, I've found.'

She heard him draw in a harsh breath, saw his mouth harden, and something knotted so tightly inside of her that it hurt. *You were my childhood hero,* she wanted to tell him. *And you don't realise it. You'll never realise it...*

'Isobel.' He uttered her name almost like an oath. 'Isobel, for God's sake, why do you put this wall up around yourself when all I'm doing is trying to understand? Is it because all this is too much of a comedown for you?'

She flinched; somehow she pulled herself together as he went on, 'When I heard those stories about you, I could not believe them.'

'It would be much easier for you,' she said calmly, 'if you did.'

She saw him struggling for words. 'I suppose,' he said at last, 'I thought that I might be offering you a fresh start with this job. A chance to prove yourself. I perhaps underestimated how difficult it would be for you, returning like this to the house where you grew up. But I trust the servants are treating you with respect?'

She thought of the footmen's tricks. Of the hurtful jibes she was meant to overhear. She threw him a bright smile. 'Oh, of course! You know, I already feel part of one big, happy family here!'

He was silent a moment. Then he said, 'I am most grateful to you for taking on this post. And I hope very much, for the sake of the children, that you'll be able to see through this project till the end.'

Never, ever would she let him guess how painfully hard her heart was beating. Never would she admit what a struggle it was, to prepare her work for the children; how she'd floundered badly this morning when he arrived in the chapel, in an effort to cover up her mistakes. She would rather die than let him realise just how useless she was.

'I suppose,' she said almost lightly, 'you would not be able to find anyone else at this stage?'

'No one quite like you,' he replied.

No one as stupid as me, she thought. The teacher who couldn't spell. She arched her eyebrows. 'Well then, I suppose I'll have to carry on. How long did you say? Six weeks? I think I can just about manage that.'

'I'm glad.' He spoke very quietly. 'And, Isobel, after that…'

'Oh, no.' She spoke quickly. 'Oh, no. You're not trapping me into anything else. As I told you before, I get bored easily. But I'm so glad you're satisfied, Mr Hamilton!'

'*Isobel…*'

But she'd already brushed past him to head for the servants' stairs leading up to the next floor and her bedroom. 'Isobel,' she heard him calling after her. 'Miss Blake. You must not go that way—'

She assumed he meant she was to use the main stairs, but that would mean going past him again and right now she just wanted to get away, so he wouldn't see what was in her eyes. Wouldn't realise the agony he'd just put her through. She reached the stairs, which were almost in darkness, and had climbed only a few when she stumbled against something bulky and solid. Losing her footing, she tried to save herself by grabbing the banister rail, but failed and found herself toppling backwards.

Then she was aware of warm, strong arms around her. Holding her.

'Isobel?' Connor was turning her to face him, his voice sharp with concern. 'Isobel, didn't you see the laundry bag there on the step?'

'No,' she whispered. 'So foolish of me…'

He was still holding her. 'Are you hurt? You're shaking.'

And suddenly, she was overwhelmed. He despised her, she knew he did. She tried to speak, to warn him that he would loathe himself if he let this go any further, but she couldn't because he was reaching to smooth back her hair, which had tumbled from its pins almost completely now, and he was hungrily drinking in her face, her lips, and she *knew*.

She knew he wanted to kiss her.

Slowly he lifted his hand to her cheek, brushing it across her skin. His fingers were astonishingly gentle, yet fierce darts of pleasure teased her wherever he touched. She felt dazed, struggling for control as he drew her close. With one strong arm around her waist, he brought her to him so that her small, high breasts were pressed against the wall of his chest.

All she had to do was push him away. But then she saw his blue eyes darkening with desire and she could feel the hard promise of his body against her, could see his tempting lips hovering…

His mouth touched hers. And her senses reeled.

How could this meeting of lips mean so much? She felt his warm, strong mouth caressing—teasing, almost—before claiming possession. Somehow his maleness enveloped her, enfolding her with desire—she knew she was in acute danger, but at that mo-

ment she wanted him to kiss her more than anything
in the world.

He *wanted* her. Despite his scorn for her, she knew
he wanted her and she exulted in it. She felt her hands
stealing unbidden up to the hard muscle of his shoulders, felt her mouth open instinctively as his tongue
explored the soft seam of her lips, then probed deep.
Honey melted her insides and she was intoxicated. She
was lost. His hand was caressing her breast now; the
nipple peaked beneath his touch in delicious torment.

'Isobel,' he was saying huskily. 'Isobel, I...'

But what he was about to say next, she would never
know, because she heard footsteps approaching and he
must have heard them, too. He pushed her away from
him so abruptly that she stumbled and caught her arm
on the newel post of the staircase and the sudden pain
made her cry out; a moment later Mrs Lett, the housekeeper, came bustling along the corridor, followed by
a curious maid.

Isobel felt sick with shame. What had they seen?
She could already hear the whispers. *'That hussy, lur-
ing Mr Hamilton into dark corners—and she's hardly
been here any time at all!'*

She nursed her bruised arm. Yes, it was dark in
this corner—thank goodness. They couldn't have seen
what was going on.

'We heard a noise, Mr Hamilton, sir.' Mrs Lett
glanced at Isobel sharply. 'And we came to see if everything was all right. If anything, or anybody, was
bothering you.' Her eyes flickered over Isobel again.

'Miss Blake stumbled over some laundry that had
been left on the stairs.' Connor spoke curtly. 'There's
no harm done, fortunately.'

He was clearly expecting the housekeeper to leave—and then no doubt he would tackle her, Isobel, again. Shame surged through her. No doubt he couldn't wait to dig again at the open wound of her time in London.

She was used to being punished for her past. But what she really couldn't cope with was the knowledge that if they hadn't been interrupted she would have melted into that kiss and would have let him do *anything.*

She couldn't forget how his face had looked dark and even dangerous as he drew her close. How her surroundings had seemed to spin around as he crushed her against his chest, moulding his hips to hers, the hardest part of him rigid against her. And then that kiss! It had caused an explosion of her senses, making her breathing tight and desperate; making her want to get even closer to him as she clung to his broad shoulders. She'd felt such an ache of need, down *there,* that she'd thought she might die if he stopped whatever he was about to do…

That cry she'd let out could well have been the sound of her throwing away the last shreds of her ruined reputation. And so, with yet another piece of her world crumbling into dust, Isobel hurried away.

'Miss Blake,' Connor called. *'Isobel!'* But she was already out of sight.

It was past eleven that night, and Staithe and his sister had retired to their bedrooms, but Connor sat on alone in his firelit study.

He had wanted to make Calverley Hall the talk of the county, the talk of London even. He wanted to silence those who whispered about men who'd made their fortunes in industry—men like him, whose money was referred to as low money, dirty money.

Roderick Staithe had inherited an ancient name, together with a large house that had been in his family for generations. Everyone knew he lacked ready cash, but that didn't trouble Staithe—he was one of the landed gentry. Nevertheless Staithe's eyes had widened as he took in the Hall and its grand rooms. The man was clearly impressed.

But Staithe's eyes had also widened at the sight of Isobel. And once again Connor thought, *I was crazy to hire her to teach those children.* Crazy and selfish. What would happen when Staithe finally realised who she was—as he inevitably would, sooner or later—and took the news back to London?

'Connor Hamilton has Sir George Blake's daughter under his roof—and you'll remember the scandal about her!'

Connor recalled Isobel's expression when he'd taunted her outside Elvie's room. He'd said, 'Is it because all this is too much of a come-down for you? Is that the problem, Isobel?'

She'd looked, then, as if he'd struck her. And for God's sake, he'd made everything far, far worse by kissing her! He'd always been proud of his self-control, but it had vanished the moment she fell into his arms. He wanted her. If he was honest, he'd wanted her from the day he saw her at the midsummer fair—and she knew it. He'd seen it in her eyes, in her flushed cheeks, in her parted, luscious lips...

My God, she's trouble. You've got to keep your hands off her.

And she, no doubt, felt exactly the same about him.

If he'd harboured any lingering memories of their earlier friendship and of what he'd believed her to be—valiant, honourable, honest—they'd been destroyed when he'd heard what they said about her in London. When he realised she was perhaps her father's daughter after all.

Yet he'd felt so damned guilty on realising he'd misjudged her relationship with Joseph Molina that he'd determined to hire her for his school. How could he have been so stupid? Stupid and stubborn, because once the idea had become embedded in his foolish mind, he'd not been able to let go of it. Just as he'd not been able to fight off the way her image was ever present in his memory, his brain...

And his body. *Don't forget that,* he told himself with ferocious self-contempt. From first seeing her at the fair, he'd been imaging how she would taste, to kiss. What it would be like to explore her slim waist and firm breasts; he guessed she would be responsive, ardent even, and he'd been right.

That kiss had been a revelation. She'd been uncertain at first, doubtless still shaken from her fall; but then she'd made a small, dazed sound in the back of her throat and the kiss had got hotter, wilder. And he'd quickly realised a mere kiss wasn't enough; dear God, he'd thought he might lose control entirely when he felt her hands clutching his shoulders and her sweet tongue melding with his, making him long to remove every single scrap of clothing she wore.

Then he remembered Viscount Loxley. He'd met him once. He was an ageing fop, raddled by years of drink and dissolution. What did he do to please Isobel in bed? And what did she do in return, for *him*? The thought made Connor wild with rage. It was crazy to desire her as he did—but he was physically aching for her even now, aching with a man's desire throbbing at his loins.

And there was something else that troubled him even more. She did not *act* like an experienced woman. Her kiss had been delicious, yes, but naïve. Shy, almost. And whenever he was with her, he still sensed that beneath her bravado, her shrugs and careless laughs, she was still the brave but vulnerable girl who used to ride almost daily to the forge. Who'd trusted him implicitly. And in return, he'd wanted to protect her, with his last breath...

Crazy of him. She knew very well she'd ruined herself with Loxley. He'd noted her expression when Staithe mentioned London—he'd seen that flare of outright panic in her eyes, before her emotion was swiftly disguised as usual by some flippant retort.

She'd looked equally guilty when he'd found her in the chapel this afternoon. 'What are you still doing here?' he'd asked, genuinely astonished.

And she'd stammered out some lame excuse. But something was very wrong.

Well, he'd hired her for the summer and somehow he had to make the best of all this and try not to let her stir up any more trouble—because he certainly had plenty of other matters to occupy him. Only today, fresh paperwork had arrived to confirm that the London investors he'd approached to back his new docks scheme had agreed to a meeting in a week's time, to discuss the finer details before concluding whether or not to put their money in his hands.

'This looks promising, sir,' Carstairs had pronounced, with what was, for him, an unusual level of excitement. 'This will be your largest project yet and worth a fortune to the firm.'

Yes, the city financiers were flocking to hear the details of Connor Hamilton's latest plans. But money, unfortunately, wasn't enough—Connor also knew that a Parliamentary committee would be gathering soon to decide whether to give final government approval to his scheme. You needed friends in high places to aspire to the heights yourself and Connor's chief ally in Parliament was Roderick Staithe.

Staithe had already informed Connor that he was going to be chairman of the committee. Staithe had also reminded Connor, several times, that he wanted a rich husband for his sister. 'Helena's taken quite a fancy to you, you know?' Staithe had winked. 'And you'll realise, of course, that if you give me the word, then I'm your man in Parliament. Just as my father was for poor old Miles.'

Connor knew that was how the upper classes did these things. He was fully aware that he couldn't enter marriage on a whim—it had to be carefully planned, for financial and social advantage. And anyway, his heart was impervious to mere sentiment, wasn't it?

But what about Isobel?

All this would pass. He'd been a fool to invite her into his life again, but in a few weeks it would be over. It was a temporary difficulty he'd rushed into without thinking and afterwards he could quietly give her a respectable sum of money and never see her again.

Yet that kiss. It still haunted him. The blood had rushed to his head, his heart had pounded at the taste of her sweet lips, and he'd wanted to take her there where they stood in the half-darkness and make love to her until the world around them faded into oblivion. An oblivion where nothing at all existed except the taste of her and the scent of her and the sound of her sobbing out his name.

He pounded his fist against his forehead. This must not happen. He paced the room, then flung himself into the chair at his desk and tried to concentrate once more on the papers he was supposed to be studying about the damned docks and the shareholders' meeting.

But all he could think was, *What about Isobel?*

Chapter Fourteen

For the next few days, Isobel didn't see Connor at all. On Sunday she went to church with Elvie and Laura, but despite another invitation from Laura she continued to eat all her meals in her room and, other than Susan, she saw hardly anyone to speak to except for the Plass Valley children.

Each weekday morning at nine, her little pupils arrived eagerly at the chapel—and they'd started to bring more children with them, from the camp. Isobel felt slightly dizzy as the numbers grew. 'They really wanted to come, miss!' declared Harry, their freckle-faced spokesman.

Some of them had to sit on the floor, but they didn't appear to mind and Isobel hadn't the heart to turn them away. But it did mean she had to work harder than ever in preparing her lessons. Arithmetic was no problem for her—she took great pleasure in teaching the oldest and brightest of her pupils their times tables and explaining various ways of becoming agile with numbers.

But the written work! That was a different matter

entirely. She had to spend hours writing out her own notes on paper and then on the blackboard, consulting the dictionary time and time again, thinking, *How on earth were you supposed to look a word up when you didn't know how to spell it in the first place?*

And, of course, the children all expected—indeed, they eagerly anticipated—some lunch. Every morning, Isobel would take her empty basket to the kitchen and fill it to the brim. Every morning came Cook's mutter, 'I don't know what Mr Hamilton's thinking of, wasting good food on the likes of them.'

Isobel always just smiled cheerfully as she turned to go. 'Thank you *so* much, Cook!'

The food always disappeared in no time and then the children would depart, leaving Isobel alone to fathom out the next day's lesson.

Then one day she had an unexpected visitor—Elvie, with Little Jack. 'Grandmother's resting,' Elvie confided. 'And I'm supposed to be resting, too, in my room. But I'm not in the tiniest bit tired, so I thought I'd come and see you, Miss Blake!' Her attention was suddenly caught by the blackboard. 'Is that word supposed to say "autumn"? But you've written "autum"— you see? Here. Let me do it for you...'

After that, Elvie called in to see her every afternoon, to show her Jack's new tricks and to help her with her spelling. Didn't Elvie think it was odd that Isobel had been appointed as a teacher when she had such glaring deficiencies? But Isobel realised the little girl had the gift of accepting people for what they were and after an hour or so in the chapel Elvie would race back to the Hall with her puppy, leaving Isobel alone. Of Connor there was no sign and all went well—until the morning that a stone was hurled through the chapel entrance.

Isobel had fourteen pupils by now and all of them were working away, their heads bent low. Because it was a hot day, Isobel had left the door open and was listening to one of the children reading when suddenly something flew through the doorway and crashed to the floor between the rows of tables.

The children screamed in terror. Isobel raced outside—and glimpsed a couple of figures running off through the trees.

There was no way she could catch them. Her own heart was pounding with shock, but swiftly she went back inside to calm the frightened children. 'It's all right,' she soothed. 'It was just somebody playing an unpleasant joke.'

Unpleasant indeed, especially as the stone had been dipped in pig manure. As the ripe smell filled the chapel, nausea washed through her as well as fear. But with all the children's eyes on her, she had to appear calm, so she went to fling the stone as far away as she could, then fetched a pail of water from the pump at the rear of the chapel and went down on her hands and knees to scrub away the filth left on the chapel floor. The children watched in silence.

Someone was getting their own back on her. Probably those footmen again.

She tried to say as much to the children. 'I'm afraid,' she said lightly after she'd finished clearing up, 'that there are some people around here who don't like me very much.'

But one of the older girls stuck up her hand. 'Miss, it's not you they don't like. It's us! Last night after dark, some men tried to set fire to our caravans. They got chased away, but tonight our dads say they're putting up a guard!'

The other children murmured in agreement. And Isobel remembered how the children had described the fight outside the alehouse. That had been about the school. Should she tell Connor about the stone through the door? But tell him what, exactly? Tell him that there were people who hated the travellers? What on earth could he do about it?

The children were clearly still upset, so to distract them she began to tell them the history tale she'd promised. It was about the Battle of Hastings, and soon calm was restored—until a quarter of an hour later, when she heard footsteps outside and broke off, her heart thumping in anticipation of yet more trouble.

Connor Hamilton walked in. Trouble indeed. Her heart began to race in a quite different way. She felt a flush of heat as she remembered that night outside Elvie's room and the kiss—though to look at him now, standing there staring at her, it was as if it had never happened. For a breathless moment she stared back, feeling utterly exposed to his relentless blue gaze as he stood in the door, arms folded. Then he said, 'Carry on, Miss Blake.'

She felt shaky. Unbalanced. How could she, she thought rather desperately, with him standing there, watching her? 'Children,' she said in a bright voice at last, 'that's enough of the story for now. But I'd like you all to draw me a picture of one of the soldiers I've just told you about.'

Harry stuck up his hand. 'I want to draw a picture of King Harold, miss, getting the arrow in his eye.'

'Very well, Harry. And I've told you, haven't I, how they looked different, the Normans and the Saxons?'

'The Saxons had long hair and beards, miss. The Normans didn't!'

'That's about it,' she agreed. Then, preparing for a battle of her own, she walked towards Connor in the doorway. 'Mr Hamilton. This is a surprise. You find us busy, as you see.'

And she smiled at him, presenting a picture of strict efficiency, she hoped. But he wasn't smiling back.

Her heart missed a beat. He stood there with the bright sun behind him outlining all his dark masculinity, his power. His eyes looked impenetrable and his dark hair was a thick, careless mane, looking as though he'd just rubbed his hands through it. He wore a white linen shirt that was open at the neck and tucked loosely into buckskin breeches; his boots were of sturdy black leather and not even polished.

And yet in sheer sensual impact he far outshone every single one of the men of fashion she'd seen in London's ballrooms. A small pulse of longing set up low in her abdomen when she saw how his open shirt revealed a hint of tanned chest and silky dark hair that she longed to run her fingers through...

Feeling dizzy, she jerked her eyes upwards to meet his. *He kissed me,* she reminded herself shakily. *That night at the Hall he kissed me and he wanted more—I saw it in his eyes, I felt it in his lips...*

Now, he just looked weary with her. 'I can see you're busy, Miss Blake,' he said. 'And unless there's something wrong with my eyesight, you have fourteen children in here.'

'Oh, dear.' She tried another of her bright smiles. 'Does it really matter? They are absolutely no trouble—'

'Why wasn't I informed?' he broke in.

She shrugged. 'I thought, actually, that it might be something for you to boast about, to your friends in London. The success of your—what do you call it?— your *charitable enterprise*.'

He drew closer. Said silkily, 'Do you think that's why I set up the school, Miss Blake? Just so I can boast?'

She suddenly heard the raggedness of her own breathing. For a minute, she couldn't even move, because her body had been almost paralysed by a helpless yearning. She drew a deep breath. 'Now, let me see,' she said levelly. 'I'm not exactly sure why you set up this school, to be honest. Sometimes, I really could swear you did it with the deliberate intention of demonstrating my exceedingly lowly place in this new world of yours.'

The children had all stopped their drawing and were staring open-mouthed. She continued to hold Connor's gaze steadily, though inside she felt exhausted. Crushed.

'I thought you might enjoy it,' he said flatly.

She caught her breath. 'Certainly, the children are delightful. But my employer—now, I'm not quite so sure about him.' She tilted her chin. 'Presumably you've come to point out that I've broken some more of your rules? You've already told me there are too many children in here. What else?'

'I've had more complaints, as it happens. Cook says that your children are eating too much and Mrs Lett says her housemaids are weary of cleaning and sweeping up here each day.'

Isobel felt her anger rising, but said calmly, 'In that case I'll do the cleaning myself.'

'*That* I will not allow.'

'Then I'll leave.'

'I'm not going to allow that either.'

She waited, heart hammering.

'I've told Cook,' he went on, 'that she's to prepare as much food for the children as you require, and I've told Mrs Lett to hire an extra maid if cleaning the chapel is proving a problem. You are to let me know, Miss Blake, if there's anything else at all that you need. I've informed all the staff that this school is a priority.'

And suddenly, something in the way he looked at her made her chest feel tight and caused her throat to ache with some inexpressible emotion. Fourteen children were staring at them, but she felt as if there were only him and her in the whole world and the only sound was the violent drumming of her heartbeat.

If she reached out, she knew she could touch the faint dark stubble on his jaw, could touch his lips and remember again how they'd felt against hers. Silky and tender, yet passionate with desire. And if she lowered her eyes it was no better—because then she saw the outline of his hard, sculpted body beneath his clothes and she remembered how he'd crushed her against him in that kiss. How her breasts had nestled against his chest and the arms that had held her were like iron...

She heaved in a deep breath. That was a mistake, too, because as she inhaled the all-male scent of him, mingled with a hint of pine and citrus, her senses exploded with longing.

'Miss!'

It was one of the little girls—Mary—with her hand stretched high.

'Miss,' Mary called again. 'I can't remember who rode horses in the Battle of Hastings. Harry says it was the Saxons, but I think he's wrong, 'cos you said it was the Normans. Didn't you?'

'It was the Normans, Mary.'

Mary poked Harry in the ribs. 'See? I told you!'

Harry poked her back and Isobel quickly went into action. 'Let me show you all a picture of the Norman horsemen,' she went on, 'in one of the books.' She turned briefly back to Connor. 'Will you excuse me, Mr Hamilton? I really need to get on with the lesson.'

'Of course,' he said. 'But let me have a quick word with you first.'

And then—*then* he told her what he wanted her to do next.

That afternoon, as Isobel struggled with her dictionary in the solitude of the now-empty chapel, Elvie burst in with Little Jack. 'Miss Blake,' she exclaimed, 'you haven't put anything on the blackboard yet, for tomorrow's lesson. Is everything all right?'

No, thought Isobel, *no, everything is very far from all right.*

When Elvie entered Isobel had been sitting at her desk, staring blankly at the wall. Now she answered, 'I'm just a little behind with everything, Elvie. You see, Mr Hamilton called in this morning and he asked me to write something about the school, for some friends of his...'

Her voice faltered suddenly. Elvie sat down beside

her and said, solemnly, 'Haven't you *told* Connor yet? How your left hand gets muddled up with your right, because of those horrid governesses you had?'

Isobel shook her head. 'Ridiculous of me, but I haven't, Elvie.'

'Then let me help you.' Elvie pondered a moment. 'There's nothing wrong with your brain, Miss Blake. You can read and remember things perfectly, can't you? It's just that when it comes to writing, your right hand won't do what you tell it to. Why not use your left hand instead? We can check any really long words in the dictionary. And I won't say anything at all to Connor or my grandmother, I promise—although I'm sure Connor would understand. Because really, you know, he's very kind!'

Kind? thought Isobel wearily. Ambitious, yes. Determined, yes. He had explained to her before he left the chapel this morning how he'd mentioned the school to several of his business friends in London—and how they'd expressed a keen interest in setting up something similar on their own estates.

'So I'd like you to write a summary for me,' he'd told her casually, 'of what you're doing here. A few paragraphs will do the job nicely.'

She'd been frozen with fear. Once again, here was Elvie to the rescue—but it was completely wrong of her to use the child in this way. Sooner rather than later, she would have to tell him the truth.

Preferably today.

It was four in the afternoon when Isobel knocked at the door of Connor's study to deliver the report she'd finally completed, but there was no reply. Then she realised his secretary, Mr Carstairs, was coming along the corridor and, after she'd explained, he took it from her with polite thanks.

'Mr Hamilton has been called away suddenly—on business, as it happens. But I will see that he gets this as soon as he returns.'

Half-dazed with this escape from what she'd thought would be a cataclysmic confrontation, she headed slowly up to her room and sat on the narrow bed, her head bowed. Already, she was missing him.

At first, she'd been truly afraid of the job she'd agreed to take on. But what frightened her most now was the effect he had on her, because whatever existed between them, whatever those emotions were, they were powerful and dangerous. His feelings towards her were coloured by the injustices he'd suffered in his past and scorn for her, of course. All that was simple enough to understand.

But what about her feelings for him?

Her childhood hero had been transformed into someone she hardly recognised and she was scared. This morning in the chapel, it had taken all her self-control to cope with his arrival, all her experience in acting the part of the flippant and foolish survivor of a ruined family. She was too vulnerable, because what she felt when she was close to him—even if he was making his disdain for her fully apparent—was a yearning so strong that it was almost out of control.

Almost—but not quite. She was determined she *would* control it. What he was doing to her was despicable, because, whether or not he was willing to admit it, he was making her a part of his retribution against the whole world for his own past struggles.

No doubt he was exacting the same revenge on everyone who had ever looked down on him. And she, Isobel, would endure all this and survive— wouldn't she?

Chapter Fifteen

'Connor's gone to London,' Elvie told Isobel the next afternoon when she called in at the schoolroom. 'And it's for a whole *week*.' The little girl was clearly downcast.

'I know,' said Isobel. 'Mr Carstairs told me. He's no doubt got a great deal of important business to attend to there and I'm sure he finds it all highly enjoyable.'

'I don't think that he *does* always like London,' Elvie said. She was looking up at the blackboard, where Isobel had started writing up tomorrow's lesson. 'Miss Blake, you've spelled "dandelion" wrong—you've forgotten to put in the "e". Grandmother says Connor has to go and talk to some nasty businessmen who've been trying to make trouble for him. But Grandmother says he's more than a match for them.'

'And I'm sure your grandmother is quite right,' said Isobel. She pitied his business rivals, whoever they were. They'd be taking on a formidable opponent.

Without Connor here, she'd told herself she ought to feel calmer—safer, even. There was no chance of him interrupting her lessons or confronting her as she hur-

ried to her room in the Hall. No opportunity either for
her to confess her many sins—chiefly, that she, Isobel,
simply couldn't spell and relied on Elvie to help her.

She was safer, maybe. But she still thought of him,
all the time.

One morning at eight, when Connor had been away
for four days, Elvie's grandmother caught Isobel as she
was setting off for the chapel. 'My dear, I believe it's
going to be a beautiful afternoon. Will you come with
Elvie and me to explore the gardens? Now, before you
say anything, I know you often work for an hour or two
after the children have gone, but perhaps we could set
off at, say, three? Would that be acceptable to you?'

That afternoon a footman brought Laura to the chapel in a bath chair that was designed for the outdoors.
Then Isobel took over—'I can manage perfectly well,'
she assured the footman—and together they ventured
deep into the wooded gardens, while Elvie skipped
ahead with Little Jack.

When Isobel had returned to Gloucestershire from
London three years ago, she'd noticed that the Calverley lands were rapidly returning to the wilds, all the
pathways overgrown with brambles. But Connor had
changed all that, swiftly. He'd put a team of groundsmen to work in the spring and now hardly a weed or
bramble or stray sapling dared to rear its head.

Connor and his money were changing everything.

'Isobel, dear,' Laura said, breaking into her
thoughts, 'I've heard that you're doing a marvellous
job with the Plass Valley children. But they must be
hard work, surely?'

Isobel suddenly realised they were almost at the river. She spotted a level place for Laura's bath chair and found herself a seat on a mossy rock so she could sit beside her. Elvie had already gone racing ahead to throw sticks in the water for her puppy.

'I don't find them hard work at all, Mrs Delafield.' Isobel smiled at Laura. 'I find them delightful, even if they are always full of energy.'

Laura said cheerfully, 'There you are! That's exactly *why* they're such hard work—all that chatter, all those ideas. But Connor has told me you appear to manage admirably.'

She's lovely, thought Isobel. But what would she think if she realised that Isobel was only getting by with Elvie's help? 'I enjoy the teaching,' she said. 'Really I do.'

'Well,' said Laura, 'I just wanted you to know I hear that you are helping the children a great deal. And perhaps Elvie and Connor also.'

This last was said so quietly that Isobel wasn't even sure if she heard her aright. And she couldn't have replied even if she'd wanted to, because by then Elvie was rushing towards them with Little Jack at her heels. 'Miss Blake! I saw a kingfisher—a real kingfisher, with a fish in his beak!'

All too soon they were on their way back and Calverley Hall came into view, its windows glittering in the afternoon sun. 'It's so beautiful,' Laura said and then broke off. 'Oh, I'm sorry, Isobel! You must find it very difficult, my dear, having grown up here…'

Isobel shook her head. 'Not at all. Even when I was a child, I realised my father was in deep financial trouble and I remember there always seemed to be a dark cloud hanging over the Hall. It was almost a relief to move out.'

Laura nodded sympathetically. 'And yet the place does cast a spell over you, doesn't it?' She hesitated. 'You knew Connor, didn't you? When he worked nearby, in the village?'

Isobel was still gazing at the Hall as she spoke. 'Yes, he worked at his father's forge and I used to pester him rather, I'm afraid. I was always turning up, always asking him questions. He worked so hard and I think everyone knew that some day he would find something bigger and better to do with his life.'

Laura nodded. 'My son, Miles, said he'd never met anyone with such energy and such determination. "Mark my words," Miles said to me, "that young man will go far." For a while, in London, Connor lodged with us and I remember that in his room he had a map of Gloucestershire on his wall. And beside it was pinned a sheet of paper that never failed to intrigue me, because, you see, it was a detailed list of all kinds of facts relevant to the place—oh, things like land prices, wheat yields, the amounts the local estates and farms sold for. I realised he must have had the local newspapers sent to him in London, every week! And he must have thought about Calverley night and day...'

Laura chattered on, not noticing that Isobel had gone very still. Very pale. Suddenly, the sunshine didn't seem as warm. And Isobel thought, *So it's as I suspected. Connor has always planned to get the Hall and all its lands.*

And now, how satisfied he must feel.

* * *

She got back to her room to find, as soon as she opened the door, that there was an almost unbearable stench. Panicking, she looked around and saw that someone had cut several large slits in her pillows and had tossed the feathers all over the floor.

The stench came from the pillows. She went over to them and realised they'd been filled with lumps of dried horse dung.

Then she saw a large scrap of paper, lying on her chest of drawers. *LADY MUCK* was scrawled across it. It must be the footmen again.

Feeling sick, she ran to fling open the windows, then put her hands to her face, her spirits lower than they'd ever been in all her life. How could she deal with all this? *How?* There was no point in reporting it to Haskins or to Mrs Lett. They wouldn't take a bit of notice.

Connor had told her to let him know, instantly, if she had trouble from any of the staff, but he was away—besides which, the person she was most afraid of in this entire place was Connor himself.

That kiss. How could she have let herself permit it? Even worse, how could she have let herself *respond* to it so ardently? She closed her eyes, found herself touching her lips and suddenly thought—had that kiss, too, been part of Connor's revenge?

The next day she realised Connor had found a new way to twist the knife in her already taut emotions. Since it was a Saturday and there was no school, she decided in the afternoon to walk to the Molinas' house, taking the grassy track through the valley. It was wonderful to see Joseph and Agnes again, but it also made her realise how she missed them. She had a few moments alone with Agnes in the kitchen, while the kettle boiled on the stove for tea. 'How is Joseph?' she asked.

'He's so much better,' Agnes reassured her. 'Ever since the roof was repaired and all the windows, too! You remember all those draughts and leaks? Mr Hamilton had them fixed. He's also been sending us fruit and vegetables from his garden and he says we're not to worry about fuel for the winter, because he will provide it. But surely you knew?'

'No,' said Isobel. 'No, I didn't.'

Agnes was gazing at her anxiously. 'Dear Isobel, are you *sure* you're all right? You know, you can come back to us any time you wish!'

Isobel smiled at Agnes. 'I'm fine where I am for the moment. My pupils are an absolute delight.'

'And what about all those servants at the Hall? Are they kind to you?'

'Oh, it's like being part of one big, happy family!'

By now Agnes was pouring out the strong tea. 'And what about Mr Hamilton? As you can guess, he's quite a favourite with us. Goodness, he's such a handsome man!'

'I actually see very little of him. And he's in London at the moment.'

Then Joseph joined them, rather to Isobel's relief, and he started telling her about his latest paintings. 'I'm getting commissions again, Isobel,' he told her proudly.

So of course Isobel had to admire his new work, then Agnes made another pot of tea and pressed her to eat more cake—'Wasting away, you are!' Agnes said darkly.

All too soon, it was time for her to walk back. The setting sun was scattering rays of red-gold light across the fields and hills, and in the distance the multi-paned windows of Calverley Hall shone like jewels. And the same old fear clutched at her heart—the dread she used to feel as the Hall cast its long shadow over her. But this time, it was her own feelings that tortured her.

Connor. How could he be so harsh one minute, then so kind the next? The Molinas couldn't praise him enough. Of course, their house was his property and it was in his financial interest to keep it sound. But to provide them with fresh produce from his garden? To promise them fuel for the winter?

She couldn't understand Connor, and she couldn't understand herself for letting him make her feel the way she did. *He despises you,* she reminded herself. Yet he made her heart race whenever he was near; he made her lungs ache with the need for air. And she couldn't forget that kiss. It was as if he'd branded her as the shameless wanton he clearly believed her to be.

She'd spent so long now, trying to cut herself off from everyone except the Molinas. From early childhood, she'd grown used to fending off scorn: the scorn poured on her for being stupid at lessons and for being the child of a drunken gambler. She'd learned to hide her feelings so no one would know how much she hurt inside. The stories that had spread about her time in London only strengthened her sense of being utterly alone. She'd learned to be resilient, she had built up a stone wall around her heart.

But that didn't mean her heart didn't ache within its defences. She didn't want the person who took that wall down piece by piece to be Connor Hamilton—

Connor, with his cynicism and his scorn for her family, and most of all for herself. She *couldn't* be feeling what she did for him—she just couldn't!

Was he, perhaps, making the Molinas comfortable so that she, Isobel, would feel she could *not* displease him? He was ruthless enough. He had to be, to have climbed as high as he had. And now, Laura had let slip that Connor had planned to buy Calverley Hall since the day he was banished. As for the school, she suspected that he'd most likely only set it up to impress his London friends and to humiliate her, Isobel—and he had no idea yet just how cruel his punishment was.

She would not *be* humiliated. She would cope somehow. But her resolution shook as she approached the Hall and realised that Connor was back. His travelling carriage was standing in the front yard. She hurried to the side entrance—the servants' entrance—to make her way up to the shelter of her room, but she was stopped at the foot of the servants' stairs by one of the footmen. 'Oh, *you* must be in trouble,' the footman said.

'Why? What do you mean?'

'Mr Hamilton wants to see you in his study, straight away.'

Very slowly, Isobel made her way towards that closed, forbidding door.

Connor stared at the paperwork that had accumulated on his desk with a mounting sense of frustration. Everyone was asking him if he'd enjoyed himself in London, but enjoyment hadn't come into it—his week had been a hectic frenzy of meetings with suppliers, investors and bankers.

And two days ago, Roderick Staithe had invited him over to his club for a meal. Staithe had spent the first quarter of an hour on trivialities, until at last Connor broke in. 'And when am I going to hear the verdict from this Parliamentary committee you're on, Staithe? When will I learn whether or not the government's going to approve my construction work at the docks?'

'Ah,' said Staithe, leaning forward confidingly, 'now there's the thing, Hamilton. Some members of the committee need a little sweetening.'

Connor's lip had curled. 'Money, you mean?'

'Good God, no!' Staithe had looked mildly wounded. 'Nothing as sordid as that. But I think several of the waverers would very much welcome a taste of the high life, on my Berkshire estate. After a few days of fine dining and champagne and gentlemen's sports, I think I can guarantee that they'll look kindly on your project.' He was stroking a large signet ring on his finger—Connor noted it bore his family crest. 'But it would all be rather expensive, so perhaps you should consider that it could be *me* you've got to sweeten.'

Connor had said flatly, 'How much?'

Staithe had looked hurt again. 'Now, Hamilton,' he'd said, shaking his head, 'surely you've not forgotten my beloved sister? Helena wants to marry you—that's the sum of it. In fact, she's got her heart set on it...'

The rest of the meal, for Connor, had passed in a haze.

The marriage was what most men in his situation would have agreed to promptly. Helena wouldn't bring a vast dowry—but Connor already had all the money he could want. What the marriage would give him was far more important—access to the upper ranks of so-

ciety and contact with even more powerful backers
for his ambitious schemes.

And Helena was eager. Connor didn't need Staithe
to confirm *that*. She was widely held to be a beauty
and she would know exactly how to conduct herself
as a rich man's wife.

But for all the rest of the week in London, while
Connor visited his foundries and assessed contracts
and met more potential investors, one person was at
the forefront of his mind. He found himself unable to
forget Isobel's bright, defiant smile. Unable to banish
the sound of her voice as she made her swift retorts
to his multiple criticisms and rebukes.

And for God's sake, he should never have kissed
her. That was a terrible mistake, but she'd tasted sweet
as honey! Those little sounds she'd made as he held
her close drove him wild and he'd imagined he almost
felt the fluttering of her heart through the thin layers
of her clothing...

But always, he realised, she was guarding herself.
Putting up a barrier. And no wonder—he'd done everything wrong, he knew that. But he hadn't guessed,
while he was in London, just how much he would
miss her.

Well, now he was back and a mountain of unopened
correspondence awaited him in his study. But the first
thing he did, once he was seated behind his desk,
was—to send for Isobel.

A few moments later, she knocked and entered.
'Mr Hamilton,' she said lightly. 'As you see, I obey
your summons.'

Chapter Sixteen

Connor felt something tug at his heart at the sight of her. Gladness? Lust? For God's sake, she was in a drab and shapeless gown, her blonde hair was scraped back in a style that was as unbecoming as possible and she probably hated him. He observed how cautiously she entered, in spite of her flippant words. He recognised the wariness in her eyes.

She would probably rather be anywhere else but here.

Yet even now his self-control was slipping. He had never wanted a woman so much—a woman he knew to be inappropriate and impossible, and who moreover didn't remotely *like* him. As she gave him her usual challenging smile, he detected the flicker of uncertainty in her eyes, saw the way her body had tensed as she confronted him, like someone expecting a physical or mental blow.

Damn it. He didn't once let his dark frown slip. One thing was for sure—she would never guess that all he really wanted to do, at this moment, was to pull her into his arms and kiss her again—and he had to keep it that way. The woman was a liability and quite possibly posed a threat to everything he'd worked for all these years, yet he couldn't seem to do anything but remember that sweet, hot kiss. And the passion lurking beneath that could ruin them both...

He stood up, keeping his face expressionless. 'Miss Blake. I trust everything has gone well for you while I've been away?'

He could have sworn he saw some emotion in those green-gold eyes of hers that might have been utter despair. But she forced a smile that somehow pierced him. Made him *hurt* for her.

'Well,' she said, 'I haven't invited every child in the neighbourhood to join the school, if that's what you fear. Even I have to realise there are some limits.'

'I meant no criticism. I merely hoped you were finding your role enjoyable.'

'Oh,' she said enthusiastically, 'everything is going so well, you cannot imagine! So far we've covered the seasons and the months, and measurements. And all sorts of useful topics, just as you requested!'

He nodded. He tried not to let his eyes wander to the elegant line of her hips and narrow waist. He wanted to say, *Have you been unhappy here, Isobel? Do you still resent the fact that Calverley Hall is no longer yours? Do you hate me for buying it? And did you miss me while I was away?*

Just then the door opened and Connor's secretary, Robert Carstairs, came in. 'Oh.' He pulled up when he saw who was there. 'I'm so sorry to interrupt—'

'No,' Isobel said quickly, 'it's all right, I was just going.'

'No, you're not.' Connor held out his hand to stop

her. 'Carstairs, come back in ten minutes, will you? And, Miss Blake, you are to stay.'

Carstairs quietly closed the door after him.

You are to stay.

For God's sake, Connor rebuked himself, did he have to make it sound like a military command? Did he have to go out of his way to be such an utter bastard to her? He saw how Isobel stood there—once more with a look on her face, he realised, that was almost fear. Hardly surprising. 'Please,' he said tiredly. 'Sit down.'

She did so, perching on the very edge of the chair to which he'd pointed, and he faced her from behind his desk. 'I'm glad,' he went on, 'to hear that the children are enjoying their lessons. But how about your week, Miss Blake? How has that been?'

She gave that little shrug of her shoulders. 'I suppose I didn't realise,' she said, 'when I agreed to take on this job that it was all to impress some grand committee in London.'

He linked his hands together and rested them on his desk. 'You're referring to that report I asked you to write?'

'Yes.'

He met her gaze steadily. 'It's true that I told some friends about the school—but only because the idea of universal and free education is one of my dreams. You can surely guess why.'

For a moment she looked vulnerable. That shadow had crossed her face again. 'Because you had to fight so hard for your own education?'

'Exactly. Isobel—Miss Blake—I'm sorry. I didn't intend this to be an interrogation.'

'No?' she queried politely. 'Then may I go?'

And he had a sudden idea. 'Please,' he said. 'Before you leave, why don't you try asking me some questions about *my* week and what I've been doing?'

Her eyes opened wide. 'You mean—ask you about your work?'

Of course. What else? he was on the verge of saying. But then, she probably imagined he'd spent the whole week in convivial dining, drinking and quite possibly womanising. Dear God, she must think him a real bastard. And why not? He hadn't done a great deal to make her change her mind.

She lifted her chin. 'It's as I suspected, then,' she said with outer calm. 'I think you invited me here to make me me feel small, Mr Hamilton. You must surely realise I would not understand one word about your business affairs in London.'

Connor leaned forward, feeling the faint glimmer of a smile curving his lips. 'Try it,' he urged. 'Ask me why I might shortly need a vast quantity of wrought iron.'

He heard her intake of breath, then she nodded and said, 'Pray tell me, Mr Hamilton. Why might you shortly need a vast quantity of wrought iron?'

He pointed to the plan laid out on his desk. 'Come and sit *here*—' he reached to drag a spare chair closer to his '—and take a look.'

She hesitated, but her curiosity was getting the better of her, because she sat exactly where he commanded and the delicate scent of lavender assailed his nostrils… *Concentrate, you fool.*

He picked up a ruler. 'This, Miss Blake, is what I've been working on. A contract to provide iron for some new docks on the Thames, just east of the city. Look.' He pointed with the ruler. 'Here's the Isle of

Dogs and here's Wapping, which is where the docks
are being built. The West India docks, here, are already completed and in use. Gradually London is
being transformed as a port, providing far bigger and
safer berths—which means no more ships moored out
in the river, waiting to be unloaded for days on end.
No more thievery, or damage to the valuable goods in
the waiting ships' holds. The Wapping docks are an
extension of the improvements already made—a great
deal of iron is needed and, if everything goes to plan,
my foundries will provide it.'

She had been gazing at the map intently, but now
she lifted her eyes to his. 'You appear to have a very
profitable venture on your hands, Mr Hamilton.'

'I've told you—it's not just about money.' His voice
had become more intense. 'Once, years ago, I had
such dreams…'

And then he stopped. And he thought, *Once, no
doubt, so did she.*

'Congratulations,' she said lightly, but he thought
she looked a little pale. 'You must have long ago ful-
filled your dreams—I'm only surprised you still take
such pleasure in new ventures.'

'I take pleasure in achievement,' he said. 'And in the
sense of complete independence that money brings.'

She nodded. 'And independence brings power.
Such a contrast, to the time when everything was
against you, when you were a boy. You've got your
own back—in truly spectacular fashion.'

He realised suddenly. 'You think that's why I
bought Calverley Hall? To get my own back?'

He saw her shrug. 'You must surely guess that's
what people say.'

He wanted to roar with exasperation. But he had *asked* for all this. She hadn't even wanted to come into his office just now! He forced down his churning emotions and kneaded his forehead. Then he said, 'You must have had dreams, too, Isobel. What were they?'

He noticed she didn't even pause to consider his question. 'I had none.'

No. No, Connor couldn't believe that! 'Isobel,' he began, 'when you were eighteen, your father took you to London and there were stories. Now, I know as well as anyone that London gossip can be vicious—'

She was on her feet. She'd gone very pale. 'And you'd like me to say those stories are untrue? I take complete responsibility for my own actions, Mr Hamilton. I do not shirk my past, I assure you!'

He tried again. 'Life's been difficult for you. You perhaps haven't deserved what's happened to you...'

'How *can* you say that?' she interrupted. Her voice was low but passionate. 'How *can* you claim to be sorry for me, when I was responsible not only for you losing your home all those years ago, but quite possibly for the death of your father?'

He rose, too, and drew a deep breath. 'I did not—I have never, ever held you responsible for the destruction of the forge. Besides which, my father was already sick and close to death when it all happened. And London? You were young. You had no one to guide you...'

And I cannot believe everything I've heard, he urgently wanted to say. *Please tell me, Isobel, that the stories aren't true.*

But all he could add was, 'What else can I say, except that you're more than making amends?'

Her eyes glinted dangerously. *'Making amends,'*

she echoed softly. She shrugged and smiled. 'But I've tried often, Mr Hamilton, to tell you that—for various reasons—I really am one of the worst possible people you could have chosen for your school. And now I want to tell you that I wish to resign.'

He watched her for a moment, then said quietly, 'If you truly want to leave, I shan't stop you. But the children would be distraught if you abandon them now. You must know that yourself. What more can I say except to beg you to stay for the children's sake?'

'Ah, but there's more. I have, in fact, managed to antagonise almost all of your staff.'

'So I've heard.'

'Really?' She sounded amused. 'And you'll have heard an *interesting* version, I assume?'

'I prefer to make my own judgements.' In fact, Haskins had come to Connor about Isobel the moment he returned from London. *We've tried to be forbearing, sir,* Haskins had intoned. *But her high-handed ways really are too much.*

Connor didn't like Haskins. He really didn't like him very much at all. Now he said to Isobel quietly, 'I want you to stay. Please.'

Again he saw the uncertainty shadow her face; told himself, *For God's sake, you fool, you ought to let her resign, for her own good and for yours!* She should take those melting green eyes and that impossibly tempting body of hers and get the hell out of here, away from the shadows of her family home and far away from the vicious gossip. Yet he wanted to protect her. Save her from herself…

He was, he realised, in big trouble. 'You signed a contract,' he added.

And something about her seemed to crumple. In a small voice she said, 'So I did.' Then she summoned one of those smiles again. 'Well, I really shall have to think about it all. Shan't I? Is it all right, Mr Hamilton, if I go now?'

Without waiting for his answer she was heading for the door—*clearly she couldn't get out quickly enough*—when, on impulse, he said, 'A moment. I don't think you answered me, when I asked you if you ever had dreams of your own.'

She gave him one of her disconcertingly direct gazes. 'Why should I have dreams, Mr Hamilton? I'm content as I am.'

And he had a sudden, overwhelming desire to prove to her that she should *not* be content. That she needed someone. *Someone like him?* She would laugh at that.

She was murmuring, 'If you'll excuse me,' and in another minute she'd be out of that door.

He found himself getting to his feet and saying, 'Miss Blake. Tomorrow is Sunday, as you'll know. And I'd like to take you out for the day.'

She looked so astonished it was almost laughable. 'A day out? When you must have a thousand things to think about?'

'All work and no play does nobody any good,' he said. 'And we'll take Elvie, of course.'

'Of course,' she said rather faintly.

'We can call it,' he went on, 'an *educational* trip.'

She nodded, clearly still uncertain. 'Where?'

'You choose.' He smiled teasingly. 'Bath? Or Wells Cathedral, perhaps?'

And Isobel suddenly said, almost hesitantly, 'Bath? The Sydney Gardens?'

'A good idea,' he approved. 'I'll tell Tom to prepare the barouche. I wonder, what time should we set out? Shall we say eleven o'clock?'

'Excellent,' she said lightly. 'So, since you're actually abandoning your plans to rebuild large sections of the country for almost a whole day tomorrow, I'd better leave you to cope with what's already on your desk.'

He smiled and she felt something inside her hurt, actually hurt, at that smile.

She was almost at the door when he called, 'Wait!', and came over to her. She felt the colour flare in her cheeks as he lifted his hand to her face. 'You have a feather,' he said softly, 'in your hair.'

Carefully he drew it out and he handed it to her, his eyes never leaving hers. She snatched it from him and made for the door, aware that he was still standing there, his face unreadable.

She hurried up to her room, trembling inside. A few more feathers had drifted to the floor, and despite the open window the air still smelled of manure.

She closed her door and leaned against it, wondering, *How much longer can I endure this?* But she was thinking not of the servants' vendetta against her, but of Connor. Most of all of Connor.

She stayed there, trying to calm her stupid, dizzy heart-rate. She told herself over and over again, *There's nothing in it. He's simply being kind. He's thinking of Elvie and feeling sorry for me.*

She didn't want his pity. As for him, what did *he* want? Money, of course, and power, to compensate for the humiliation of his upbringing. Yet sometimes, she saw such bleakness in his eyes, almost despair—

as if there were wounds in his past that just couldn't be healed.

She felt she could deal with him best when he was being harsh and autocratic. She could then summon her usual mask of defiance and bravado; it was her shield against a hostile world. But when he was kind, she felt her defences fall. He'd once been her only ally, but she'd lost him. And all she wanted now was for him to respect her again, for him to actually *like* her and laugh with her as they'd once done...

Who was she trying to fool? No one, least of all herself. She wanted a lot more—and that was impossible.

A day of pleasure tomorrow? She was dreading it.

Chapter Seventeen

Elvie couldn't stop dancing with excitement when Isobel went to collect her the next morning. 'An outing!' she kept exclaiming. 'With Connor!'

A maid had already dressed the little girl in a sensible flannel gown, but Isobel quickly searched Elvie's wardrobe and found her a short-sleeved pink gingham frock instead. 'The sun is going to shine all day,' Isobel promised her, 'and we'll take a shawl for you in case it gets chilly later.'

Since she'd moved in here, Isobel had worn nothing but sombre browns and greys. But today, on sudden impulse, she put on one of the few outfits she'd saved from London, but never worn since—a blue day dress with a dark blue spencer, demure but stylish. To go with it, she chose a straw bonnet with a blue ribbon—and when they went down to meet Connor in the courtyard, she thought she saw his eyebrows lift in approval. 'Miss Blake,' he said, 'you look most elegant.'

And Isobel felt her own heart do a little dance of pleasure, because Connor looked wonderful in a well-cut coat of olive-green kerseymere. As ever, his hair

was a little too long for fashion and was already ruffled by the light summer breeze—but somehow it only
emphasised the chiselled lines of his strong face and
she found her senses singing in answer to his smile.

Elvie was already running to the open carriage in
excitement, the ribbons of her large sunbonnet fluttering. *She is happy,* Isobel thought suddenly. *And I
would be happy, too, if only I didn't keep wanting
too much from life.* Like wanting Connor. Like wanting her past to be obliterated. But 'if onlys' were for
fairy tales—everyone knew that. *I will enjoy today,*
she vowed to herself. No matter what happened afterwards, today would be special.

Tom sat up high to take the reins of the open carriage and Elvie sat between Connor and Isobel. Little Jack had been left with the other dogs for the day.
Elvie chattered merrily to Connor almost all the six
miles to Bath and, by the time they'd reached the
Sydney Gardens, the sun was high in the sky and the
tree-shaded walkways were crowded with visitors.
Tom took charge of the carriage and horses, while
Connor held Elvie's hand and gave Isobel a quizzical
glance. 'Since this was your choice, Miss Blake, what
would you like to see? Where would you like to go?'

'I don't know,' she said honestly. 'You see, I've
never been here before. I just heard that it was beautiful.'

'Then shall I be your guide?'

'Yes!' cried Elvie. 'Yes, Connor. Show us everything!'

And he did. He showed them the formal flowerbeds and grassy lawns, Merlin's Grotto and the ruined
castle by the waterfall, and—Elvie's favourite—the

Punch and Judy show. Connor hoisted Elvie onto his strong shoulders so she could see the puppets above the crowd and she kept looking down at Isobel to exclaim, 'Can you see them? Can you see how the naughty dog's run off with the sausages? Little Jack would never do that!'

'I wouldn't be too sure.' Connor winked at Isobel, while Elvie shook her head and insisted, 'No, he wouldn't, Connor! You're wrong, you're wrong!'

An elderly couple passing by smiled and said to Isobel, 'What a lovely family you have.'

She started to say, 'They're not my...' but then stopped. 'Thank you,' she said quietly.

They bought some hot pies to eat by the boating pond, then Connor took Elvie into the famous Labyrinth. Elvie clutched Connor's hand tightly as he led her into the hedge-lined maze and Isobel saw how the little girl was almost ecstatic with delight. *Elvie is lucky to have him.* And some day, Isobel thought suddenly, he would surely have children of his own...

Of course he would. He was the owner of a thriving business empire; he would want a family, he would want heirs. It was inevitable that he would marry. Connor had always been ever-present in her thoughts and dreams since she was a girl, but she had to remind herself that once this summer was over, his memories of her would vanish as swiftly as those fireworks that were starting to blaze above the park in the sky, even though the light was only just beginning to fade.

For a while they sat to watch the fireworks, then Isobel took Elvie for one last look at the lights twinkling around Merlin's Grotto. But as they walked to rejoin Connor, Isobel pulled up. Connor wasn't alone.

Roderick Staithe was there; he was talking to Connor, but as Isobel slowly approached with Elvie's hand in hers, Staithe's eyes devoured her. Connor looked grim-faced and Isobel felt very cold suddenly.

'Well, well,' Staithe chuckled. 'This is a lucky meeting. Saw you in the distance, Miss Blake, in that pretty blue gown of yours. A teacher, eh? Now, Connor, what kind of trick was *that* to play on my sister and me that night we visited you? Why on earth didn't I recognise this young beauty instantly? Miss Isobel Blake, as I live and breathe. Your servant, ma'am!'

His words were tainted with mockery and when he took her hand and bowed over it, Isobel almost snatched it away.

'So you've managed to get yourself back in your father's house, Miss Blake,' Staithe went on. 'By hook or by crook, as they say. And Connor's a sly dog. A mighty sly dog.'

Connor was stony-faced. Isobel stood there, her heart hammering, with Elvie's hand clutched tightly in hers. Then Connor said, 'I told you, Staithe. It's growing late for Elvie and it's time we returned to Calverley Hall.'

'Of course. A cosy set-up.' Staithe's face had grown a shade darker as he looked once more at Isobel. 'No wonder, Hamilton, that you're neglecting your business in London to rush back to Calverley—'

He broke off, because Connor had stepped forward almost menacingly. 'I neglect nothing.' His voice, unlike his demeanour, was clear and calm. 'And watch what you say, Staithe. You understand me?'

Isobel saw Staithe's face grow suddenly pale. Then

he gave a stiff little bow and walked off. Connor turned to Isobel and Elvie, and said, 'It's time to go home.'

Connor was an expert at hiding his feelings. All the way back to the carriage he held Elvie's hand and chatted lightly to her about the fun they'd had today, while Isobel followed.

But his mind was actually reeling. Staithe had come up to him when he was on his own, with a gloating expression on his face.

'Your secret's out,' he'd said. 'Saw your pretty teacher with you and Miles Delafield's child, half an hour ago. She's Sir George Blake's daughter, isn't she? And despite that demure expression, I've heard she's taken after her father in more ways than one. She's got his appetite for mischief, especially in the bedroom— I've heard that Viscount Loxley taught her some pretty tricks and rumour has it that if he wasn't up to the job himself, he'd pay his footmen and watch.' He'd chuck-led. 'Now, I could take offence at what you've been up to, for my sister's sake. But we all have our little secrets, don't we? Though I must say I'm rather sur-prised that you let her openly associate with Miles's daughter...'

Connor had wanted to punch him to kingdom come. 'Keep your filthy mouth closed,' he'd said flatly.

Staithe had raised his eyebrows. 'You're not try-ing to actually defend her, are you? You're not going to tell me those stories aren't true? Really, Connor!'

It was at that precise moment that Isobel had re-turned with Elvie.

You're not trying to actually defend her, are you?
Yes, he realised. Yes, he was. Isobel had thus far

made no attempt to defend herself, but he could *not* believe those filthy stories about her.

He'd had a word with Tom earlier and told him to hire a horse for himself and set off ahead of them back to Calverley. So it was Connor who now harnessed up the horses, while Isobel settled Elvie inside the carriage. Even as Isobel wrapped her securely in the big shawl she'd brought, the little girl was almost asleep; Connor, on looking round and realising it, swiftly came to help Isobel lay her carefully on the upholstered seat, wedged in with cushions. She didn't stir.

'Join me up at the front,' he said to Isobel. 'Keep me company.'

'I'm fine here,' she said hurriedly. 'Next to Elvie...'

'Join me,' he repeated.

Isobel did so without another word. And they set off.

Isobel's mind was in turmoil and she felt slightly sick. What had Staithe said to Connor before she arrived? Too much, she feared. *'Saw you in the distance, Miss Blake, in that pretty blue gown of yours. A teacher, eh?'*

Whatever Connor was thinking, he said nothing.

She silently gazed ahead as the horses trotted on. The countryside was perhaps at its loveliest at dusk, she thought. As the sun began to sink behind the distant hills, she could see a flock of crows gathering in the woods and the fields of ripening wheat glowed like gold in the last of the day's sunshine. Connor's silence was giving her time—too much time—to reflect.

It had been so easy to see him as a rich and ruthless man out for total revenge on the world and on her, too. And yet she felt deep inside her that he was still the same person who'd been her friend in the past, who had provided a refuge at the forge, even if only for an hour or two, from the unhappiness of her home. Brave, loyal, laughing Connor. But then everything had gone so very wrong. And suddenly she wanted to weep for what they had both lost.

He spoke at last and it was as if he was reading her thoughts about the distant past. 'I don't bear a grudge, you know, Isobel. For the way your father treated me.'

She turned to him, feeling suddenly passionately angry on his behalf. '*I* would bear a grudge! You should hate him for what he did to you and your father!'

'Life's too short,' he answered, 'to waste it on revenge.'

She caught her breath. *Don't you realise the revenge you're inflicting on me? By hiring me and by putting me through this?*

Just then a pheasant landed noisily on the road ahead of them, making the horses start. Connor quickly steadied them and Isobel said, 'You drive well.'

'I learned most of what I know about horses and driving from old Tom. You'll remember he often brought your father's horses down to the forge for shoeing and his carriages when they needed repairing.'

'Until my father stopped paying the bills.'

He glanced at her. 'Exactly. Isobel, I was glad to realise Tom is still here. But what happened to all the others?'

She shrugged. 'They'd already started leaving even before my father died. As you'll know, the whole estate was bankrupt by then.'

She waited, pulse hammering again, for him to say

something about London. About Staithe, and oh, God, those false stories about her and Loxley...

He said, 'You must have been sorry to lose the Hall.'

She remembered her loneliness as a child. Her father's rages and her mother's tears. 'Oh, you know,' she said with forced lightness. 'One adjusts. But tell me more about yourself and what happened to you when you left Calverley for London.'

Another carriage was coming towards them and he slowed a little until it passed. Then he began. 'The city, I found, was filled with clever and ambitious men, all of them anxious to make money. But a few of them also wanted to make the world a better place—and Miles Delafield was one of them, full of ideas, but full of integrity, too. Those iron foundries of his—what a sight they were, to someone fresh from the countryside! I used to think you could see a new world growing before your eyes, once you got used to the flames, the steam, the heat. You could see the molten iron being shaped for everything our new generation requires, Isobel. The men labouring there were brave and strong, and I was proud to stand alongside them.'

'How sad that Miles died,' she said quietly.

'Yes.' All of a sudden she saw the light had gone from his eyes. 'He left the business in my care, and he left Elvie and Laura in my care also. London is at the heart of the business world, of course, and you must wonder—everyone must wonder—why I chose to buy a home in Gloucestershire.'

They'd reached the crest of a hill and he carefully pulled the carriage to a halt and glanced in the back, where Elvie was still sound asleep. 'Look around you,' he said.

She knew exactly what she would see. The view from here was wondrous at any time of day, but at sunset, on a clear summer's evening like this, it took one's breath away—the lush meadows, the wooded hills.

And Connor was continuing. 'This was my home, too, remember? I lived next to a forge, not in a mansion like you, but this was still a place I loved. I never forgot the fields and the woods and the river. And most of all—I never forgot *you.*'

Something burst and exploded inside her then, evaporating her strength, leaving behind just an aching, a melting, a longing. She realised his hands were reaching out to gently cup her face; his palms were warm and strong; his fingertips were caressing her cheeks; she suddenly longed to feel them on her breasts and she had to bite on her lip to suppress the hunger that had been building in her for so long.

He's going to kiss me again, she thought, and her lips tingled; she felt a desperate craving to be closer, closer yet—but at the same time she thought she saw despair and frustration in his eyes.

Her heart plummeted. She guessed then that he hated himself for wanting to kiss her. What awful things had Staithe said to him about her? Or did Connor know too much already?

'Isobel,' he said. 'For God's sake, tell me the truth about London. I must know…'

And at that very moment Elvie woke, calling out Isobel's name. Isobel was already rising from her seat. Connor reached out for her. 'Isobel—'

'I must go to her.'

He bowed his head. 'Of course.' His voice sounded flat, almost despairing.

She hadn't realised she could *hurt* so badly. Her limbs were heavy as she went to sit beside Elvie, holding her tight. The way he'd touched her just now. The way he'd *looked* at her...

The moment of dangerous intimacy with Connor was over and it was as well, she told herself. Elvie's awakening had saved them both from a perilous situation. He'd asked her for the truth—but why should he believe her, when nobody else did? How could she expect him to?

Staithe's poisonous leers should have reminded him of that—and Connor ought to be grateful for the warning.

Their journey had been uninterrupted after that. Once he'd pulled up the horses in the Hall's courtyard, Connor handed over the reins to a groom, then walked round to the carriage door to lift down Elvie, who clung to him sleepily. 'Today has been *lovely*. Thank you, Connor. It's been the bestest day ever.'

'I agree. The best.'

'Can we go there again soon? Please?' She yawned, snuggling into Connor's strong arms.

'I'll be taking you and your grandmother to London soon, little one,' Connor replied, 'and that will be even more exciting for you. You'll see great palaces, and marching soldiers, and lots of entertainments— maybe even Astley's Amphitheatre or Vauxhall Pleasure Gardens, if you're really good.'

'I still like today best,' murmured Elvie. 'I *loved* today...' Her voice trailed away and within moments she was asleep again.

Connor turned to Isobel. 'Come with me, will you?'

She followed in silence as he carried Elvie inside and up to her bedroom on the first floor. Elvie gave a sleepy sigh as he laid her on the bed.

Isobel stepped forward. 'I will see to her.'

'No.' Connor shook his head decisively. 'You've done enough. Summon her maid and I will escort you to your room. I wish to speak to you, in private.'

He wasn't even sure what he was going to say. To confront her about the whole, horrific story of her time in London, as everyone—including Roderick Staithe—knew it? He remembered first hearing it all. Feeling sick with disappointment and betrayal, he'd believed it—but on meeting her at the midsummer fair, everything was different. He'd resurrected his belief that Isobel was still the girl who'd been his loyal friend. Even when she'd tried to warn him she wasn't fit to be in charge of children, he'd ignored her. But was that because he really believed her to be innocent, or because he wanted her so badly?

Why wouldn't she defend herself, or even try? Whatever the truth of it, this lethal attraction that drew them together was addictive and dangerous and plain impossible—for both of them. He cursed his own stupidity viciously under his breath. But he longed to taste her sweet lips once more and to hold her lush body in his arms and caress her until she cried out in a delirium of passion.

And it was no good. Everything had been tainted today by that ill-fated meeting with Roderick Staithe.

You don't know me, she'd whispered to him that day at Calverley's midsummer fair. *You really don't know me.*

He wished he did—but all the way up to her room she'd said not a word. He let her lead the way, even though they were going there on his orders. She was unwilling; he could see the tension in her shoulders, see it in the way she held her head. She never once looked round to see if he was still following, not even when she opened the door. But as she went in, she stepped back with a shocked cry.

'What is it?' Connor demanded sharply. 'What's happened?'

She was unable to speak. She'd put her hands up to her face. He pushed past her—and immediately saw an oil portrait of her mother and father hanging crookedly on her wall. It had been completely defaced. Crude ink scrawls denoted a scowl on her father's face and a ridiculous grin on her mother's.

He exclaimed, 'What the…?'

'It's nothing.' She was moving swiftly to take the picture from the wall and clutch it to her. Her voice shook, but she tried to shrug. 'Just another stupid, childish trick.'

'But that picture! It wasn't in here before, surely? Where can it have come from?'

'I imagine it was found up in one of the attics.' She was meeting his gaze squarely now, but he saw that she looked very pale, very fragile. And suddenly he registered what she'd said a moment ago—*just another stupid, childish trick.*

He stepped closer to her. 'You said "another". Do you mean this sort of thing has happened before?'

She nodded.

'Then why, in God's name, didn't you tell me?'

'I thought—I hoped they would soon get bored.'

'Who are "they"? The servants?'

'I assume so.'

'Then I will deal with it,' he said. 'Immediately. And there's something else, Isobel. I tried to ask you on the way home today about what really happened in London, because I cannot believe—'

She dropped the picture. There was no glass to break, but the frame had fallen with a great crash. He picked the thing up and shoved it outside the door, then he came back to her. 'Isobel. We really need to talk.'

'Are you quite sure?' She'd arched her brows quizzically, but she looked as if her bright façade was about to crack open. 'I did warn you, you know, that I was in no way suitable for the role you've cast me in. I did my best to tell you that you were making a huge mistake.'

He said in a low voice, 'I wanted to believe that you'd been wronged. I wanted to believe I was right to think you're still the girl I once knew. Please tell me that you haven't changed, Isobel. I'm begging you.'

And just for a moment, he saw something in her eyes—a welling up of emotion too strong to be contained, a vulnerability that pierced him to his soul—and he put his hands on her shoulders and drew her remorselessly to him, and...

She pulled herself away. '*Another* mistake, Mr Hamilton. A very big mistake. But I hope—' her voice suddenly shook a little '—that whatever happens in the future, we can still tell ourselves that today has been a lovely day, a perfect day, if only for Elvie's sake.'

'*I* wasn't pretending,' he said. 'About any of it.'

And he saw, again, that he'd silenced her completely. She looked stricken. Damn Staithe and his vicious gossip. Damn Viscount Loxley and Isobel's brute of a father. Damn them all to hell and back.

'I wish you a good evening, Miss Blake,' he said at last, and left her.

For Isobel over the next few days, the children were her salvation. She loved the time she spent with them, and they were eager for everything she could teach them. There were only two more weeks of the school to go—but she felt that in some of her pupils at least, she'd kindled a desire for knowledge, even if she did still have to rely on Elvie's corrections to her own atrocious spelling.

But if the children were a pleasure, Connor was her own private, never-ending torment. Elvie told her on the Monday that he'd gone to London and it was as well, Isobel thought silently. Though three days later he was back, according to Susan the maid—but Susan also said he was either closeted in his study or out visiting his farms.

Isobel steeled herself to see him the following Sunday, when Laura had invited her to attend church. But again—just when her nerves were stretched to breaking point—he wasn't there. Some matter had demanded his attention out at one of the farms, Laura explained, so he'd decided to ride over there straight away.

Elvie, Laura and Isobel had been driven to the church in Chipping Calverley by Tom. And Isobel had time to reflect during the journey that in the past week, there had been some drastic changes at the Hall.

It was Susan who first alerted her. 'Three of the

footmen have left, miss—ever so sudden! Mr Haskins and Mrs Lett are saying nothing, but we're guessing it's the master himself—Mr Hamilton—who's sent them packing and none of us below stairs are sorry in the least. We never did like them.'

Susan said no more, but Isobel guessed the maid had worked it out for herself—just as she had. Connor had identified those responsible for the unpleasant tricks played on Isobel and got rid of them.

That wasn't all. From then on, the rest of the Hall's staff—footmen, maids, grooms, even Mr Haskins and Mrs Lett—had become almost embarrassingly polite to her. She guessed Connor must have rebuked them all, but instead of being glad, she felt a hot rush of shame. Connor would have told them to treat her with respect—but she didn't *deserve* respect. Surely Connor's encounter with Roderick Staithe in the Sydney Gardens had convinced him of that?

She didn't even attempt to listen to the Reverend Malpass's dreary sermon, but instead reminded herself that there was only a week to go before the Plass Valley families would move on to their next destination, the apple harvest in Somerset. Then the lessons in the chapel would come to an end and she would no longer be needed here. What next?

She would go back to the Molinas, she supposed. But—not to see Connor again?

She couldn't face it. She *had* to face it. What a mess she'd got herself into. She wasn't sleeping well and, often by the time morning came, she was exhausted. It was partly because she'd been up half the night poring over various English primers, trying to prepare the next day's lesson. But it was also because of Connor.

It was criminally wicked of her to have ignored her body's warnings. Criminally wicked to have blinded herself to the fact that whenever Connor was near, her brain turned to a soggy mess of indecision and she couldn't think of anything or anyone except Connor. Whenever he was near, something happened to her—it was as if her willpower and her common sense melted away and her brain became full of wild imaginings. She couldn't forget the expression in his voice and in his eyes when he'd said last week, after their outing to Bath, 'I never forgot the fields and the woods and the river. And most of all, Isobel—I never forgot you.'

She'd been shaken to her core. But Connor had believed those awful stories about her and so did everyone else. A man of his position and pride could not allow himself the weakness of taking her as his mistress—and as for marriage, it was out of the question. He needed someone of suitable rank and reputation, not a disgrace like her. A disgrace who had let herself fall into his arms—and who couldn't spell into the bargain.

She still felt hot with shame when she remembered her London Season. The social gatherings that her father, with ever-increasing desperation, had ordered her to attend. *You must find yourself a rich man, damn it!* She'd felt lost and terrified, but above all she'd felt an overwhelming longing to escape and find Connor. After every hideous party or second-rate ball, she'd imagined telling Connor about the absurd and often cruel people she'd met, so he would listen and make light of the hurt she was enduring. And with his help, she would feel better. Healed.

At his side, she used to feel ready to face the world. But now there was nowhere to run.

She would cope. She'd *always* coped. Yet she'd never hurt in this way before. Never felt so completely unable to survive her heart's impossible yearning. She had to leave—*now.*

The Vicar's sermon was drawing to an end. Elvie, who'd been trying her hardest not to wriggle, sneaked her hand into Isobel's and squeezed it. And Isobel smiled down at her, but she had already made her decision.

She had to tell him everything and put an end to this charade.

During the past week, Connor had plenty to distract him from his troubling thoughts of Isobel Blake. Two days after the trip to Bath, the news had arrived that his docks project had received a setback—the Parliamentary committee whose approval was meant to be a mere formality had raised several objections.

'Why?' Connor had gone over it with Carstairs. 'Damn it, why?'

Carstairs hesitated. 'Isn't your friend Roderick Staithe on the committee, sir? Perhaps he and his companions there require a little encouragement?'

Yes, thought Connor in frustration. It would be Staithe, of course; the wretch had hinted as much during their brief encounter in the Sydney Gardens. Staithe had been angry to see Connor with Isobel. Doubtless Staithe would, if he felt like it, gladly resurrect those allegations about Isobel that in his blackest moments Connor feared might be true.

But Connor *never* believed them when he was with

her. He was always freshly convinced of her integrity, her honesty. And that kiss! It was as if she'd never been touched by any man before. He couldn't forget how she'd trembled in his arms, responding meltingly to his caresses as if every touch was opening up new emotions in her. Connor had felt he was tutoring an innocent, a sweet, delectable innocent. He remembered that afterwards she'd been shaky and unbalanced, her lips still swollen with need. He'd been shaken to his core and he'd been so hard for her it had hurt.

He had to get the approval of Staithe's damned committee. But Staithe wanted him to propose to Helena. How the hell could he, when his mind was full of Isobel?

He'd been in London for three days and made progress of a sort with his investors. He was back by Friday and had promised Laura he would accompany her to church, but as he was getting ready, news arrived that a fence had been damaged up by the Five Acre Coppice, putting the livestock there at risk.

It was one of the stable boys who gave Connor the message.

'Who brought it?' Connor demanded.

'I dunno, sir.' The boy blushed. 'He didn't stop to give his name. Just rode off again.'

It was the tenant farmer who should have been informed, not Connor, but Connor decided to go there anyway. At least, he thought, the ride in the fresh air would help clear his head. He got to the coppice to find that, yes, the fence was down—a few posts were over. But something was odd. It looked as though the posts had been *pulled* out.

Five Acre Coppice was in a remote part of the estate

and the fields here bordered thick woodland. Connor thought he heard muffled voices from behind some trees and, as he looked round, his senses taut, there came the sound of heavy footsteps. Five men, all of them in rough farm garb and heavy caps, came running up and pulled him from his horse. They started punching and kicking him, and as Connor went down, still fighting, the blows came from all directions.

So did the abuse. 'Take *this,* damn you, Hamilton, for encouraging the gypsy vermin. And *this.* And *this…*'

After returning from church, Isobel went straight to her room, then closed the door and leaned against it. She was weary of leading this false life. She was exhausted emotionally by the effort of pretending that Connor Hamilton meant nothing to her, when she could never be anything to him. Both of them were being harmed by it.

Pausing only to remove her pelisse and bonnet, she set off downstairs and almost ran into Haskins. 'Ma'am.' He bowed his head stiffly. 'May I be of assistance in any way?'

She really could not get used to this false civility— my goodness, Connor must have given all his staff a mighty telling-off. 'I'm looking for Mr Hamilton, Haskins. Do you know if he's in his study?'

'He rode out this morning to see to a minor problem on one of his farms, ma'am. I can let you know when he's back if you wish.'

'I'll tell you what, Haskins. I shall wait in the parlour for him and from there I'll be able to hear the minute he arrives. You see, I really need to speak to him, because—and you'll be *extremely* happy to hear this—I'm going to tell him that I'm leaving.'

His jaw dropped. By then she was already setting off to the parlour. But she never got there, because at that exact moment the big front doors crashed open and four grooms lurched in, carrying between them some kind of heavy burden.

She saw the blood on their clothes, she saw their shocked faces and she realised they were carrying the body of a man.

Connor. Oh, God, it was *Connor*.

Chapter Eighteen

When Connor finally opened his eyes, he was in his bedroom lying between cool sheets. His head felt bruised and tender. The clock on the wall told him it was four o'clock; the afternoon sun was streaming through the window and he winced at the brightness of it, but only for a moment, because already some-one had gone to close the curtains and a female voice said calmly, 'I fear the light is too strong for you. Is that better, Mr Hamilton?'

Isobel. He could see her more clearly now and he re-alised she was dressed as usual in a plain, high-necked gown with her blonde hair pulled back and coiled at the nape of her neck, though the usual stray tendrils caressed her skin...

'How long have I been like this?' His voice was thick, gravelly almost; he realised his jaw ached and it hurt to talk.

She hesitated, then came closer. Her expression was still calm, but her eyes, he saw, were troubled. 'You've been sleeping for three hours, Mr Hamil-ton. The doctor has already been and he will return later. You're a little bruised, but he said there's nothing broken. He also said you must rest. And that was an order.'

A little bruised. Well, that wasn't too bad, since he'd feared at the time those men had meant to kill him. He'd fought them hard, but had been outnumbered, and it was through a mist of pain that he'd heard the sound of horsemen galloping up and a shout of alarm—'It's Mr Hamilton, lads. They're kicking the living daylights out of Mr Hamilton!'

It was the local farmer, William Purslove, with his two sturdy sons. They'd leaped off their horses and had dealt blows left, right and centre until Connor's assailants ran. Farmer Purslove had crouched at Connor's side. 'Mr Hamilton, sir. Can you hear me? Are you all right?'

'Yes.' Pain had racked him everywhere; he'd tasted blood. 'Yes, I'm all right.'

And then he'd been enveloped by blackness.

It was funny that Isobel should be the first person he saw when he finally opened his eyes. She was standing over his bed now, still looking grave.

He tried to speak again. 'It was because of the children,' he said, enunciating each word carefully.

She was pouring something into a glass before handing it to him. 'This is barley water. Cook has made it specially. And, yes, you are right—I'm afraid it was because of the children.'

He was thinking of the words those men had used as they'd punched him. *Bloody gypsies.* Kick. *Riffraff.* Kick. *People like you—* a punch to the stomach *—giving them ideas above their station.*

She waited until he'd drunk, then took the halfempty glass to put it on a side table and sat on the chair by his bed. And she told him about the verbal threats that the children had reported to her and the stone through the chapel door. 'I regret very much,' she said, 'that I didn't tell you this earlier. But I thought the incident of the stone was directed at me.'

'You suspected that it might be the servants again?'

She hesitated, then bowed her head in agreement.

Connor clenched his bruised hands as they rested on the bed sheets. 'You and the children must be protected,' he said almost harshly. 'I will ensure that at least two of my groundsmen are within sight of the chapel and within calling distance, every day.'

'Very well,' she answered calmly, 'though you should be resting, not making plans.' She hesitated. 'But since we're talking about the school, Connor, there are things I must tell you.'

He heaved in a deep breath and winced, because breathing hurt his bruised ribs. 'You are *not* going to tell me you're leaving those children without a teacher. Is that understood?'

He saw distress clouding her face. 'I tried to tell you from the beginning that I'm truly not much use as a teacher—'

'And I,' he interrupted, 'beg to differ. You know very well I interviewed several applicants, but I asked you, Miss Blake, to fill the post, because in my opinion you were ideal for the job.'

Her green eyes widened. 'Perhaps my memory's a little at fault. But are you now claiming that you *asked* me?'

He suppressed a sudden laugh, not wanting to hurt his ribs again. Then he said, quietly, 'I'm sorry. The thing is, I saw this as a way to give something back to those who would never get the opportunities that I had.'

'And you also saw it as a way to pay *me* back. For the sins of myself and my family.'

Her voice was calm, but he could see a tiny pulse beating in her throat. He'd already noticed her breasts rising and falling beneath the tight fabric and he couldn't help but remember again how slender and yielding her body had felt against his, that night they kissed... 'Never your sins,' he said. 'Never.'

'Well, that's how it feels to me,' she said almost lightly. 'And unfortunately, in appointing me, you really made a huge mistake.'

He braced himself, thinking of her past, remembering Staithe's recent, lewd insinuations. He prepared himself to ask—no, to *demand* the truth—but then he realised she was talking again. She was saying, 'Yes, you made a mistake, because there's something even you can't fix.' She looked very pale. 'I should never have agreed to be the children's teacher—because *I cannot spell.*'

For a moment he was unable to speak. And then—then, he burst out laughing. 'Oh, Isobel. Is that all?'

Her eyes were shadowed. Her hands were clasped tightly in front of her as she said, 'I would have thought that was rather a crucial skill for a teacher.'

'Isobel, listen to me.' He was still laughing, even though it hurt like hell. 'Do you think I care if your spelling's poor? We're not coaching children for Eton and Oxford here! No doubt you've learned to cope with what you claim is your weakness—'

'I'm afraid it's more than a weakness,' she insisted stubbornly. 'You see, I'm naturally left-handed, but I was told it was unacceptable and I was made to use my right. I think that was when my problems began.'

He was astonished. 'What the hell does it matter whether you use your left hand or your right? *Unacceptable?* Do you really think I believe those old superstitions about witchcraft and sorcery? What did your mother say?'

'My mother led the campaign to mend my ways. Every time I was caught using my left hand I was locked in an empty bedroom and made to copy sections of the Bible with my left hand tied behind my back.'

He had a moment of revelation. 'That room. The one Mrs Lett wanted you to take, when you arrived here. Was that the one you were locked in when you were small?'

'Yes.'

Oh, Isobel. He felt something inside him actually hurting for her. He steadied himself and said, 'You've coped with it and that's the real point. Everything I've observed in the chapel—your writing on the backboard, the children's slates—it all seems *fine* to me—'

'That's because Elvie helps me,' she interrupted.

He stared at her. 'What?'

'Elvie has realised I can't spell and she helps me.'

Just for a moment Connor was stunned into silence. Then he said, 'I really don't care. Because however you've done it, you've made the children happy and you've made Elvie happy. You and that idiotic little dog have brought back the child I used to know. You're good for Elvie and you're good for the travellers' children, and you're good for *me.*'

'No,' she whispered. She'd risen to her feet now and was facing him. 'There's still more I must tell you...'

And her voice trailed away, and he thought, *She is going to tell me about London.* He saw she was bracing herself to speak and he was mentally preparing himself—when suddenly he heard voices in the distance. He recognised them as belonging to Carstairs and the doctor, and they were coming nearer. Before Connor could do or say a thing, Isobel had hurried to the doorway at the back of his room that led to the servants' stairs and vanished, leaving behind her the faint scent of lavender.

Connor was still swearing under his breath when the doctor came in with Carstairs. Connor lay back wearily as the doctor felt his pulse. 'A touch of fever, I think,' the doctor pronounced. 'Mr Hamilton, you need to rest, sir.'

'Then leave me alone,' said Connor, 'and stop fussing over me.'

The doctor insisted on an examination of his bruised ribs and head, but then he moved back to Carstairs's side and Connor heard them talking in hushed voices by the doorway.

'Plenty of liquids. A little laudanum to aid his sleep...'

At last the voices faded and he heard the door close quietly.

Connor lay back on his pillows. Isobel couldn't spell! Her lessons with her succession of governesses must have been hell. She must have been desperately unhappy and insecure—yet she'd never told him the half of it.

She'd been incredibly brave and he realised now

that she still was—she was also honourable and loyal and caring. No wonder those scruffy urchins hurried so eagerly to the school in the chapel every morning— they loved her patience and kindness, as well as her delightful sense of humour. So she couldn't spell? What the hell did it matter, when he found, in her company, that he was able at last to see beyond the shadow cast over his life by his own poverty-stricken upbringing?

Something about Isobel healed all of them—the children, Elvie, Laura. For him, Connor, she did something else. He couldn't forget how he'd felt when she fell into his arms that night when the Staithes were his unexpected guests. Couldn't help but remember how sweet was the scent of her hair and skin, and how that kiss had sent desire roaring through him.

So she had a questionable past. What happened to her in London had stained her reputation, causing men like Staithe to sneer at her and women like Helena to cold-shoulder her. If the stories were actually true, so what? She had been young and lost and alone. Someone should have been there for her—in fact, he, Connor, should have been there for her.

Yes. *He* was perhaps the one who had treated Isobel Blake most unfairly of all. And right at this moment, something flickered in him that was much more disturbing than mere lust.

It was the desire to hold her and to protect her against the whole world—because, quite simply, he couldn't bear for her to leave his life again.

Thanks to the doctor's potions Connor slept heavily that night, and by nine the next morning he had risen, washed and dressed. Apart from a slight pallor, the bruises on his ribs and jaw were the only outward sign of his ordeal.

The doctor came at eleven and reported satisfactory progress. 'Though that doesn't mean,' he warned, 'that you're to be up and about at your usual pace, Mr Hamilton. And have you reported this incident to the authorities? Whoever was responsible needs to be punished severely!'

'I've heard,' replied Connor, 'that the culprits are being dealt with.'

It was true. Tom the groom had come up to his room an hour ago to quietly tell him that Farmer Purslove and his two sons—the men who'd come to Connor's rescue—had recognised his attackers as some unemployed local ruffians who had been making threats against the travellers for weeks.

So the Purcloves had got together a few comrades last night and together, Tom told him with glee, they'd surrounded the culprits outside their usual drinking haunt and given them a good beating. This, Connor knew, was the justice of the countryside and he was content to leave it at that.

He spent the rest of the morning in his private rooms, sparing himself the prospect of the servants' concerned glances and whispers. Soon after lunch—which was brought up to him—Carstairs came with the day's post; Connor ripped open a large envelope from London and swiftly spread out the sheets of paper on his desk. They were covered with column after column of figures; he skimmed them and glanced at the totals on the final page, then read the accompanying letter.

Damn it. *Damn it.*

Carstairs was watching, looking anxious. Connor pointed to the papers. 'According to these figures from the London accountants, it looks as if my plans for the new docks would bankrupt every single one of my investors.'

And those accountants had been highly recommended. They were supposed to be the city's finest.

He told Carstairs to bring up the heavy file of documents from his study downstairs and began to investigate. But he was tired—hellishly tired—and his head and ribs were aching afresh. As he sat behind his desk, he felt his head gradually sink on to his folded arms, until at last he slept, and when he woke he saw that dusk was falling outside.

Hauling himself up, he stretched his cramped limbs and lit two candles. Then he realised that someone had been in and left him a tray of bread and cold meats together with a tankard of ale. He drank the ale gratefully—his throat was parched—then he rang for Haskins and ordered, 'Send Miss Blake to me.'

He was standing by his window staring out into the gathering darkness when he realised she had appeared silently in the open doorway of his room. Her eyes had flown to his desk.

'I see,' she said, 'that you haven't taken much notice of the doctor's orders, Mr Hamilton. I thought you were told to rest.'

He went to close the door before looking, like her, at the scattered papers that had given him such a pounding headache. 'Just a little light reading.' He gave a faint smile.

She nodded, but her answering smile was tense. 'You wished to speak to me?'

He gestured her to a chair and he sat, too, by his desk. 'I did intend to rest.' *Hell, his head was pounding again.* 'But I felt I had to talk further with you about our conversation last night. I realise there's only a week left of your contract, but I wanted to emphasise, Miss Blake, that I feel you've done an exceptional job.'

'Ah, the school.' She spoke calmly, but he could see the apprehension in her eyes. 'As I've told you a number of times, you really made rather a mistake in hiring me.'

He was watching her gravely. 'I think that as ever, you underestimate your own capabilities. I understand, Isobel, that you might need a little more time than some people for written tasks—but where teaching young children is concerned, that's perhaps no bad thing, because it means you can sympathise with them. As far as I'm concerned, the school has been a great success—'

He broke off, aware of the way she was looking at him. She said quietly, 'Even after what happened to you yesterday?'

'Yes,' he said. 'Even after yesterday. There will always be fools and bigots around—and those men have been dealt with.' He realised he was fingering his bruised jaw. *Damn it, I should have shaved, I must look like a ruffian myself.*

'Isobel,' he went on, 'there was something else I wanted to talk to you about. You see, I have an apology to make.'

Chapter Nineteen

Sometimes Isobel thought she was hopeless at reading people—yet in that moment she could almost feel the heat of some nameless emotion blazing through Connor with a strength that frightened her.

He reached from his chair to take her hand, and immediately she felt a treacherous surge of exhilaration stealing through her veins. Even when he let go, she felt the longing for him pulsing silently through her.

'I hope,' she said as lightly as she could, 'that this apology of yours doesn't involve the signing of yet another contract?' She was trying to put up a bold front, because right now Connor Hamilton was breaking down every single one of her defences, leaving her as exposed as if he'd flayed her.

He said, 'Soon I must return to London.'

Oh. Was that it? She felt, stupidly, as if she'd just been pushed off a cliff edge. 'But of course. Duty and business call you back there, no doubt.'

'Partly that. But first of all I need to apologise for what happened seven years ago. I need to apologise for turning my back on you.'

She was staring at him, wide-eyed.

He went on, 'After the forge was destroyed I stormed off, bearing what I imagined was a huge burden on my shoulders. But leaving Gloucestershire turned out to be the making of me. Whereas you, Isobel, were left alone with your father. Left, in other words, without anyone to turn to.'

She felt herself struggling. What was he trying to say? What was he trying to *do*? Soon he'd be off to London, no doubt for longer this time. And for her the pain of missing him would be worse than ever.

'And what precisely,' she replied, her voice still light, 'could you have done for me? Let me guess.' She pretended to think. 'I know! You could have dressed me up as a boy, Connor. And then, I could have ridden to London at your side and got a job in one of those iron foundries you talk about, making—girders? Is that the right word?'

He couldn't help but laugh. 'Girders. And rivets and bolts. And you wouldn't have stood the heat and the noise for more than a few minutes.'

I would, thought Isobel blindly. *I could have done anything, Connor, if you'd been there with me.*

'So.' She shrugged. 'I couldn't work in a foundry. I couldn't have worked as a clerk for you, because I can't even spell. So what, I wonder, am I good for?'

And she was suddenly utterly shaken and was glad she was sitting down; because the way he was looking at her made her heart kick at her ribs and then ache almost unbearably. There was nowhere to hide from him here. She was, she guessed, being betrayed by her tainted blood, her father's blood; she felt scraped raw by the shame of her own appalling weakness.

And she just couldn't stop looking at his mouth. Couldn't forget the yearning his lips had awoken in her that had never really died out and still she felt the searing shame thudding through her veins. She crossed her arms in familiar defence and bowed her head—only to look up with a jolt as he said at last, in a low voice, 'What are you good for? Oh, Isobel. You're worth far more than the way I've treated you.'

And she was shaken to her core again—because he looked utterly crushed. He was in despair. Only his emotion wasn't directed at her, but at *himself*.

She said, faintly, 'You were kind to my friends, Agnes and Joseph Molina—'

'Of course,' he interrupted harshly. 'Of course I was—and my reasons were completely selfish. I was a bastard to force you into this job. I've been a selfish bastard all my life.'

Whatever she expected, it wasn't this. 'No! You care for all your workers. You care for the Plass Valley children. Most of all, you care for Elvie, you've done so much for her...'

He stared at her and she felt suddenly chilled by the depth of bitterness and self-recrimination in his eyes. 'It's my duty to care for her,' he said, 'because it was my fault that her father died.'

She felt herself freeze with shock. Stunned, she managed at last, 'Miles Delafield died of a heart attack, Connor. No one was expecting it, no one could possibly be blamed...'

'I could,' he said flatly.

And he told her. He told her how last summer, in London, they'd had almost more orders than they could cope with and Miles and Connor were busy from dawn till dusk—only then trouble arose at their foundry in south Wales.

'I knew Miles was close to exhaustion,' he said, 'but I left him in London in charge of everything and went to Wales to sort out the problems there.' His eyes were almost black with suppressed emotion. 'By the time I got back, five days later, Miles had died. They told me he'd been working all hours of the day and night, without me there to help him—and it was *my fault.*'

She realised it was now quite dark outside and above the wooded hills in the distance a pale moon was rising. The two candles on Connor's desk cast flickering shadows on the strong lines of his face, etching the pain she could see there. The dreadful hurt, the guilt.

'How could you have known,' she whispered at last, 'that Miles was going to be taken ill?'

'I *should* have known. I knew before I set off for Wales that he was doing far too much.'

Isobel couldn't help it—she put her hand over his. 'Wouldn't he have done that anyway, Connor, whether you were there or not? And your journey to Wales. If you'd not gone there, what would have happened?'

'We would have lost an important contract. And over a hundred of our Welsh foundry workers would have lost their jobs.'

'Then you had no choice,' she said firmly. She withdrew her hand. 'Miles would have known that. And Miles might, sadly, have suffered his heart attack anyway.'

He gave her a ghost of a smile. 'Such pearls of wisdom. It's no wonder the Plass Valley children listen to your every word.'

Suddenly she was acutely aware that they were here

alone in his private domain and it was getting late. His words had been light, but his eyes blazed into her, scorching her. She could feel the all-male strength of him only inches from her, and it was up to her to put a stop to this. *Now.*

'I'm quite good at talking, Connor,' she reminded him. 'I used to turn up at the forge—remember?—and plague the life out of you. *What's this for, Connor? Why are you doing that, Connor?*'

'You didn't plague me,' he said quietly. 'Isobel, you must have had an abominable childhood, but you never complained.'

'I was fed. I was clothed and had a roof over my head—there were even servants all around, until my father stopped paying them and they left.'

'Your father—God, Isobel, you don't resemble him in the slightest!'

'Now, how do you know that?' she tried to joke. 'Give me some money, and see how I take to the card tables. And how do you know that if I had servants, I wouldn't hound them without mercy? I simply haven't had the opportunity to be a typical aristocrat!'

'You wouldn't be anyway,' he said. 'You *couldn't* be.'

She was silent a moment, looking down at her hands, which were clasped in her lap. 'When we met,' she said at last in a low voice, 'at the midsummer fair, I believe you despised me. Didn't you?'

He rose to pace the room before turning to face her. Isobel saw his eyes were filled with—what? Regret? Compassion? *Desire?*

'I think I was blind,' he said quietly, 'not to see you as you really are.'

Her heart hammered. So who did he think was the

true Isobel Blake? She said, 'Perhaps you were actually right, in your low estimation of me. Have you thought of that?'

And then, before he could think what to say, what to do, she rose to her feet. 'Connor, I need to leave, for your sake. Having me here in your home isn't doing you any good at all. It's making you enemies—you see how they attacked you?—because not only do people dislike your school, but they hate me, on account of my father, and they will hate you, too.'

'Damn it, Isobel!'

He was clenching his fists while her eyes flew wide open.

'Damn it,' he went on, 'I will not let you push me away! You—yes, *you*—are doing me all the good in the world. I cannot bear to let you go. I will *not* let you go.' And, with his eyes never once leaving hers, he leaned forward and gripped her by the arms.

She tried to ease herself away, but he only pulled her closer. He was warm and strong and solid—he was *Connor*—and it was shockingly easy to pretend that they were different people and that this really could mean something…

A path which could only lead to absolute disaster.

'Don't let yourself in for more regrets.' She did her best to speak lightly. 'You weren't perhaps so very wrong in your opinion of me in the first place, you know.' Her heart and lungs were bursting to say, *But you are wrong, you don't know me, nobody does!* But she just couldn't. She couldn't afford to open herself to the lacerating hurt of his inevitable rejection.

He was still gazing at her, his eyes dark with emotion. 'And what do you think *is* my opinion of you, Miss Blake?'

She laughed. 'The correct one, I imagine. Now, listen—this is so foolish. You were injured yesterday and the doctor ordered you to rest, and you must be hurting everywhere...'

Her voice trailed away as he reached out to put his hand under her chin and tilted it up so her eyes were forced to meet his. 'Yes,' he said quietly. 'I do hurt. Everything hurts. But you can make the hurt better. You can make *me* better.'

And in that moment she felt her breath grow ragged and she realised that she needed what was happening far too much. She needed *him*. Her body remembered his lips against her skin, remembered how he had kissed her throat, her bared shoulders, her mouth. Those memories of pleasure came in an almost painful rush, making her breasts achingly tight and heavy beneath her confining gown, making her legs hopelessly weak.

'I need you,' Connor whispered.

And she surrendered.

He pulled her to him and he kissed her. It wasn't a gentle kiss—he kissed her with all the roaring, pent-up desire he'd been feeling for this woman for what felt like a lifetime.

And she kissed him back. He was aware of her lips yielding; he registered anew the softness of her mouth, the suppleness of her slim body clasped against his as she flung her hands around his broad shoulders, as she adjusted her stance to let his thigh press between her legs. He kissed her and kissed her, allowing her only the occasional gasp for breath, and he heard as well her tiny moans of desire and they drove him wild.

Their mouths still locked, he found himself stumbling with her towards the wall until her back was pressed against it and he briefly stopped kissing her to fumble with that tantalising line of tiny, tight buttons running from her waist up to her neck. She flung back her head and gasped as he pressed his mouth to her silken throat, then he shoved aside the delicate silk slip beneath her gown and found her high, rounded breasts. Pressing his lips to their sweet upper curve, he caressed one tender nipple until it hardened to his touch.

She was arching towards him now, her fingers digging into his back. Her breathing was jagged; she was gasping his name as he pulled her closer, his mouth finding her lips again and delving with his tongue deeper, deeper into her softness. And then he was sweeping her up in his arms and carrying her through to his bedroom, where he laid her down very carefully then said, 'You do want this, don't you?'

'Yes,' she whispered. 'Please, yes.'

Please, yes. His gaze was steady on hers as he slid off his shirt, his boots, his breeches. The sight of his sleek, rippling chest made her heart thud with fresh desire, because he was all male, all muscle and sinew and long limbs. He was beautiful.

He was Connor and she'd never wanted anyone else. Whatever the cost, whatever the consequences, she wanted to have this one night with him to remember. He sat on the bed beside her, his gaze still on her, and she reached out to touch the long, dark bruise along his ribs. And the thought of the pain it must have caused him wrenched her heart. She reached to kiss his skin there, licking at the slightly salty taste, and then he was putting her hands aside, but only to slide her gown from her shoulders, along with her silk slip.

She gasped and caught her lower lip between her teeth as his strong hands began to trail a tender path from shoulder to waist to hip, melting away her fear and creating a new and delicious tension in her as he pushed down her clothes and tossed them aside. Then he was pulling her close again and she gasped as she felt the silky, satiny hardness of his arousal against her stomach.

He was kissing away her low cry, while his hands continued to explore her curves; he was stroking her, teasing her, cupping her breasts in his hands, circling their stiffened peaks until she was moaning with frustration. She tangled her fingers in his thick dark hair, reaching for his kiss, finding herself wantonly pressing against him, her thighs loose.

He caught her wrists and moved away. 'No,' he murmured. 'Not yet. Isobel, I want you to remember this for ever.'

Then he was lowering his head to her breast, alternately biting softly and sucking until she was writhing and helpless, her whole body spinning in a gathering vortex of need. She cried out in protest as he lifted his head. 'Connor...'

Her own hand, she realised, was sliding with a will of its own down his chest to his taut abdomen; and further, then, to the silky line of dark hairs that led to his pulsing manhood. He gave a low, husky laugh then kissed her mouth, his tongue parting her lips almost roughly and delving deep. And she yielded to him, saying with her kiss what she could not say with words, as she let her legs instinctively wrap around him.

He is healing me, she thought, suddenly feeling his hardness nudging between her thighs. *Healing me of my past...*

There was a sudden brief moment of pain and she froze, almost afraid. But then she was gasping, wanting more, because his hand was down there between her legs, finding the little nub of pleasure there and coaxing it with his fingertip. And she opened to him like a flower, awash with longing, exalted by the sensations pouring through her. She was moving by instinct now, joining his powerful rhythm; and as the heat built in her body, she could feel it in him also and the wild pleasure pounded through her. At last he thrust hard one last time and she gasped out his name and was tumbling over the edge, whirling in a starfilled void where she was alone except for Connor and her fierce, fierce joy.

'Isobel?' His voice came as if from far away. 'Isobel?'

'Mmm?' She sighed. He had gathered her close and her naked breasts felt soft and vulnerable against his hard chest.

'*Isobel.*' His voice came again, harsher now. 'This is important. Didn't you care what people thought of you? Why haven't you tried to defend yourself, against those stories about you and Loxley?'

She drew away a little, cold again. 'I found it easier to say nothing after a while. Since nobody at all believed me when I told the truth.'

'But I was the first just now. As I guessed I would be.' His voice was almost hoarse with emotion. 'Yet you allowed those—those *lies,* about you and the Viscount—'

'They weren't all lies!' She was pulling herself up now. 'I lived with him for two whole years and so my reputation naturally was ruined. And you're right— tonight has all been a terrible mistake. For me *and* for you.'

Feeling suddenly sick with dismay at what she'd allowed to happen, she stumbled from his bed and started pulling on her frock with fingers that just wouldn't work.

'Isobel.' He'd risen, too, was reaching for his breeches and shirt. 'What happened in London—you were so young. To move in with Loxley—it cannot have been your fault. But tell me how it happened. Don't I deserve the truth?'

She stared up at him, aware of her heart fracturing into more and more pieces with every moment that passed. 'Very well, then. As you already know, I was just eighteen when my father took me to London. During my calamitous coming-out, my father despaired of ever finding a rich husband for me. He was ill by then—quite how ill I didn't realise. Anyway, during a drunken night at one of London's lowest so-called gentlemen's clubs, he decided to auction me.'

'*Auction* you!'

'Indeed. I was taken to the club by my father's mistress, Mrs Sparlet—it was late and I had no idea what was happening, but I was told it was a matter of urgency.'

She heaved in a deep breath. 'My inebriated, dying father was waiting for me. He led me by the hand into a room full of drunken men and offers were invited.

What, exactly, was the highest bid? I cannot remember at all, but the man who bought me was Viscount Loxley.'

Again Connor let out a low hiss of anger. But Isobel raised her hand to silence him.

'Viscount Loxley,' she went on, 'was twenty years older than I was. At first I was terrified. I knew his reputation, I knew his past affairs were the talk of the town. But do you know, Connor? He never touched me.'

'Never?'

'No. He took me home that night to his mansion near Hyde Park and he gave me a set of rooms of my own, and a lady's maid, and he told me he despised my father for what he'd done to me.'

She looked up at Connor. 'Loxley asked me straight away if there was anyone else I wished to stay with—a friend or relative. I said that I had no one except my father and I would rather die than go back to him. Loxley listened and after a while he told me that he had no children, but he wanted to look after me as if I were his ward and he my guardian.

'I stayed with him. And he kept his promise—he was always kind, always respectful. My father died soon afterwards. Loxley told me of his death and he also told me the Calverley estate had been repossessed by his bank—and I said that I didn't care. I didn't care in the least!' For the first time her voice was heated, then she continued more quietly.

'By then, I'd realised Loxley's health was poor. It was a lung disease—he was becoming very weak. So I used to sit with him and tell him Gloucestershire folk tales I remembered from my childhood, or play card games with him for pennies.' She half-smiled at the memory.

'I was with him for two years. Towards the end, when he was seriously ill, he told me he was arranging to make me safe. *"I'm going to make sure your future is secure, Isobel"*—those were his actual words. But I never learned any more and soon afterwards he died.

'During my time with him, I saw few people apart from his servants—he had become almost a recluse. Of course, I'd guessed that evil gossip would have spread about me. I knew that many would have assumed I was his mistress. I didn't really care at the time, because with him, I felt safe. But on his death I was quite alone. Everyone, without exception, believed the worst of me. Who could blame them?'

She was almost calm now—told herself she was past caring. 'Of course I shouldn't blame you, Connor, for believing it also. Tonight has been—fun. Is that what one is supposed to say? And then, I think, the next thing to say is—best to pretend it never happened. Don't you agree?'

She was buttoning her dress as she spoke, then putting on her shoes. Before he could stop her, she'd gathered up the rest of her things and swept out.

And she left by the servants' door.

Connor cursed himself roundly and solidly. The knowledge of how she must have suffered, and how she'd had to bear her suffering alone, was like red-hot needles piercing his skin.

As a girl, she'd had abominable parents and she'd had no one to turn to—except, perhaps, him. After that came London. She'd endured a round of parties and balls which she must have hated, before her dying father, in drunken desperation, offered her up to the highest bidder.

She was bought by Loxley. Connor hadn't heard about the auction, but he'd heard she was living with the notorious Viscount and had believed the worst, along with everyone else. But this summer he'd met her again at the fair, and—swept up by his eagerness for his new school—he'd big-heartedly decided to let bygones be bygones and to give her a second chance.

Generous of you, he told himself now, with great bitterness. *When all the time you'd been planning— what? To get her into your bed?*

He'd been not only a fool, but an unjust fool. Yes, there had always been incidents that made him doubt the stories of her time with Loxley. For instance, the way she closed up on any talk about her past. Her obvious shock when he even touched her, let alone kissed her.

And what untold harm had he done to her now?

After Loxley's death she'd found friends in Joseph and Agnes Molina and had been happy with them. Until he, Connor, came along, to wrench her from her peaceful existence—and all the time, he'd been wanting her for himself.

Isobel Blake, he realised now, was exactly what she had always been: brave and stubborn and passionate, with a huge sense of justice. And how must she be judging him, this minute?

She was probably deciding that she had thrown her innocence away on someone utterly undeserving of her.

Her mixture of vulnerability and courage gripped him so badly that his own bruises were nothing compared to the almighty ache at his heart. He could go to her now and explain. But what on earth could he say? *I'm sorry I believed those lies about you, even for a minute.* That wouldn't be enough. It never would be enough—but he had to at least try, because he wanted her. He needed her. He loved her.

Tomorrow. He would give her the chance to calm down and rest, then he would go to her tomorrow and try again. He didn't go back to his bed; instead he sat in the chair by the window, staring out into the night and thinking about Isobel.

Chapter Twenty

Isobel rose earlier than ever the next morning and went straight to the chapel in the cold light of dawn. During a long sleepless night she'd thought about running away, but that would be cowardly—best to carry on for the last few days of her contract, as if nothing had happened. Because nothing *had* happened really, except that she knew now how wrongly Connor had judged her—like everyone else. She'd hoped that he of all people would believe in her—but she'd expected too much.

Slowly she set out everything for the morning's lesson and all the while she felt the enveloping joy she'd experienced last night seeping out of her as the sun's rays filled the chapel with harsh reality.

What on earth had she hoped might be the result of this?

Yes, he'd made love to her—if love was the word. They were physically drawn to one another and had been from the start—there could be no denying *that*. And last night, dear God, she had blatantly encouraged him, so it was no wonder he'd accepted her willing embrace! Embarrassment flooded her body at the memory of what she'd let him do.

He'd bedded Isobel Blake, the daughter of his old enemy and also the scandalous young mistress of Viscount Loxley. Or so the gossips loved to whisper. Connor must know as well as she did that what had happened between them could never happen again— he was an extremely rich man of business now and it was his duty to shore up his company's position, to strengthen his connections both in commerce and in public life.

He had to marry well. He could not afford to have his name dragged through the mire by a connection with her.

Somehow she got through the morning in the chapel—after all, how could you remain absorbed for long in your own mess of a life, when over a dozen eager faces were listening to your every word? Afterwards she walked back slowly to the Hall, praying she wouldn't meet anyone. But as she headed for the side entrance, Haskins approached.

He must have been watching for her. 'Yes, Haskins?'

'Mr Hamilton would like to see you in his ground-floor study straight away, Miss Blake.'

Probably, she told herself wearily, to send her packing with a pay-off, so he could put an end to their mutual embarrassment over last night.

He was working at his desk when she entered the room, but he rose and went to shut the door once she was in. She realised with a sudden burst of pity that he looked terribly tired and that bruise on his jaw hadn't faded in the least.

'Isobel,' he said. 'About last night. We need to talk, you and I.'

She feigned mild surprise. 'We tried that last night. And it didn't exactly help, did it, Connor?'

His expression remained grave. 'We must talk,' he repeated.

She shrugged, her smile still fixed to her face. *So you can tell me that, though you respect me very much, and so on, and so forth, you don't want me in your bed or in your life?*

But she nodded. Like a lamb to the slaughter.

He offered her a chair, but she shook her head. 'I've got four more days of teaching the children,' she said, 'and then my contract ends—much to the relief, I'm sure, of your staff and yourself. You know the old saying, Connor—all good things must come to an end...'

Her voice tailed off as he closed the distance between them and gripped her shoulders. 'Isobel,' he said almost violently, 'Isobel, I don't *want* this to end. I don't want you to go. Do you hear me?'

She felt the breath being punched from her lungs. She tried to laugh, but it came out all wrong. 'You're surely not asking me to be your mistress? Now, that would *really* astonish people. First you buy Calverley Hall and then you take over its disgraced former heiress—you truly can't be serious!'

'I don't want it to end,' he repeated, his voice raw. 'I can't bear to lose you.'

For a moment she couldn't move. She couldn't breathe. His hands on her shoulders trapped her in a surge of impossible longing; his eyes were dark with passion. His shirt was open at the neck and he *still* hadn't shaved; his hair was wild and those shadows beneath his eyes implied he hadn't slept a wink. Just like her.

And he looked utterly, heartbreakingly desirable.

This was going to take all her strength. This was going to be the biggest and hardest battle she'd ever fought. With her stomach twisting itself into hard, painful knots, she forced herself to say, 'Connor. I realise, even if you don't, that last night was a huge mistake, which you're going to regret every time my name is mentioned. So let's forget that it ever happened, shall we? Fortunately I have only a few days left of my contract, so we can perhaps put last night down to an episode of foolishness between two adults who ought to know better.'

'*Foolishness?*' He exhaled sharply. 'Is that really how you think of everything that's happened between the two of us?' She saw how his hands had clenched into fists. There was something dark and agonised in his gaze and he looked as if she'd torn him wide open.

Which was how she herself had been feeling since that day at the midsummer fair, only now it was worse; now she felt as if being close to him was like a knife being turned in her heart and she didn't think she could bear it. Not any more. She pulled herself away.

'I think,' she said quietly, 'that it's best if I go now, don't you? And leave you to the real business of your life. Those new docks you're going to build.' She was glancing at the papers on his desk.

He was dragging his hand across his unshaved jaw. 'It's uncertain,' he said at last, 'whether I'll get the contract now.'

'Really?' She lifted her chin. 'I'm sure you'll manage it somehow. After all, you usually get exactly what you want.'

'*Isobel*—' He broke off as there was a knock at the door and a footman entered, clearly not seeing Isobel at first.

'Tom the groom has just called, sir,' he said, 'and says he wants to speak with you— Oh!' He'd noticed Isobel. 'I do beg your pardon, Miss Blake...'

'I'll come,' Connor said. He turned to Isobel. 'I'll only be a few minutes. Isobel, will you stay here?'

She looked very pale. 'I'd really rather not—'

'Please,' he said.

The business with Tom didn't take long, but it was still longer than Connor wanted. Old Tom was desperately eager to tell him that his attackers, after the beating they'd taken, had packed up and disappeared from the district. But all Connor was thinking as he finally made his way back to his study, was, *Please let her still be there.*

What a mess he'd made of everything. She still obsessed him. Even dressed in her usual drab gown, she looked utterly lovely. Her sweet face, her soft skin, her voice, her scented body—they all haunted his dreams. He suddenly wished that they were meeting for the first time, without all the clutter of their previous lives to untangle. With an enormous effort of willpower, he pulled himself together and went in.

And he realised she was sitting at his desk, looking through the papers spread out there.

She sprang to her feet as he entered, looking agitated. 'Connor, these calculations. I noticed them last night, on your desk upstairs. Did you realise they're wrong?'

'*What?*'

She was pointing at them. 'Whoever wrote them out has made errors in the totals. They're not easy to spot, but they're enough to make the final figures completely wrong.'

He was staring at her, then at those lethal papers that proved his plans were completely uneconomic. Clearly she was interpreting his silence as hostility.

'I'm sorry,' she went on very quietly, 'I realise it's no business of mine, but as I say I spotted a couple of errors last night and couldn't help but look at them more closely just now. May I show you?' She was pointing at the columns of tightly written accountants' figures. 'For example, there are errors *here* and *here*, with at least another one on every page. You know I'm hopeless at spelling, but I think I told you I'm rather good at arithmetic. I've started writing down where the numbers are astray. Take a look—you might find it interesting. But now I must leave you to your work—'

He broke in. 'Isobel. Can you possibly sort through it all for me, *now*? This is really important. These figures relate to my docks contract. I'm due to set off for London this afternoon, because tomorrow I have to present my cost estimates to my investors and then to a committee set up by Parliament. I was going to check them myself, but if you'll do it first, I can see if my own calculations match yours.'

She looked rather shaken. 'It will take me a little while. Not the maths, but the writing it down—I cannot do it as neatly as you might require...'

'It doesn't matter in the slightest! As long as your figures are legible, and correct, that's really all I'm concerned about. Please, Isobel, do what you can. This is important.'

She nodded slowly, and sat at his desk with her back to him. He paced the room while she worked, mentally lashing himself. After all his false assumptions about her, his complete misjudgement of her, he expected her to *help* him?

She had no family. She'd lost her home, which he'd dragged her back to, and forced her to work for him. She'd done everything and more to adapt to her new situation in life. She'd been respectful to him and Laura, and lovely to Elvie and the traveller children—and what had he done in return?

He'd seduced her. She was going to find it hard to forgive him for the many other ways he'd wronged her. The trouble was that Connor really couldn't imagine, now that Isobel Blake had come back into his life, how he was going to live without her. And in the meantime, there was something else that troubled him deeply. The accountants who'd prepared those figures had been recommended by Roderick Staithe.

Isobel sat there with a pencil in her hand, her emotions in turmoil. When Connor had said *I can't bear to lose you* she'd felt such a huge rush of longing that it had taken every ounce of her physical and emotional strength to stop her stupid self from rushing headlong into his arms.

How can you be such a fool, Isobel? She glanced swiftly up at him; he'd stopped pacing and was staring out of the window, his profile harsh and almost haunted. And she realised she had no defence against this man. None at all. But she did know that his feelings for her could ruin him.

She realised suddenly that he was looking at her, his eyes shadowed by an emotion she couldn't read. 'Isobel. If this is too difficult for you—'

She said, 'This isn't difficult. This is easy.'

It was everything else in her life that lay in ruins.

Drawing in a deep breath, she pulled the sheets of paper towards her. Yes, the actual calculations were simple enough for her; she was gifted, she could do them in her head. But Connor needed it all written down, and she was afraid that in her awkward scrawl, he might not be able to make any sense of it.

Then she remembered something Elvie had said to her. *'There's nothing wrong with your brain, Miss Blake. You can read everything perfectly—can't you? It's just that when it comes to writing, your right hand won't do what you tell it to. Why not use your left hand instead?'*

So she did. Connor wouldn't notice—and anyway, hadn't he told her he didn't even care? She worked on, and he didn't interrupt, but he lit more candles on his desk for her as the light faded.

Connor watched and waited. He was thinking, *How could I have been so blind to misjudge her so? How can I make amends? But—why didn't she try to defend herself by telling the truth to everyone?*

He could see she was working her way swiftly through those daunting sheets of numbers, using her left hand, creating column after column of workings-out on the blank paper he'd provided. At last she turned to him, her gaze steady.

'I was right,' she said. 'These costings you have

been given are faulty. They overestimate the cost of your requirements by almost a thousand pounds. It's been done skilfully.'

He felt a thump in his chest. 'You're saying the errors are deliberate?'

'Yes. Let me show you.' She pointed. 'Where the numbers have been carried over to the next page, some of them have been shifted to the left, by one column—not all of them by any means, or it would have been easy to spot. But enough to make a big difference to the total. Somebody knew exactly what they were doing.'

She indicated her own figures then and he scanned them swiftly. She was absolutely right. 'Thank you,' he said.

She shrugged. 'I'm sure you have highly skilled staff who could have done exactly the same.'

'In London, yes.' He was shaking his head slowly. 'But what's been done here is nothing less than sabotage. And I'd rather as few people as possible know about it.'

Especially as the person who'd had these figures prepared and sent to Connor post-haste was Roderick Staithe. With an accompanying note.

I thought I'd let you know what you're up against, Hamilton. My experts have worked out the costing of your offer of iron for the docks based on your price per ton. And, as you can see, it comes to far more than your rivals' figures.

I'm afraid you'll have to lower your price or lose the deal...

Connor was meeting Staithe in London tomorrow. Staithe would say jovially, 'Seen the figures, Hamilton? Not good, are they? I'm afraid the Parliamentary committee is going to take some persuading to back you, once they catch sight of these!'

And Connor could guess, too, what Staithe would demand in return for bringing the committee round. Staithe had Connor neatly lined up as an extremely wealthy brother-in-law. Tomorrow Staithe would doubtless ask for a substantial sum of money for himself and a proposal of marriage for Helena. And Staithe was going to be disappointed all over again.

He was about to tell Isobel, who was still sitting silently—tensely—at his desk. For God's sake, she deserved to know *everything* about all this! Only then from outside came the clattering of a horse's hooves and the shout of a groom. Connor went quickly to the window to look out into the lantern-lit courtyard. 'It's Carstairs. He was still supposed to be in London. He must have urgent news.'

Isobel stood up slowly. She'd been at his desk for two hours, working non-stop—she looked exhausted. And he realised he'd never wanted anything, or anyone, so much in his entire life.

'I must go,' she was saying. 'Mr Carstairs will want to see you straight away.'

'Yes.' He was shrugging on his coat. 'But stay here. We will talk. We *must* talk.' He went out, leaving the door open—she could already hear Carstairs's voice.

'Mr Hamilton? This is urgent, i'm afraid.'

Out in the corridor Carstairs spelled out the news to Connor immediately. 'We've got trouble,' he said. 'These rival bids have suddenly appeared for the docks contract and it all rests on the Parliamentary committee that meets tomorrow. I'm afraid you may no longer be the foremost choice.'

Connor's reply was harsh. 'Staithe chairs the committee and he's trying to foul up my bid.'

'But why on earth—?'

'It's rather complicated. The point is, Carstairs, there's been some dirty work here and I'll have to go to London straight away to sort it out.'

'*Tonight?*' Carstairs looked appalled. 'But, sir. Your injuries, from the other day. Are you sure you're sufficiently recovered?'

'Absolutely sure.' Connor glanced at his watch. 'I'll just get a few things together for the journey. Tell the grooms to get my horse ready, will you?'

Carstairs left and Connor turned to go back into his study. He needed to talk to Isobel. He needed to say to her, *Please. Stay at the Hall, at least until I get back from London, because I have so much to say to you...* But she'd gone. She must have slipped away like a ghost while his back was turned—and he had no time, now, to find her.

Connor uttered one of the few prayers of his life. *Let her be here when I get back. Let me be given a second chance.* Although, he thought bleakly, he would be lucky if he hadn't earned her everlasting scorn—because he'd not believed in her.

London

The next morning shortly before eleven, Connor rapped on the front door of Staithe's house in Clarges Street, Mayfair. The butler looked surprised—'It's rather early, sir!'—but Connor announced that he'd wait.

Shortly afterwards, Staithe came down the stairs in a silk dressing gown. 'Hamilton,' he drawled. 'I didn't think you would prise yourself away from your rural idyll so quickly.'

Connor thrust out the papers containing the false figures. 'These were wrong. If they'd been presented to the committee this afternoon, they would have lost me the contract for the docks. But I rather think that was what you intended, wasn't it?'

Staithe raised his eyebrows. He looked rather pale. 'Be careful, Hamilton. These are harsh accusations.'

'And they are true. Why did you do it?'

Staithe hesitated, then sighed. 'This is all rather unfortunate, wouldn't you say? If only you'd been a little more co-operative in the first place.'

'If only I'd offered you a bribe, you mean?' cut in Connor. 'To get your committee on my side? Remind me. What's your price?'

'I want,' said Roderick Staithe, 'you to marry my sister and give me fifty thousand pounds, plus a twenty per cent share in your London foundry. And then there's the matter of Miss Isobel Blake. Get rid of her. Expose her for the whore she is.'

'No.' Connor was surprised at how calmly it came out. '*No* to everything. But most of all to your demand that I get rid of Isobel Blake.'

Staithe leaned forward. 'Are you forgetting about her sordid life with Loxley? Believe me, you'll be a laughing stock if you persist in dallying with her.'

'I'm not dallying with her. I'm going to marry her.' Connor folded up the sheets of calculations and put them back in his coat pocket. 'I'm also going to visit the members of your Parliamentary committee and show each of them these false figures your accountants concocted. I'm going to tell them it was all a ruse for your own advantage and I'm going to warn them you should not only be kicked off their precious committee, but you should be thrown out of Parliament, too.'

He set off for the door. Staithe hurried after him. 'Hamilton. Wait. *Listen...*'

Connor walked on without a backward glance, out into the street where he paused and looked around. The sky above the splendid white houses was clear and blue, and sparrows chirruped in the leafy trees.

Yes, he was going to visit Staithe's Parliamentary allies. But before that, he was going to ask a few discreet questions. He was going to make enquiries about Viscount Loxley's relatives—and Loxley's will.

He remembered again what Isobel had said. *'"I'm going to make sure your future is secure, Isobel"—those were his actual words.'*

Connor had already found out the name of Loxley's lawyer, who had an office in the Strand. He hailed a cab and settled back for the ride, a glint of steely determination in his eyes.

He had a feeling he was going to rather enjoy all this.

Chapter Twenty-One

It was some days later and Isobel had given her final lesson in the old chapel. The children had brought her gifts: posies of wild flowers and cakes their mothers had made. Mary read out a poem she and Harry had written about their time at Plass Valley and after that they all left one by one. Isobel waved to them until they were out of sight.

She rose early the next morning and walked into Chipping Calverley to take the public stagecoach for the six-mile journey to Bath. Alighting in the centre, she found her way to an agency whose address she'd carefully copied from the *Gloucestershire Herald*— an agency that specialised in providing suitable companions to the genteel ladies of the town.

On showing the manager, Mr Jennings, a note of recommendation that Laura had written for her, Mr Jennings, clearly impressed, talked with her a while, then told her that she might very well suit an elderly widow in the town, Mrs Gregory. Since Mrs Gregory lived only ten minutes' walk away, he suggested they go to visit her and the meeting was a success. Isobel found Mrs Gregory to be kind and charming—a little like an older version of Laura. There was no formal interview—instead they chatted over cups of tea and Mrs Gregory suggested that Isobel should move in and take up the position of companion in three days.

By the time Isobel got back to Calverley Hall, it was late, but Laura was still up and waiting for her.

'I'm extremely sorry that we're losing you, my dear,' Laura said. 'But you no doubt know what's best. Unfortunately it could be several more days before Connor can return from London. Won't you at least stay until he's here again? I'm afraid he won't be very pleased with me for assisting you in this!'

'He will understand,' said Isobel quietly, 'and I'm very grateful for your letter of reference. I shall miss you and Elvie. Thank you for the friendship you've always offered me.'

On her last afternoon at Calverley Hall, Isobel packed her few possessions, then walked up the familiar path to tell the Molinas her news.

'Will this lady in Bath be kind to you?' Agnes asked anxiously and Isobel assured her that Mrs Gregory couldn't be kinder.

But Agnes didn't ask Isobel about herself. Agnes could no doubt read everything she needed to know in Isobel's eyes. Agnes would guess Isobel hadn't been sleeping and she would be right, because nights, for Isobel, were the worst. She tried not to think of Connor, but every night she dreamed of him. All she knew was that he was still in London—living his other life. His *real* life.

She didn't expect him to get in touch with her again. Why on earth should he? He would have realised— just as she did, on overhearing that conversation he'd had with Carstairs—that she was a hindrance to him and worse.

The new docks meant everything to him—not just the money, but the jobs and welfare of his workers. Roderick Staithe had the power to wreck the entire project and Connor had no alternative but to keep to the promise he must have made long ago—to marry Staithe's sister.

Even if he didn't love her? Yes—because that was the way the rich and powerful lived their lives. Everything was done for profit and social advancement. Helena Staithe was beautiful and well born. And with her at his side, Connor's industrial might would go from strength to strength.

Isobel understood. Yet she couldn't forget being in his arms that night and being loved by him. She didn't *want* to forget. The memory was part of her life now and Connor was part of her being.

Mrs Gregory's elegant town house in Bath was very close to the Assembly Rooms. There were four servants: a butler, two maids and a cook, and all of them were pleasant and respectful to Isobel. Within a few days she'd grown used to Mrs Gregory's gentle routine and learned what she was expected to do: to provide company, to listen to the old lady's memories of her youth, to help sort her silks for her embroidery and drive out with her in her carriage when the weather was fine.

But Isobel still had too much time to spare. Too much time for her own memories.

And then, one September afternoon as she sat with Mrs Gregory in her sunny parlour, she heard the clatter of a horse's hooves in the cobbled street outside. Moments later somebody was knocking at the door. Mrs Gregory, who was rather deaf, didn't hear it, but Isobel did. She heard the butler's voice; she heard the abrupt tones of the caller—and her heart began to thud as if it would burst.

Swiftly she hurried to the hallway and said to the butler, 'Thank you. I will see to this.'

Connor stood there, his eyes dark with emotion. She was aware of the blood draining from her face and felt her pulse race, making her dizzy.

'Isobel,' he began. 'Laura told me you were here. I know you left Calverley of your own free will and I realise you would rather not see me any more, but I have things I must tell you. Can we be private somewhere? Could we perhaps go for a walk in the Sydney Gardens?'

She closed her eyes briefly. *And open herself up to more hurt? Fresh pain?*

But Connor himself was hurting. She could see that in the set of his mouth, the darkness of his eyes—and she couldn't bear it. *One last time, Isobel. Summon up your strength one last time.*

She drew a deep breath. 'I'll just tell Mrs Gregory. She needs some more silk threads for her sewing. I can get those for her on the way.'

Her memories of the day in the gardens with Connor and Elvie all but overwhelmed her as he led her down one of the paths away from the crowds, then turned to face her. He said, 'That night, Isobel. The night we were together, at Calverley Hall. To me it felt so right. I realised it was what I longed for, to be with you. But I know now that I made so many mistakes. I rushed you into it. No wonder you regretted it—'

'Regretted it?' She couldn't help it; the words tumbled out. 'Oh, Connor! How could I?'

His expression changed then. Instead of despair, she saw something that was almost hope in his eyes.

By now they'd reached a secluded section of the woodland path, where there was a stone bench overlooking a waterfall. No one else was around. He made her sit next to him on the bench and said, 'I had to go to London, Isobel—I had no choice. And while I was away you said goodbye to the children and you said goodbye to Laura and Elvie. You packed your things and you left, though Laura told me she begged you to stay...'

'Because I was no good for you, Connor!' The words wrenched at her heart. 'Don't you see?'

'No!' He sounded angry. Bewildered. 'I don't see *at all.*'

She was looking straight ahead at the waterfall, whose foaming cascade tumbled over glistening rocks. She said at last, 'I heard Mr Carstairs talking to you. He said that Roderick Staithe had the power of decision over your docks project—and I know Staithe expects you to marry his sister in return for his support. I expect that Helena will make you very happy—'

'No one will make me happy,' he said abruptly, 'except for you. I want you, Isobel. Haven't I made that clear?'

'For your sake, Connor, that's not possible! Staithe would drag up the old stories about me and try to ruin you.'

'No, he wouldn't.' He suddenly grinned mischievously. 'While I was in London, I gathered a few willing witnesses to prove that Staithe is a cheat and a liar.'

'Connor—how?'

'Those figures you looked at for me proved it. He's resigning from Parliament today, as a matter of fact. If he does start spreading stories about you, I can make sure that he's in even worse trouble. Believe me, I'd enjoy it.'

Did she dare to hope? Could she *afford* to hope? She wanted to reach out and touch him, but instead she asked carefully, 'So your docks are safe? Your workers' jobs are safe?'

He smiled again. 'Of course they're safe. I think you've *always* rather underestimated me, Miss Blake. Just as you underestimate yourself. Now, you asked me why I'm here.' She'd slipped her hands away, but he took them again.

'I want you,' he went on, 'to come to London, to be at my side when I tell people about the school for the Plass Valley children. As you know, I've been talking to some other businessmen who are interested in setting up similar schools. I thought that together, you and I could explain how it worked and what we achieved.'

'But—'

'I know you're going to tell me you can't spell. In spite of that, you've succeeded beyond my hopes. Forget your spelling! As I've told you before, it's your ideas and your personality that are the key factors.'

'I see,' she said. Her voice was very small. 'And that's why you're here?'

'That,' he said, 'is only a small part of it. *This* is the real reason why I'm here.'

He was reaching into his coat pocket and holding out a small leather box. With unsteady hands, she opened it—and saw an exquisite diamond ring. He took it from her, put it on her finger and kissed her palm. 'Marry me, Isobel,' he said.

She felt something aching in her chest. 'Now *this*,' she responded with an effort at lightness, 'is taking things a little too far, Mr Hamilton.' Her voice had a catch in it, but still she tried to smile. 'Do you truly want to ruin yourself?'

Suddenly she felt his arms round her, drawing her close. 'Isobel,' he was saying. 'Isobel.' He was tenderly stroking her hair back from her face. 'I mean it. I want you to be my wife.'

'But those things you heard,' she cried desperately, 'they actually did happen, Connor! My father put me up for auction and Viscount Loxley bought me. Yes, I was his companion, not his mistress. But who will believe that?'

'Everyone,' he said, 'by the time we've told them the truth.'

'But I tried to, believe me!' Despair coloured her voice. 'I told you, I think, how Loxley promised he was going to do something to make me safe. But I never knew what and, after the funeral, various relatives of Loxley's—cousins who'd scarcely ever visited him—declared me to be a harlot. When I tried to defend myself, I was thrown out of the house, without money, without friends or family. That was when I met

Joseph Molina and he invited me to live with himself and his sister, back in Gloucestershire...' Her voice faded a little. 'Only then, Connor, I learned that you were buying the Calverley estate. I thought of moving away again. But I didn't.'

His arms held her more tightly. 'You should have told me *everything,* straight away! On the day of the midsummer fair!'

She looked at him steadily. 'I suppose that by then I believed I'd lost you for good. Perhaps by not even *trying* to tell you what had really happened to me in London, I was trying to protect myself from any further hurt.'

'You mean—you feared I might not believe you?'

'Yes.' *But it didn't work,* she was saying to herself. *It didn't protect me, Connor, from what I feel for you.*

'How brave you've been,' he said. 'How misjudged you've been. Oh, Isobel. I should have been there for you.'

'Many, many parts of my life have been good. When I was a girl at Calverley, I used to love riding to the forge, to talk to you. It was my escape. My refuge. When you left...' Her voice grew quieter. '*That* was the bad time. And realising my name had been blackened beyond redemption by Loxley's relatives— that was bad, too. But I found happiness with Joseph and Agnes Molina, in their farmhouse.'

'Only then I returned,' he said almost fiercely. He was still holding her. 'I blundered into your life again. Isobel, I've misjudged you, so badly. But I'm trying to make amends. That's why I was so long in London. You see, I tracked down Loxley's lawyer.'

Her eyes widened.

'I found,' he went on, 'that Loxley, a few weeks before he died, made a codicil—that's a legal amendment to his will. Yes, most of his money and property was left to those cousins of his—but he left ten thousand pounds to you. And I found out something even more important.'

He was drawing a sheet of paper out of his pocket and unfolding it. 'This is a copy of the declaration by Loxley in the codicil. It says, *"To whom it may concern. I wish to make it clear that I took Isobel Blake into my house in order to protect her and keep her safe. She has been my loyal companion—nothing more—and is entirely an innocent. I wish her to be regarded as my legal ward and will shortly be making arrangements to this end."'*

'His legal ward?' Isobel felt rather dizzy again.

'That's correct. Unfortunately, he died before his wishes could be formalised. But his intentions are there—together with his declaration of your innocence.'

She was shaking her head. 'Oh, Connor. Why did no one *tell* me?'

'I rather think that, having met Loxley's relatives yourself, you can probably guess.' Connor's expression was grim now. 'How do you think they felt, on realising Loxley had not only left you a large sum of money, but was also declaring that he wished you to be considered his ward? They were his executors—so after his death, they pretended the codicil had never existed. Then they blackened your name thoroughly, to prevent the chances of anyone ever listening to you.'

He flourished the piece of paper. 'I discovered this copy of the codicil at the lawyer's office. I got Loxley's lawyer to confirm that the original had never been revoked and is therefore still as valid as the day it was written. You could bring charges against Loxley's relatives, Isobel.'

'No.' She was very pale again. 'No. But I want justice done, Connor.'

'That's exactly what I thought. So I visited them.'

'The relatives?'

He nodded. 'Yes. I told them that if they give you the ten thousand pounds and make it quite clear that Loxley's relationship with you was that of guardian and ward, then they won't find themselves in trouble with the law.'

'But everyone believes the worst of me anyway. How can that be changed?'

'Quite easily.' He grinned. 'You're going to be my wife. By the time you come to London with me, as my bride, I'll have made quite sure that the declaration in the codicil has been made public knowledge. Anyone who raises any doubts will have me to deal with. As for Loxley's relatives, I think it would be rather entertaining to force them to acknowledge you in public. I could even suggest to them that they invite you to their house—'

'I shall not go!' Her chin had tilted stubbornly.

'No.' His grip on her hand tightened. 'But the invitation would speak for itself. And the main thing is that I've got *you,* Isobel. That's all that matters in the world to me.'

He was silent a moment, then he went on, 'Do you know, when I returned to Calverley this spring, I went to look at the place where the forge once stood. There was a small patch of garden at the back, where my father used to grow vegetables and roses. I expected it to be an overgrown wilderness. But someone had tended it and the rose bushes were in full bloom.'

'I started going there after you'd gone,' she told him almost shyly. 'And when I came back here with the Molinas, I visited it every week, to look after those roses.'

'But why?'

'It was for your father and for you. You see, I always hoped you might come back.'

He took a deep breath and pointed to the ring on her finger. 'You've not given me your answer yet, Isobel. I want you to marry me. I want you to be my wife.'

She was shaking her head. 'Impossible! My father was a disgrace and so am I.'

He laughed. 'Do you think I care? You give me strength and joy, and a belief in myself. I used to long for your visits to the forge, because you were inquisitive and caring, and above all courageous. And I love what you've become.'

'All of it?' She raised her eyebrows in a hint of mocking disbelief. 'You do realise I can be rather difficult?'

'Of course! I've seen it! You're outspoken and rebellious—and I've seen you fighting mad at times, especially in defence of those children. But since I'm so tolerant, and so relaxed...' he paused as she let out a gasp of merriment '... I'm sure we'll get on together extremely well. Isobel.' His voice became serious again. 'You've had to fight the whole world on your own, but you have never stopped being strong and loving, and honourable. I'll be the proudest man in the world to have you as my wife—and together, we'll fight off anyone who dares to suggest otherwise.'

He kissed her, oblivious to anyone else who might be around. As he caressed her willing mouth with his, clasping her close, she responded ardently; and when they finally—reluctantly—drew apart she was filled with renewed desire for this man to whom she'd given her heart.

'Happy?' he murmured, still holding her close.

'I didn't know I could be so happy.' Her voice still trembled with passion; she managed a shaky smile. 'I don't know how to say it and you might even laugh, but—'

'Try me,' he offered.

'I think,' she said very quietly, 'that I've always loved you, Connor. You've always been my hero. Only it hurt me so much, when I thought you believed those things about me—'

'Hush,' he interrupted. He traced the outline of her lips with his forefinger. 'Hush, darling Isobel. I've made bad mistakes, but I hope you can forgive me. And as for the rest of the world—it can go to hell, as long as I have you.'

Suddenly she threw him a teasing look. 'Now, I cannot believe you would give up your iron foundries!' He began to speak, but swiftly she reached to put her fingertip on his mouth. 'And I wouldn't,' she went on softly, 'for one minute, expect you to. Because your work is your life, Connor. Your work is *you* and your dedication to it won't have to alter in the slightest because of me. But I want you to let me be by your side, supporting you, helping you whenever and wherever I can.'

'And loving me,' he said, reaching to cup her cheeks

and tilt her face to his. 'Loving me, always, Isobel. That's the most important thing of all.'

He took her in his arms in a silent acknowledgement of all that had happened to the two of them. A moment of mutual forgiveness and hope. Then he kissed her again; and he didn't stop until they heard the sound nearby of someone clearing his throat. Connor looked up as a man said politely, 'Begging your pardon, sir. Madam. But it's starting to rain, you know.'

It was one of the park keepers—and he was right. Overhead the sky was rapidly darkening; heavy drops of rain were beginning to fall and not far away was a rumble of thunder.

Connor sprang to his feet and grinned broadly. 'Thank you,' he said. 'But you see, I've just asked this lady to marry me—and she said yes!'

The park keeper nodded his head approvingly. 'Now *that's* worth getting a bit soaked for, I'd say. Best get that lovely lady of yours somewhere nice and dry though, sir. And look after her, won't you?'

'I will,' Connor promised. 'Believe me, I will.'

Epilogue

July the following year

The gardens of Calverley Hall glowed with colour in the warm summer sunshine as Isobel wandered along the paths with her basket, snipping off fragrant blooms. Elvie followed close behind with Little Jack—who wasn't so little now.

'There are some lovely pink roses here, Isobel,' called Elvie, 'that I think Grandmother would love for the morning room! And we could put some yellow ones in the hallway for Connor, so he sees them when he comes home today. Because he *is* coming home, isn't he?'

At that very moment they heard the sound of a carriage rattling along the drive and Elvie clapped her hands with delight. 'It must be him now!' And she went charging off towards the house, with a devoted Jack at her heels.

A little later Connor found Isobel in the rose garden, sitting on a stone bench. 'You're back, Mr Hamilton,' she said, lifting her radiant face for his kiss. She wore a light green gown whose colour shimmered in the dappled sunlight beneath the trees and highlighted her vivid eyes.

He drew her up into his arms and held her there after he'd kissed her, breathing in the scent of her hair, her skin. 'I'm here, Mrs Hamilton,' he said. 'Where I belong.'

'But how long for?' she teased. 'I know you. How long before you're charging off to London with some amazing new scheme firing up your brain?'

'I've decided to take a holiday,' he announced. He linked his arm through hers and together they started strolling along the path. 'I've left everything in London in extremely safe hands and the work at the docks is progressing on time and on target.' He smiled down at her. 'Have you missed me?'

She let a mischievous smile play around her mouth. 'Do you know, I have, rather. I think I'd better warn you that you'll realise how much, once we're alone tonight.'

His hand was suddenly round her waist and he pulled her to face him. 'So I'll need all my energy, will I? We'd better ensure Cook provides a special feast.'

'Especially,' she added, 'since I'm eating for two.'

He drew her closer, suddenly protective—anxious almost. 'And is everything going well? Did you keep your promise that you'd see the doctor if anything at all worried you?'

'Everything's *fine,* Connor. Don't I look well?'

'You look,' he said, 'absolutely wonderful.'

Her smile then was like the sun, warming up all the cold places inside him, healing all the old hurts. He would do the same for her, he vowed. He would take away all the shadows of her past. They would heal each other.

Their wedding last October had been a simple affair, with only a few guests—Laura and Elvie, Agnes and Joseph Molina, and Robert Carstairs. That was how they'd both wanted it. But Connor also arranged a wonderful party for his staff; a party which was all the better, people quietly agreed, for the fact that Haskins and Mrs Lett were not present. They had been replaced by a new steward and a new housekeeper, both of whom met with everyone's approval.

Once the winter was past, Connor had taken Isobel to London to his house in Mayfair and, though she was nervous at first about meeting his friends and business partners, they had been in raptures over her.

'So beautiful. So charming,' they all said. 'Connor, you're a lucky fellow!'

Roderick Staithe, after resigning his seat in Parliament, had retreated to the country and of the incident years ago that had caused Isobel such anguish no one spoke a word, because Connor had dealt with Loxley's relatives in his usual efficient manner.

The ten thousand pounds was now hers. And within a week of Connor and Isobel's arrival in the capital, Connor had arranged for them to attend a grand *soirée,* at which Loxley's relatives would also be present. Isobel hadn't wanted to go in the least, but Connor had promised to be at her side throughout. 'And they won't stay long,' he'd laughed. 'Believe me.'

They didn't. There were six of them; they bowed or curtsied one by one to Isobel, saying, 'Mrs Hamilton. Our cousin Viscount Loxley's charming young ward. How good you were to him in his final months! It's such a pleasure to see you again.'

Connor was right; they left very soon afterwards

and from then on not a word was heard of the slanders they'd spread. Connor and Isobel had already decided to give Loxley's bequest to a new charity involved in setting up schools for children in the poorest parts of London. And if anyone remembered the stories about Isobel, they certainly took great care never to mention them in Connor's presence.

Isobel was looking up at him now. She was slightly anxious, he realised. 'Do you *feel* married, Connor?' she asked.

'Why, yes. Don't you? Why do you ask it?'

'It's just that I can't believe my own happiness. Really.'

He laughed. 'Difficult as it may be, you're going to have to get used to it, Isobel—for ever. And that is a definite promise. I may even get you to sign a contract.'

He cupped her cheeks, kissed her lips with a warmth that thrilled her whole being, then took her hand and led her towards Calverley Hall.

They were both home, at last.

* * * * *

If you enjoyed this story check out these other great reads by Lucy Ashford

THE CAPTAIN'S COURTESAN
THE RAKE'S BARGAIN
THE OUTRAGEOUS BELLE MARCHMAIN
THE CAPTAIN AND HIS INNOCENT